Should Have Been Me

A fake dating small town romance

A Pembrooke Novel

Jessica Prince

For the women who had their hearts broken and imagined getting their revenge by dating someone older, hotter, and richer. This one is for you.

Let's Connect

By signing up for my newsletter, you're guaranteeing you'll stay up to date on all new releases, cover reveals, giveaways, sales, and all the other exciting book news I have coming!

I pinky-promise to use my emails only for good, not to spam you, and make sure each one is enjoyable for everybody.

Sign up on my website at www.authorjessicaprince.com

Discover Other Books by Jessica

Bombshell
Knockout
Stunner
Seductress
Temptress
Vamp

<u>HOPE VALLEY SERIES:</u>
Out of My League
Come Back Home Again
The Best of Me
Wrong Side of the Tracks
Stay With Me
Out of the Darkness
The Second Time Around
Waiting for Forever
Love to Hate You
Playing for Keeps
When You Least Expect It
Never for Him

<u>REDEMPTION SERIES</u>
Bad Alibi
Crazy Beautiful
Bittersweet
Guilty Pleasure

Wallflower

Blurred Line

Slow Burn

Favorite Mistake

Sweet Spot

THE CLOVERLEAF SERIES

Picking up the Pieces

Rising from the Ashes

Pushing the Boundaries

Worth the Wait

THE COLORS NOVELS

Scattered Colors

Shrinking Violet

Love Hate Relationship

Wildflower

THE LOCKLAINE BOYS

Fire & Ice

Opposites Attract

Almost Perfect

CIVIL CORRUPTION SERIES

Corrupt

Defile

Consume

Ravage

<u>GIRL TALK SERIES</u>:

Seducing Lola

Tempting Sophia

Enticing Daphne

Charming Fiona

<u>STANDALONE TITLES</u>:

One Knight Stand

Chance Encounters

Nightmares from Within

<u>DEADLY LOVE SERIES</u>:

Destructive

Addictive

Pembrooke Playlist

"Where's My Love" by SYML
"Stick Season" by Noah Kahan
"Dial Drunk" by Noah Kahan
"The Fire" by Christ Stapleton
"Who's Afraid of Little Old Me" by Taylor Swift
"Gasoline" by Halsey
"Nightmare" by Halsey

Chapter One

Jolie

"No, no, no. This isn't right."

I tried my best to keep from rolling my eyes or letting out the frustrated sigh that had been building in my chest for the past three hours, creating a pressure like I was holding in a sneeze. This was all part of the job. The shitty part, of course, but luckily, I loved what I did, and ninety-seven percent of the time, the brides I worked with *weren't* egotistical bridezillas.

But Lexi Parsons fell in with that three percent, and she was driving me and my two best friends, Ryan and Tarryn, crazy.

Ryan and I had met on the first day of third grade. I'd been nervous about entering a new class and had kept to myself, trying to summon the courage to make friends when

Daniel Boyd, this doughy little jerk who was known to be a bully, started calling me ugly. Ryan had waited until recess, then punched him in his fat stomach so hard he barfed all over the see-saw. She might have gotten into trouble if she hadn't threatened to tell the rest of the kids in our class that he got beat up by a girl, a slight he had too much pride to admit. It was one of those bestie meet-cutes for the ages, and we'd been inseparable from that moment on.

Tarryn came into the picture our freshman year of college when she stumbled into our dorm room drunk off her ass after a welcome mixer, carrying an entire platter of magic brownies that she kindly offered to share. We'd spent the rest of that night forging an unbreakable bond by getting stoned while eating our body weight in choco-late, watching *Labyrinth* on Ryan's laptop, and bonding over the pure genius that was David Bowie. RIP.

Despite all odds, we'd managed to mature since those days and, a few years after graduating, had decided to start a business together. And much to the surprise of the rest of our graduating class, we were pretty damn good at it. Three's a Charm Events was a one-stop shop for all your wedding or party planning needs. We had a gift for making any bride-to-be's Pinterest board dreams come to life.

Ryan had always had a gift for things like spreadsheets and organization, and had developed a real hard-on for calendar apps, so it made sense that she handled the actual planning side of the business.

Growing up, photography had always been a bit of a hobby of mine. When I joined the yearbook in high school, that passion had grown, and I'd proudly announced I was going to college to become a professional photographer. My mom and dad had always been supportive, if not a bit more realistic than I was, so my dad had lovingly suggested that maybe a degree in business with a minor in photography would be a more stable choice. At the time I remember thinking they just didn't get it, but after one summer working at a portrait studio taking pictures of families in hideous matching sweaters and screaming toddlers who liked to bite, I decided maybe my dad had a point.

After graduating, I'd taken a desk job that offered decent pay and health insurance, thinking that was the grownup thing to do, but I had started to slowly wither away beneath those hideous flickering fluorescent lights like a houseplant deprived of sunlight. The cubicle life was *not* for me. I wasn't good at watercooler talk and couldn't stand the misogynistic undertones that were still a disappointing part of corporate America. That was abundantly clear when I told my boss off in front of everyone in my cubical pod for talking to my tits and calling me sweetheart and honey.

I ended up quitting before they could fire me, because *of course* the one with the vagina was the *hysterical* one who acted out of line. Not the perv with the wedding ring and a penchant for licking his lips in that skeevy way that made all women cringe.

Tarryn had been in a similar boat, and one random Wednesday night, over a couple bottles of wine between the three of us, Tarryn and I lamented our woes. We were deep into the second bottle when Ryan told us the idea she'd been bouncing around to start a business, and how she thought it was something the three of us could do together. I believed in the plan that we had come up with, and I knew I could mix my degree in business with my love for photography and create my dream job as the official photographer for Three's a Charm Events.

Tarryn's love for gardening had started back in college when she'd tried her hand at growing her own weed in her dorm room and she turned out to be pretty damn good at it. And though she used that skill as a way to make enough money by selling to undergrads that she never had to take out student loans, she didn't really have the temperament to become some sort of queenpin or criminal mastermind, so she shifted her focus to plants that wouldn't get her arrested. Now she was the in-house florist for the business.

We spent years nurturing our little company, caring and cultivating it until it blew up into something none of us had ever expected. Three's a Charm was *the* event planning company everyone in and around Pembrooke, Wyoming wanted to use. We were booked out months in advance and only taking referrals to keep things from getting out of hand. We'd expanded the business, hiring a receptionist and an assistant to handle the administrative tasks so we could focus on the events themselves.

Being our own bosses was the ultimate dream come true, and most mornings I woke up excited to go to work. Ninety-seven percent of the time.

"He needs to look at me more *adoringly*," Lexi stressed, her displeased gaze bouncing between me and her new husband. I wasn't sure the man was capable of looking at her any differently than he already was. From what I'd experienced during their engagement shoot and now today, he only had one facial expression—stoic. Or maybe it was constipated.

Either way, it was a look that went well with his total lack of personality. Even the man's voice was boring as hell, a monotone that made you struggle to stay awake when he spoke. If beige were a person, it would be this dude.

It had been like this since I arrived earlier to start taking photos of the bride and groom, along with their wedding party, preparing for the big day. In the bridal suite, I'd tried to get a few candid shots of Lexi and her friends getting ready, but she'd micromanaged the whole thing, from posing her bridesmaids to standing at my shoulder and instructing me on how to take photos of her maid of honor as she was getting her hair styled, talking about lighting and shadows like she knew better than I did, despite me being the professional photographer and her being a Pilates instructor.

Candid had quickly flown out the window, which was disappointing, because I knew most new brides would like to go back and look through those shots to see the genuine emotion on their faces. It was like a frame by frame of everything they were feeling in the moment. Instead, she'd have a bunch of tight-smiling friends and family and, at the end, one ill-planned Charlie's Angels pose—insisted upon by the bride, of course—that looked more awkward and cringey than fun.

I could already imagine the call I was going to get from her in a few weeks' time when I sent her the proofs. So any time she was preoccupied, I made sure to get better photos so I had a mix of what she wanted and what would end up looking best.

I held the camera up, the shutter clicking rapidly as I

took several more pictures than usual, hoping that would strengthen my odds of getting what she wanted. But I wasn't feeling confident. If Lexi wanted a man who stared at her adoringly, she shouldn't have married the human equivalent of soggy cardboard.

The guy hadn't shown any emotion during the ceremony, simply standing at the altar blank-faced, staring off into space before mumbling his vows after the officiant poked him in the arm to wake him from his trance.

I lowered the camera, forcing my lips to stretch into a smile. "I think we got it. These look great. Really, really great."

I heard a snort in the earpiece I was wearing to stay connected with Tarryn and Ryan. It was something we'd implemented early on when it became clear we needed to stay in constant communication during our events to ensure that things flowed smoothly and we didn't have to run all over the place looking for each other.

"Uh-oh," Tarryn said with a chuckle. "She said 'really, really great'. You know what that means."

The bride let out a derisive harumph as she headed in my direction. She pointed at my camera and wiggled her fingers at me. "Let me see that. I'm not sure I believe you."

"Keep your cool, Jo," Ryan warned into my ear. "You can't go off on the bride, even if we all want to. I've got you covered. Just give me a second before you go nuclear."

My back molars ground together, most likely making my smile look demented as I tightened my grip on the camera to keep her from snatching it out of my hands. That camera was my Precious, and I'd go Gollum on any bitch who tried to touch it. I would choose it over anyone. It cost more than my first car, and I would be damned if I let this chick get her grubby paws on it.

Just then, the DJ's voice sounded over the speakers that been strategically placed throughout the ballroom, tucked behind fake plants to keep them hidden from view. "Ladies and gentlemen, dinner is about to be served, so please make your way to your assigned tables."

"You're going to love these, I swear," I assured the bride, hoping to loosen the tension in her jaw, but also because it was the truth. I was damn good at my job, and I'd make these images shine if it took every last ounce of my talent. "Go. Enjoy your dinner."

The rest of the wedding party, clearly having had enough of their bossy friend, broke off from the group photos I'd been taking and headed toward the tables like cattle being called to feeding time, not that I'd blamed them. I'd seen Lexi smack a Tic Tac out of one of her bridesmaid's hands and yell at her for trying to eat before the ceremony. I was sure they were starving. Lexi had no choice but to grab her new husband's arm and pull him toward the rest of her guests.

I was grateful for the reprieve, no matter how small it was. I headed toward the reception area at a much slower pace, spotting Ryan standing at the DJ booth, ever-present clipboard in hand as she rattled off instructions.

"Thanks for the assist," I muttered so she could hear me through the earpiece. Her head turned in my direction, and she shot me a quick thumbs-up before getting back to work.

The woman was a machine. In all honesty, the main reason Three's a Charm was so successful was Ryan. She lived and breathed for our business and was the one who steered the ship, keeping the rest of us in line. She was the visionary. Not only was the company her idea, but it was also her creative genius that made the events we put on spectacular, which was why we were so damn popular in the first place.

Whatever gene made a person brilliant at their chosen profession, Ryan had two of them. She could envision things that would never cross my mind. She had single-handedly created some of the most beautiful weddings I'd seen and was the cause of countless happy brides all over.

I moved along the outskirts of the crowd, shooting

photos of people talking and laughing, capturing the excitement only a happy occasion such as a wedding could garner.

As much as I loved my job, being around so much love and romance on a regular basis stung a bit. It was a reminder that my own plans for my dream wedding and happily ever after had gone up in smoke.

Ever since I was a little girl, I'd been in love with the idea of love. I was that little girl forcing one of the boys in her kindergarten class to play the groom in her fake wedding, or wearing my mom's pretty scarf as a veil and a pair of her high heels as I pretended to walk down the aisle. I recited my wedding vows in front of the mirror while holding my collection of slap bracelets half curled as a bouquet.

I kept a scrapbook of cut-out magazine images of dresses and flowers and cakes. Hell, I'd been planning the day for as long as I could imagine. There was always a groom in those fantasies, of course. He just happened to be whatever celebrity I'd crushed on as a little girl, then, as I got older this dark-haired, well-built dude dressed in a tux who had no face.

At least that had been the case until Barrett Cohen.

On that thought, I shook off the melancholy that had slithered over me and got back to work.

By the time the limo took off with the happy couple

and the last of the guests staggered home, Ryan, Tarryn, and I were dead on our feet.

We sat at one of the empty tables as the crew moved around us, breaking everything down and converting the room back to its original state. It was tradition that, at the end of every wedding or event, we gave ourselves a few minutes to decompress and toasted with a shot of something eighty proof.

"Another one in the books, ladies," Ryan said, holding her shot glass up. "Not all of them can be easy, but we still managed to pull off a gorgeous wedding."

"Hell yeah, we did." I threw the shot back, wincing at the fiery path the liquor took down to my stomach.

"I mean, once we finally convinced her this place wouldn't allow live geese in the fountain in the lobby, no matter how special the bride thought she was," Tarryn added.

I shook my head, my shoulders slumping. "Are we even sure that groom was human? I'm pretty sure he was a robot."

Tarryn poked me in the arm on a laugh. "Pretty sure I saw him plugged into an outlet in the corner at one point. Must have needed to charge his batteries."

Ryan downed her shot and plunked the glass onto the table as she rose to her feet and stretched her back out. "Yeah, well, it's done, and so am I."

Tarryn and I stood as well, the three of us moving on autopilot through the ballroom and out into the fresh night air. "See you guys at the office tomorrow," she said as we broke off in the parking lot, heading in different directions.

"I'll bring coffee and donuts," I called out as I beeped the locks on my car.

Ryan nodded, looking as tired as I felt. "Sounds perfect. See you in the morning. Love you, crazies."

"Love you back." Tarryn and I chorused.

My heart felt a little lighter as I climbed into my car and started the engine. I might not have romance in my life, but I had my best friends and, for now, that was enough.

Chapter Two

Jolie

The soft glow of the lamp on my entryway table lit enough space for me to see as I dropped my keys in the bowl beside it and hung my purse and jacket on the hooks on the wall by the door.

The silence of the house was broken when my cat trudged over to greet me with a low, husky meow.

"Hey, Smoosh," I said as I bent down to pick up my little princess. She let out a contented purr as I nuzzled my face into her downy fur. When I decided a few months earlier maybe it was time for me to get a pet, I headed to the shelter thinking I'd get a cute little puppy. But the moment I set eyes on the gray and white Exotic Shorthair, I knew I'd found the one. I'd fallen in love with her smooshed in face and big yellow eyes and took her home with me that day. Since then she'd been the best companion. Affectionate without being clingy, she enjoyed her own space. Sure, she could be a bit of a diva at times, but I chalked that up to her being gorgeous and knowing it.

"Did you miss Mommy? I bet you did. I missed you too. I had to spend the evening with a bridezilla and her android husband when I would have much rather stayed home with you."

She began to squirm, her way of communicating I had reached my allotted thirty seconds of cuddles and it was time for me to put her down.

She trotted off to parts unknown as I headed in the opposite direction toward my bedroom. I was so tired, the fluffy white comforter and cozy down pillows of my bed were calling for me to flop down and not get up for at least twelve hours, but I knew better than to go to bed with my makeup on. Especially my 'event makeup' that was heavier and smokier than what I usually wore day to day.

Kicking off my heels, I picked them up and carried them to my closet, returning them to their rightful place on the shelf. The instant I opened the closet door, my gaze shot to the garment bag hanging in the very back corner. Usually I was able to forget it was there, but on nights like this one the wedding dress I never got to wear but couldn't bring myself to donate or sell had a habit of mocking me.

It was coming up on a year since Barrett ended our relationship and called off our wedding, and while the pain had dulled, the reminder of that humiliating time in my life still tended to crop up when I least expected it. That was the problem with dating someone who grew up in the same small town. They didn't just fall off the face of the earth after a breakup like you'd hope.

I'd known Barrett pretty much my whole life, but it wasn't until a year after I graduated from college and moved back home to Pembrooke that we got together. As a kid, he'd been painfully shy and awkward, this scrawny little thing with braces and acne-prone skin that other kids teased mercilessly. There were a few times I'd tried to initiate a conversation with him or include him in a game of kickball during recess, but he always ducked his head and ran off before I could get a full sentence out.

I felt really bad for him, and when I left for college, I remember thinking I hoped things got better for him. Then one day, years later, I was standing in the middle of the Drunken Moose, a popular bar and grill that had been lovingly shortened to *the Moose* by locals, waiting to pick up my to-go order when I felt a tap on my shoulder.

It had taken me several seconds to place the handsome man smiling down at me. His eyes finally garnered recognition. That tall, leanly-muscled, well-dressed man looked nothing like the shy wallflower I remembered from years earlier.

I smiled, giving him a hug and telling him how great it was to see him. He'd returned the sentiment before asking me out to dinner the following evening, and from that moment, we'd practically been inseparable. That had been the start of something magical.

I'd fallen head over heels for the funny, charming, still somewhat nerdy man, and for the first time, the groom in all my daydreams finally had a face and a name. I spent the next three years counting my lucky stars. I had the best friends a woman could ask for, a new business that was doing better than we ever could have imagined, and the man of my dreams.

Then it all got even better when he'd pulled out a beautiful solitaire diamond engagement ring one night and asked me to be his wife.

I spent the next year of my life pouring over that scrapbook I had kept since I was a little girl. With the help of Ryan and Tarryn, we'd planned my fairy-tale wedding. It was tricky, trying to figure out how to throw a wedding we were all in, but we were determined to make it work.

We were only a few weeks out from the big day

when Barrett informed me it wasn't what he wanted. Or more to the point, *I* wasn't what he wanted.

Now, I know people say there had to have been warning signs, but if there had been, I was clueless to them. I genuinely thought we were happy and were going to build a beautiful life together. There was no lull in the bedroom, no lack of conversation. We weren't living two separate lives that happened to take place under the same roof. We were both in, one hundred percent—at least as far as I knew. So it went without saying I'd been crushed when he came home one night and informed me it was over. Just like that.

He packed his things like he hadn't just reached into my chest and ripped out my still-beating heart. Then, as he started for the door, suitcases in hand, the son of a bitch actually had the audacity to look back and inform me that he'd grab my engagement ring with the rest of his stuff later in the week. Something inside me had shriveled and died when he said that.

I'd loved that ring. I thought I would wear it for the rest of my life, or at least until one of the kids we were supposed to have had asked to have it for their partner. I'd always romanticized the idea of passing my wedding ring down and having it go from generation to generation.

Instead, after a call to my girls when I told them the

whole ugly story, we'd loaded up in Tarryn's car and headed out to Pembrooke Lake. We sat on the shoreline, a bottle of vodka passed around, and as the sun sank low, dipping behind the jagged ridges of the mountains that surrounded the lake, I stood up and headed for the water. As soon as it was lapping at my toes, I slipped the ring off my finger and launched it as far as I could, sending a rather loud *"fuck you"* into the air for Barrett as it plunked into the water and sunk down to the dark depths.

Ryan and Tarryn had hooted and cheered behind me, chanting my name like I'd just sent a baseball sailing right out of the stadium for a World Series winning home run.

It had been a bonding moment for all of us, as well as a cathartic release for me. And the amount of joy I got at seeing the anger on Barrett's face when I told him he'd have to fish his precious ring out of the goddamn lake if he wanted it so badly had been priceless.

I buried myself in work in an effort to forget, but that was easier said than done, given what I did for a living. It hadn't helped when, only a couple weeks after he dumped me, he'd been spotted in town with Leighton Cavanaugh on his arm. Pembrooke's very own resident mean girl. She'd been a self-centered, spoiled little brat in high school, grasping hold of her popularity by using fear over kindness, and she hadn't gotten much better the older we got. She was still a grade-A bitch with a streak of entitlement that ran miles long.

When I found out he'd moved on to her before the body of our dead relationship was even cold and in the ground, I might have had a little purging party in which I created a playlist of Taylor Swift revenge songs while drinking wine and burning the rest of the shit he left behind.

Flipping off the light in my closet, I shut the door firmly and headed for the bathroom. Once my skin was freshly cleansed and moisturized to a dewy glow, I slipped out of the skirt and blouse I'd been wearing all day and into my comfy sleep shorts and a matching tank before climbing into bed.

Just as I leaned over to flip the lamp off, my phone pinged with a text alert. With a furrowed brow, I grabbed it off the nightstand and saw a text waiting from my sister-in-law.

Charlotte: *You awake?*

I checked the time before replying back.

Me: *Just got home from a wedding. Better question is why are you awake?*

Charlotte and my older brother, Dalton, lived halfway across the country in a small town in Virginia called Hope Valley. I missed my big brother like crazy.

Fortunately, I got to see him at least twice a year, once when I would visit them in Hope Valley, and once when they came to Pembrooke. However, Charlotte was extremely pregnant at the moment, so travel was out of the question for her, a bummer because she was the best sister-in-law a chick could ask for. In fact, most days I was sure I liked her more than I liked my own brother. Needless to say, Dalton had seriously lucked out when he landed her.

The moment the message showed as read, my phone sounded with an incoming FaceTime call. Charlotte's face appeared on the screen as soon as I answered, her smile so big it was pulling at her cheeks as she waved wildly.

"Oh my god, I miss your face so freaking much!" she exclaimed.

I let out a little laugh and propped myself up against the headboard. "I miss you too, crazy. Why are you awake right now? Isn't it like, two in the morning over there?"

She blew out a raspberry and crossed her eyes exaggeratedly. "Yeah, but this little one has decided it's time to do a clog dance all over my bladder," she explained as she caressed her swollen baby bump that was even bigger than the last time we FaceTimed. "So I decided to skip sleep and make myself an ice cream sundae instead." She waggled her eyebrows and shoved a heaping spoonful of ice cream with all the fixings into her mouth.

I smiled, the bleak mood brought on by my wedding dress gone thanks to one phone call from my sister-in-law. "I take it Dalton's asleep?"

She licked her spoon clean before answering. "Yeah, I figured I'd give him the benefit of sleep since I'm going to put him to work later when I make him paint the nursery."

My head fell back on a deep belly laugh. "Didn't you finish the nursery last week?"

Her nose scrunched up adorably. "Yeah, but when I walked in earlier today I decided I hated the color. I think I'm nesting, and I can't do that in a room with pale yellow walls." Her expression turned thoughtful. "I'm feeling a really soft sage green. What do you think?"

I shook my head as my shoulders shook with silent laughter. "I think Dalton's head is going to explode, but what Mama wants, Mama gets."

"Exactly." She narrowed her eyes and pointed at me through the screen of my phone. "See, I always knew you were the smarter Prescott sibling."

"Thank you for noticing," I said with a tiny bow.

My brother's gruff, sleep-raspy voice carried through the speaker. "Jesus, do you have any clue what time it is?" A second later, his shirtless form popped on the screen over her shoulder, his overly-long hair a mess and his beard flat on one side from where he'd been sleeping on it.

"Ugh, gross! Put on some clothes before I go blind!"

His deep chuckle resonated through the air and a sharp pain shot through my chest. Man, I missed him. I missed them both, but I had a special bond with my big brother, in spite of the distance separating us.

I had hoped when he retired from the military he'd come home, but through some of his connections, he ended up getting a job as a certified badass for a company called Alpha Omega. It was through that job he'd met Charlotte. She'd been a confidential informant on a case dealing with police corruption, drugs, and murder. Dalton had been tasked with protecting her when the shit hit the fan. Charlotte had been the one to fight the draw, but my brother was a smart man. He knew what he wanted, and he went for it, full-tilt. It was something right out of a movie or romance novel.

"Good to see you too, little sis. But is there a reason you're keeping my pregnant wife up so late?"

I placed a hand on my chest in feigned offense. "Hey, this wasn't my fault. It was *your wife* who started blowing up my phone."

The look he gave Charlotte created an uncomfortable knot it my chest. Concern marred his brow, pulling at the center of his forehead, but there was also adoration shining in his eyes. It was how he'd been looking at Charlotte from the very beginning, and the reason I'd pushed so hard for them to get together the first time I met her. He cherished her. It was written all over his face.

It was just another reminder of how stupid I'd been to think that what I had with Barrett was forever, because I couldn't remember him ever looking at me the way my big brother looked at his wife.

Like she was the meaning for his very existence.

"The little one keeping you up, baby?"

I watched in fascination as her features went soft. She brought her hand up to give his beard an affectionate scratch. "It's all right, Cowboy. I was having an ice cream craving anyway." She lifted her spoon with the other hand, but before she could tuck it into her mouth, Dalton leaned forward and stole the bite for himself.

Just like that, the tenderness in her expression was gone. For such a tiny little thing, my sister-in-law could be fierce as hell, and the death glare she shot him was enough to send any other man scurrying. "You keep stealing my ice cream and you'll be sleeping on the couch for the rest of this pregnancy," she warned, making me laugh.

"I'd take that threat to heart," I said through a big smile. "I'm pretty certain she means it."

Dalton shot me a wink. "Please, my wife is obsessed with me. She can't get enough."

My eyes stopped mid-roll when a jaw-cracking yawn forced its way out of my mouth. "As much as I love watching you guys argue, I need to get to sleep. The wedding tonight kicked my ass, and I still have to go into the office tomorrow."

Charlotte's bottom lip jutted out in a pout. "Fine," she huffed. "I guess I'll let you go. I just miss you like crazy."

"That makes two of us," Dalton added. "You need to get your ass to Hope Valley for a visit, little sis. It's been too long."

I smiled huge, warmth spreading through my chest. My romantic relationship might have gone up in a burst of flames, but I still had more love that I could possibly ask for. My support system was mighty.

"I miss you guys too. You know how it is during wedding season, though. We're slammed right now, but I'll be there when that little nugget is born, I promise."

My brother hit me with a stern look. "You better."

I drew an X on my chest over my heart. "Cross my heart. You know I wouldn't miss it. I need to solidify my place as the favorite immediately."

It might have just been my brother and me, but Dalton and Charlotte's circle of friends and loved ones in Hope Valley was huge, not to mention Charlotte's twin sister. I had a ridiculous amount of aunts and uncles to contend with, and I refused to be shoved to the back burner just because I lived half a continent away.

"I love you guys. Talk soon."

"Love you back," Charlotte said enthusiastically.

"Love you, sis," Dalton added.

I tapped the screen, ending the call, and dropped the phone back onto my nightstand before flipping off the light.

I might have been exhausted, but that call with my family had been good for my heart.

Chapter Three

Vaughn

I stood in front of the large picture windows in the living room. My hands were tucked in the pockets of my slacks, my jacket unbuttoned. It was basically the most casual I ever got, at least that used to be the case. I was sure that would change, just like everything else in my world had lately.

The spotless glass overlooked a pristine lake tucked into the valley and surrounded on all sides by the foothills and jagged mountains that made up Pembrooke.

The house was large for only one person, almost obscenely so. Every appliance, every finish from the light fixtures to the cabinet handles, were top of the line. The state-of-the-art ZLine with seven burners, a porcelain cooktop, and Italian hinges would be any professional chef's dream. But the odds I'd ever touch the damn thing were slim to none.

The home was built to resemble a large cabin built of glass and wood and dripping with luxury. It would be most people's dream home, yet for me, it was just another investment. One I'd live in, but an investment all the same. I could have rented or stayed in a motel, saving myself the seven figures this place was going to cost me, but the idea of living right on top of other people, no matter how temporary, set my teeth on edge. This worked best for me. It might not have been my forever home, but once I was finished here, I'd find a way to make money off it. That was what I did.

As I stared out at the view that would have undoubtedly moved most other people who didn't see things in the concept of dollar signs such as I did, the realtor's voice finally came back into focus.

"As you can see, the view from every room in the house is stunning. You won't find panoramic views like this anywhere else around town."

That was just one of the reasons the price tag on this house was so ridiculous. The community it had been built in was small, boasting its exclusivity with only seven of these McMansions that lorded over the small, quaint town below.

Most of the other houses were owned by people who

chose Pembrooke as their vacation spot, not their forever home. They either came here in the winter to ski or in the fall to see the leaves turn before returning to whatever city they called home. I would be the only resident of this tiny neighborhood who lived here full-time. That was the real selling point for this place—the solitude.

I wasn't exactly a fan of people, so living up on the mountain, twenty minutes outside of town, without a single neighbor to bother me, sounded like heaven.

A dislike of neighbors was why my last residence was in a penthouse apartment in Denver.

I let out an annoyed sigh as the realtor kept going on. It wasn't her fault I was so short of patience, of course. But every single one of my days was packed from the moment I woke up until I went to bed. There were no such things as breaks or vacation days in my world; it was how I preferred things and also the reason I managed to become a millionaire before the age of forty. So having to listen to her give her standard pitch was burning precious time I didn't have to waste. Also, I wasn't exactly known for having much of a poker face when it came to my moods, which worked fine for me, since being an asshole generally kept people away.

"Of course, I have several other listings for you to consider. If this isn't what you're looking for, we can try somewhere closer to town. I'm confident we can find you—"

I held my hand up to cut her off. "This is fine. I'll take it."

She sputtered for a few seconds. "You'll take it? But—Mr. Cavanaugh, this is only the first house I've shown you. Wouldn't you like to see other properties?"

Not particularly. Dragging this process out any longer actually sounded like my nightmare. And anything closer to town—to people—was out of the question. It was bad enough I'd chosen to disrupt my entire life this way. It felt like I'd shoved a stick into the spokes of a rapidly spinning wheel for the hell of it, and now I was dealing with that inevitable crash that came afterward. To say I didn't like change was a massive understatement. I preferred routine and liked to know what was coming from one moment to the next. However one phone call from my dad, telling me he was sick, had shoved my carefully curated world off-kilter. If I was going to stay here, I was going to need my privacy.

I would be here for my father in the ways I knew how. I'd granted his request to reconnect. But I drew the line at actually being a member of the community. Even if I had been once before. That was a long time ago, and I wasn't looking to reflect on the past.

No thanks.

"That won't be necessary. Just write up the contract offering asking price. I'd prefer to close as soon as possible."

Her mouth opened and closed like a goldfish several times as she tried to process what I'd just said. "I—Okay!" she finally said enthusiastically, barely able to contain her excitement for the fat commission she was about to make. "That's—I'll get right on that."

I let out a grunt, bypassing her extended hand on my way to the door. I wasn't one for pleasantries. I had things to do, so I didn't see the need to stick around for a bit of small talk with a person I didn't know the first thing about.

I headed for my Mercedes G-Wagon parked right by the front door in the large half-circle driveway, climbed in, and started it. I caught a glimpse of my realtor from the corner of my eye as she stepped out of the house, her hand in the air, mid-wave, but I was already driving past, my mind already occupied with the laundry list of things I had to get done.

As if she sensed it was the most inconvenient time possible, my dash lit up with my mother's name as the ringing of my cellphone connected to the car's Bluetooth echoed through the speakers.

I didn't have time for her particular brand of shit, but I knew if I didn't answer, she'd keep calling until I couldn't stand it any longer and finally picked up. Best to get it over with.

I hit the button on my steering wheel to connect the call. "Mother," I said in a flat voice, using the only moniker she deemed acceptable.

Estelle Cavanaugh didn't tolerate casual endearments such as Mom. It was Mother or nothing.

"Please tell me you've come to your senses and left that podunk town in your rearview mirror."

If there was any question as to why I was the way I was, all a person needed to do was look to Mommy Dearest for the answer. If I was cold and unfeeling, my mother had a block of ice where her heart should have been. She survived solely on logic and common sense and didn't have time for such things as emotions. It was one of the reasons her marriage with my father hadn't lasted.

Where Estelle was an emotionless robot, Hershel Cavanaugh was all heart. Detrimentally so, in some cases.

The two of them had grown up here, but my mother always had aspirations of getting out. Honestly, if it hadn't been for the fact that my mother had accidentally gotten pregnant, they probably wouldn't have lasted as long as they did. My father had loved my mom in spite of her lack of empathy and overall caring, while she'd simply tolerated him until, one day, she couldn't any longer.

I was seven when my mother informed my father she couldn't pretend to love him any longer. She sat me down and explained the situation in that succinct, clinical manner of hers that would have confused most other kids, but I was used to it by then, and asked me who I wanted to live with. Even at such a young age, I already knew my tender-hearted father needed me more, so I chose to stay with him.

He was a good dad, I had to give it to him. He tried his hardest. He'd always done what he thought was best for me, but my mother came calling when I was thirteen years old and informed him it was time for me to come live with her because he was making me too soft—her words—and he hadn't the means to fight her on it, especially since he'd already remarried and had another child by then. While he'd chosen to live a normal life most people could be happy with, albeit, paycheck to paycheck, my mother had spent the years away building her empire, and her legal team would have cut my poor dad off at the knees.

So once again, my world had been rocked.

I didn't bother letting my annoyance show. It wasn't as if Estelle would care. "You already know the answer to that question, so I don't know why you bothered asking."

"You're wasting your life away in that place," she insisted for the millionth time since I'd informed her of my plan to relocate to Pembrooke in order to help care for my father and get him back on his feet.

"You act as if everything is on hold. That's not the case. All the work I do can be handled remotely. The only thing that's changed is my address, and that's temporary."

Her harrumph of displeasure filled the car. "Until you get sucked in and find yourself stuck."

I shook my head in exasperation. I always knew my mother's heart was callused, but there had been a part of me that thought maybe, deep, *deep*, down, a hint of feeling was still in that useless organ in her chest. I guess I had been wrong.

"He's sick, Mother. I know you hated this town and might not have been in love with him, but I thought you'd manage at least a bit of compassion for the man you were married to and had a child with."

"It's not like he's dying. He'll be fine. Eventually."

A bark of derisive laughter scraped its way up my throat. It was a wonder I was a functioning member of society at all, given the cyborg who raised me. "I wonder if you'd be so blasé if the shoe were on the other foot and *you* were the one diagnosed with cancer."

I imagined her face right then, her skin smooth as glass, not a wrinkle in sight, because her lack of all emotion prevented any expression from crossing her face other than boredom.

"I'm just saying, Vaughn, you have a company to run and responsibilities in Denver. It isn't like Hershel is on his own. He started a whole other family."

It wasn't the first time she'd made a snide remark regarding my father remarrying and having a second kid. Only she made it seem as though he'd abandoned his original family in order to start a new one, all but throwing me over for his new daughter. That hadn't been the case at all, but I'd been young and impressionable, and I'd let her words form a kind of scar tissue over my heart that began to harden it, especially toward my dad.

It had taken me years to realize it had been a manipulation on her part, but by that point, the damage had been done. I was an adult with a very busy life of my own. The strained relationship I had with my father was something I pushed to the back burner, forgetting most days in my pursuit of money and power.

At least until that phone call a few weeks ago.

Finding out he was sick had . . . changed things. It

refused to stay on the back burner any longer. I couldn't compartmentalize our relationship like I had before, and to my surprise, a bit of that calcified hardness around my heart chipped away.

I didn't have the desire to get into this with her, not again, so instead of arguing, I asked, "Is there something else you needed, Mother, or were you just calling again to bitch about the fact I didn't do what you wanted?"

"Language," she clipped through the car's speakers. It was downright laughable how she thought she had a leg to stand on to scold me on the language I used. Even after she'd all but ripped me from my father's house, she hadn't done much mothering. She was too busy working and networking to spare me the time. From thirteen until I moved away for college at eighteen, I'd basically been taking care of myself.

I never understood why she fought to get me back, let alone went through with the pregnancy in the first place. There wasn't a maternal bone in that woman's body.

"As always, Mother, it's been a pleasure talking to you, but I have to go. I'll look forward to your next lecture in a few months' time."

With that, I disconnected the call and let out a heavy sigh. Then for the millionth time in the past few weeks, I questioned what the hell I'd gotten myself into.

Chapter Four

Jolie

I took back every kind, loving, adoring word I'd ever said about Smoosh. *I took it all back.* She wasn't a sweet, perfect cat. She was the fucking devil.

My yellow rubber kitchen gloves were shredded into ribbons, the tattered pieces hanging down my forearms in ruins. I suppose it was my fault. I should have known the material wouldn't hold up against her claws, but I hadn't expected her to lose her ever-loving mind and turn into a psychopath at the sight of her kitty carrier.

Until a handful of minutes ago, I had no idea that cats could actually scream. Now I did, and it was a sound that would haunt my dreams for the rest of my life.

My arms stung, the ribbons of razor-thin claw marks

stretching up from wrist to elbow, beading with ruby-colored blood as I slowly crept around the back of my couch on my tiptoes. I did my best to keep my voice low and calm, crooning gently in an effort to calm her down. "It's okay, Smooshy. It's okay."

The low, menacing rumble she made caused the tiny hairs on my arms and legs to stand up.

"It's not the end of the world. It's a checkup."

She hissed, sending a shiver down my back as I imagined the evil cat from *Pet Sematary*. I'd been way too damn young to watch that movie, but when my mom had warned me against it—rightfully so, since I was a gigantic baby when it came to scary movies—my rebellious streak had kicked into overdrive, like it always did. Of course I'd snuck to watch it, and of course, it had given me nightmares for weeks. And thanks to my once-beloved cat giving me that creepy reminder, it was pretty much guaranteed I'd be sleeping with the lights on tonight.

I slowly lowered myself onto all fours, my heart beating like crazy as I sank down to peek under the couch, silently praying that Smoosh wouldn't lunge from underneath and claw my face off. Her big yellow eyes blinked at me from the shadows. Yep, just like the scary movie.

This was my nightmare.

"The carrier isn't going to hurt you," I insisted, reasoning with the unreasonable. "It's to keep you safe. And the vet is super nice." She made that terrifying rumble again. I tried smiling, not that it would do any damn good. "If you're a good girl and stop hurting Mommy, I'll give you a treat. How does that sound?"

Apparently, it sounded like bullshit to her, because when I tentatively reached out, she batted at my hand, wolverine claws engaged. The furry little asshole.

"Ooh! You little—" I cut myself off, reining in my temper before I could say something I wouldn't be able to take back. Part of me was convinced that Smoosh could understand most of what I was saying, and in spite of the physical pain she'd exacted, I didn't want to hurt her little feline feelings.

God, I was ridiculous.

"That's it. No treats for a week. And you only have yourself to blame, missy. This behavior is totally uncalled for."

Just then, a brisk knock sounded on my front door. I knew who it was without having to look, and as the knob turned, I could see everything happening in slow motion in my head, like a flip book telling me what was about to happen, but there wasn't enough time to stop it.

The door opened on the sound of Tarryn's voice.

"Hey, lady. I got your text. You need help with the little furball?"

I shot up from my place on the floor between the couch and the coffee table, my hair whipping above me. "Close the door!" I shouted, but it was too late.

As if sensing her freedom from the cat carrier, Smoosh ran so fast she was little more than a streak of gray and white lightning on her way out the front door.

"What the—?" Tarryn stumbled back at the scream my cat emitted on her way to freedom. It was the same scream she'd used when she'd clawed my arms and gloves to shit when I tried to shove her ass into the carrier.

"Catch her!" I nearly collided with my friend on my way out of the house, panic gripping my chest in a tight fist. There was no way in hell I was going to catch Smoosh with how fast she was running . . . straight toward the road . . . that cars were actively driving down.

"Smooshface Prescott," I called out as sternly as I could, using her full name the very way my own mother used mine whenever I screwed up royally. "You get your fluffy ass back here right this instant!"

Any hope I had of that working went right out the window as she darted across the front lawn, getting closer to the street just as a big, black, Mercedes G-

Wagon came around the corner, the shiny, impeccably clean paint job shimmering under the sun.

"Shit," I breathed as my heart dropped right into my butt. "Shit, shit, shit!" I waved my arms frantically, praying to catch the driver's attention, but they didn't appear to be slowing down at all. In fact, I was pretty sure they were going faster than the speed limit as it was.

"Hey! Slow the hell down!" I shouted at the top of my lungs, the air sawing in and out of my chest almost painfully as I imagined the very worst. "Smoosh, get out of the road!"

I let out a started yelp as my cat darted right into the middle of the blacktop and froze like a deer in the freaking headlights in front of the massive car. The sound of brakes squealing filled the air as my heels dug into the ground, stopping me short as I slapped my hands over my eyes. I couldn't watch my poor little baby get flattened like a pancake.

A tiny scream erupted from my throat as everything went silent. I wasn't sure what I was supposed to hear, but the only sound was my own heart whomping in my ears for what felt like an eternity before I heard a deep, bewildered, pissed-off voice barking, *"What the fuck?"*

My hands fell from my face, and the first emotion to run through me was relief that my cat wasn't lying dead in the middle of the road. Instead, it looked like she'd climbed the man from the G-Wagon like he was a tree and was currently clinging to his shoulders like a koala.

The second thing that struck me was: *hot dayum*, but that's one sexy hunk of man.

Vaughn

In what had been a series of shitty days since my relocation to Pembrooke, Wyoming, this one was turning out to be at the very top of that shitty heap. You know those days where you wake up and nothing seems to go right? That was the day I was having, and it all started when I woke up at five o'clock this morning, thirty minutes after I was supposed to be out of bed.

Waking up every morning at four thirty was the only way I could guarantee I'd have time to get in a workout before my day officially started. If I wasn't up before the sun, I was already late. However, the storm that went through some time in the night while I was sleeping had apparently knocked out the power, knocking out my alarm clock.

It was my internal alarm that had me shooting up from a deep sleep at five, but without time to hit my home gym, I already felt like I was starting the day off on the wrong foot, which set the tone for the hours to come.

I had a day full of conference calls and Zoom meetings, so after a scalding shower to wash the cobwebs left from a jarring wake-up, I moved to the closet and donned one of my suits. At thirty-eight, I should have been sick and tired of the routine of twisting a tie into a perfect Windsor knot and slipping monogrammed cufflinks into my cuffs morning after morning, but dressing for business every single day was something I was used to.

My mother liked to tote me around from time to time when she felt the need to play the strong, successful single mother, and during those times, a suit and tie were a requirement. Just as they were with the private schools I'd been forced to attend since leaving Pembrooke. At thirteen—hell, even at fourteen and fifteen, those suits had been my goddamn nightmare, but I eventually became accustomed, and now they were like a second skin.

I donned the expensive Italian fabrics that had been tailored to my body's specifications like armor. Each business day was like a battle, and I went in prepared.

However, when I headed into the kitchen for a cup

of coffee, I discovered not only did the expensive-as-hell coffee maker get knocked out with the power, but a surge had seemed to fry it, because the son of a bitch refused to turn on.

A man could go into battle with his armor on, but if he didn't have a necessary weapon, it was useless. I somehow managed to slug my way through my first call without the aid of caffeine, but that was the extent of my brain function.

Desperate times called for desperate measures, so I called my assistant, who was still back in Denver, and had her push my next video conference by an hour so I could run to town for a cup of coffee. As I guided my car through the sloping backroads that led from my house to the town below, I questioned my need for solitude for the very first time.

At least in my penthouse I could have used an app to get something delivered, but, even though Pembrooke was caught up on recent technology enough to offer DoorDash and Postmates, I lived too far out for anyone to make the drive.

I'd hired a service to come in and stock my fridge and pantry with food and paid a chef to meal prep every Sunday, so as I drove down the main drag of downtown Pembrooke, I was seeing it all for the first time in more than two decades. What struck me hardest was just how familiar it still felt. Memories started flooding my brain like a dam had just busted.

The corner store and barber shop directly across the street from the salon were just as they'd been when I was a boy.

The Drunken Moose was right where it had been when I was a kid and my dad would take me there once a week to eat wings and watch whatever game they had playing on the television. He called those evenings our *guy time*, and kept them up even after he remarried and my stepmother had my half-sister.

Until I saw that familiar sign, I'd forgotten all about those evenings.

Guilt shot straight through my chest like a bullet piercing my skin.

How could I have forgotten about them?

I shook off the shame that coated my skin like a clammy sweat and guided my car through the streets that'd been locked in time, preserved for the past twenty-five years. This wasn't the type of town to have a Starbucks on every corner or a big-box store where you could stop to get anything from groceries to clothes to a new set of tire chains. The people here liked things at a much slower pace. It was one of the reasons my mother hated it.

Sinful Sweets had been one of my favorite places

back in the day, having served the best cupcakes and sweets a kid could want, and I recalled every time my father brought me in for a treat, he'd get himself a cup of coffee.

The bakery was still there, only now it was even bigger and had been retitled to Sinful Sweets Café. As soon as I pushed through the heavy glass doors, I recognized the old mixed in with some new. The shop hadn't been redone so much as expanded. On one side was the familiar bakery and coffee shop, while the other side had the café with a kitchen and seating for eat-in dining.

It was barely seven in the morning, and already, both sides were quickly filling to the point discomfort had my skin tightening over my bones and muscles. I needed to get my coffee and get the hell out of there, so I moved toward the bakery side and joined the line that had already formed.

Just then, the door behind the front counter swung open and the redheaded woman who moved through was one I would have recognized anywhere—mainly because I'd had a crush on her from the time I was old enough to appreciate women until the day I was forced to leave. Chloe Delaney had run this place for as long as I could remember, and if I liked people, I might have said it was nice to see she was still at it.

I moved to the counter when it was my turn,

ordering a large black coffee from the woman I used to have a crush on, and noticed her smile was still as bright; she was still a knockout, even all these years later.

My muscles tightened as recognition sparked in her eyes. Her gaze narrowed on me as she slid my coffee across the counter. "I'm sorry. Do I know you?" she asked, clearly trying to place me.

If I'd been a nice person, I would have reminded her of who I was. Instead, I dropped my change in the tip jar and took a step back. "Don't think so," I lied, holding up my cup. "Thanks for the coffee." I turned on the heel of my leather Ferragamos and headed out the way I came, ignoring the curious looks from the people around me. It had been a while, but I knew all too well that nosiness was a small-town thing. I was the mysterious new guy they'd never seen, and I was sure it was only a matter of time before tongues started wagging.

I climbed into my car without sparing a look to a single person and started back toward my house with barely a free minute to spare before my next meeting.

I'd brought the cup to my lips, taking the first sip of coffee that was a hundred times better than I'd expected it to be, when all of a sudden, something darted out into the road.

I slammed on my brakes with a curse, sending the coffee flying, the scalding hot liquid spilling down the front of my crisp white shirt and into my lap, the heat of it peeling layers of skin off with it.

"Fuck, fuck, *fuck!*" I shouted, gripping the wheel with both hands as I whipped the car to a stop and threw it into park before shoving the door open, all while trying to pull the fabric of my shirt away from my skin to keep it from causing any more damage.

I made the mistake of climbing out, and shit went from bad to worse.

"*What the fuck?*" I managed to shout just before I was attacked.

Chapter Five

Jolie

It took me a moment to rip my focus off the man and all of his . . . man-ness, because there was a *lot* of it. Something hit me just then, like an elbow right to the gut. That faceless figure I had been imagining as my groom for years had been big—not just tall, but broad—and he'd had thick, dark hair.

Barrett had been tall, but that was where the features he'd shared with my faceless apparition had ended. He was lean, more like a swimmer or a runner, and his hair was light brown. But this man . . . well, he looked like he was built to pick women up and throw them over his incredibly impressive shoulders for a living. Where Barrett's hair had been the color of toffee, this man's was the color of a full, rich espresso, and looked thick enough for a woman to really grip while he went downtown. And *damn*, but the dude could wear a suit.

Oh shit! A suit that Smoosh was currently clinging to for dear life with those razor claws of hers.

"Shit, shit, shit," I panted as I closed the distance between me and the stranger, who was batting at my cat like she was attacking him. Meanwhile, she was wrapped around his shoulders and face like a cat-fur scarf. "I'm so sorry," I cried once I reached them.

"Get it off!" His voice was muffled beneath Smoosh's considerable fur. It might have been short, but it was thick as hell, and it looked like she was trying to suffocate the poor guy. "Getitoff, *getitoff*!"

I was trying, really, but the man's flailing was making it difficult. "Smoosh, bad!" I scolded, reaching up and grabbing her around the middle. I gave her a tug, earning another one of those death screams as she dug her claws into his suit even deeper. Given my job, I'd seen my fair share of tuxes and suits, and I knew how to spot expensive fabric and high quality from a mile away, and the one this guy was wearing—that Smoosh was currently destroying—probably cost double my monthly mortgage payment.

That sound must have freaked the man out as much as it did me, because his flailing became more frantic. "What the hell is that?" I couldn't see his face, thanks to my cat, but I could hear the panic in his voice. "Is this thing about to kill me? It's trying to kill me, isn't it?"

I tugged again, but the dude was so tall, it was difficult to get a good hold on her. "Just be still. And maybe crouch down for me. That's it. A little lower," I guided when he bent his knees so we were face to face—or face to cat fluff.

I wrapped an arm around her middle and really pulled. "Ah, fucking *fuck*! It's clawing the shit out of me! Get it off, goddamn it!"

"I'm sorry. I'm sorry! Just hold on. I've got her." Holding Smoosh by the middle with one arm, I used my hand to pry her claws out of the man's wide shoulders. "Almost got her . . . *there*!" I let out a breath of relief once I managed to extract Smoosh's claws from the expensive material and curled her up to my chest.

Just then, Tarryn came running up, the cat carrier swinging wildly from the handle she was gripping. "I got this!" she exclaimed proudly, hoisting the plastic bin that had caused all the problems to begin with. "Holy crap! That was insane! Your cat's totally nuts, babe."

From the sounds she was making, I knew Smoosh was gearing up for another meltdown, and I didn't want to risk her getting free again. "Hurry up. Open the door!"

She flung it open, and I shoved the feline in, despite

her wailing, slamming the door closed and latching it on a relieved breath. "Thank God that's over," I started as I turned back to the man, able to see his face for the first time. "I'm so so—" The apology died on my tongue, because holy chiseled perfection, Batman! This dude didn't just have a body of sin packed into an expensive suit. He was freaking *gorgeous*.

His features were sharp and masculine, from his high, cut cheekbones to the straight ridge of his nose to a jaw that looked like it had been carved from marble. But his eyes hit me dead center in the chest and stole all the air right out of my lungs. I'd never seen eyes like his before. They weren't blue or brown, but an insane combination of both, somehow. The color around the pupil was a gorgeous blue that reminded me of the clear turquoise waters of the Caribbean ocean, but the iris was rimmed with a band of burnt umber. His eyes reminded me of oxidized copper, trailing from dark to light, and were so unique, that even the rage in them just then didn't detract from their beauty.

I shook myself out of my stupor and cleared my throat before trying again. "I'm really sorry about my cat messing up your suit, but thank you so much for stopping. I don't know what I would have done if something happened to her."

Unfortunately, when he opened his mouth and

spoke, all that awe-inspiring beauty was clubbed to death like a caveman going to town on a woolly mammoth.

"I'll tell you what would happen. The world would be a better place for it. That feral creature needs to be put down," he declared, lips curled back from his teeth as he brushed fruitlessly at the front of his clothes—like brushing the cat hair off would undo the damage her claws or, what looked like an entire cup of coffee, had already done. "Do you have any clue how much this suit cost?"

"Uh . . ." I'd forgotten all about Tarryn standing there until that moment. She cleared her throat uncomfortably and reached to take the carrier from my hand. "I'll just go put this little hellion in your car."

I offered her a grateful smile over my shoulder before turning back to the six-foot-three wall of muscle and pissed-off energy standing in the middle of the road with me.

I curled my lips between my teeth to keep my snippy retort at bay. "I don't suppose offering to pay for dry cleaning would make the situation any better?"

His nostrils flared on an exhale, reminding me a lot of an angry bull. An angry bull that just so happened to have the prettiest eyes I'd ever seen. "You really think dry cleaning is going to be able to fix *this*?" He waved his hands down his front.

"In my defense—or, well, my cat's defense—we didn't do the coffee."

I could have sworn I heard a low growl from deep in his chest. "I spilled the coffee all over myself when I had to slam on the brakes to avoid hitting that menace to society over there!"

I slammed my hands on my hips indignantly. "Hey! Don't call her that. It was an honest accident. She was just scared about going to the vet and tried to make a break for it."

His eyelids narrowed, and a voice in the back of my head started chanting, *warning. Warning.* Something told me this wasn't the kind of dude you wanted to get into a shouting match with, but I'd be damned if I let him insult my cat. I was the only one who got to do that.

"Or maybe it just realized it was living with a bad pet owner and realized it would be better off on its own."

Oh no he didn't. I sucked in a huge gasp of affront. "Excuse you? I'll have you know, I'm a *great* pet owner."

He crossed his arms over his chest, and even through all the layers, there was no way to miss the noticeable bulge of his biceps. The man was seriously jacked. *Gah!* Why were all the gorgeous ones the absolute worst?

"Is that what you call letting your psychotic cat get loose, run into traffic, nearly cause an accident, then destroy thousands of dollars of Italian wool?"

"I said I was sorry!" I exclaimed. "And if it makes you feel better, I'll even get your stupid car detailed." I crossed my own arms, mimicking his stance and narrowing my eyes in a vicious glare. It was one thing to insult Smoosh. Okay, I got it. She went a little bananas. But it was a whole other can of worms to accuse me of being a crappy cat mom. I was *fantastic*, thank you very much. "Besides, the only reason she climbed you the way she did was because she felt safe with you. She's not really a people person, so the fact she wouldn't let you go obviously means she liked you." Not that I could understand why. The guy was being completely unreasonable.

"Well, the feeling's definitely not mutual."

As if she heard this jackwad, Smoosh let out another one of her screams that made my molars clamp together.

"You're irresponsible, and no one should have ever allowed you to have a pet."

Was this dude for real? What an asshole! "And you're a raging jerk who probably gets off on being a storm cloud over everyone's day."

He let out another one of those gruff rumbles that hit me in my lady parts. *Seriously, God. Why?* "I should report you for animal neglect."

My blood was officially at a full, rolling boil. I couldn't remember a time in my life where I'd ever been so heated, especially over a stranger. But this guy had to be the rudest person I'd ever crossed paths with. "And I should report you for being a raging hemorrhoid."

He let out a scoff, and for a split second I thought maybe I saw the corner of his mouth tremble like he was trying to suppress a smile, but that couldn't have been the case. There weren't any lines around his mouth or eyes indicating he even knew how. I was willing to bet he'd never smiled a day in his miserable life.

"Jesus, that's your comeback? How old are you?"

I'd never done anything in my life to warrant a brush with the law, but I was fairly certain punching this jackass in the mouth would have been totally worth the assault charge. But I'd been saving to buy a special zoom lens and didn't want to have to blow my money on bail.

"I'm old enough to know when a miserable jerk isn't worth my time. Thanks for not squishing my cat, asshole," I said as I started moving backward toward my car. "Have a miserable day. Hope to see you again never."

I was officially rescinding my offer to have his suit dry cleaned and his car detailed. He could take care of it himself. And I really hoped that coffee burned like hell when it spilled on him.

It was the least he deserved.

Chapter Six

Vaughn

Things hadn't gotten any better as the day progressed. My car reeked of coffee and my chest still bore the signs of that earlier spill.

When I got home after the whole debacle with that menace of a cat and stripped out of my ruined suit, throwing four grand right into the garbage—literally— the skin on my chest and abdomen had been an angry, mottled red and felt like the top three layers had been melted right off, thanks to that piping hot coffee I hadn't gotten to enjoy. I'd spent the rest of the morning feeling like my skin was on fire.

It had faded as the hours passed, and thank Christ there were no blisters, but my chest was still flushed a bright pink and sensitive to the touch, which was only irritated further by the seatbelt I had strapped over me as I made the drive from my place to my father's.

I would have rather tied a cinderblock to my nuts than attend a family dinner, but the recent struggle to tell my father no when he made a request was getting harder and harder to do. I'd moved here to be closer to him, after all, and as much as I would have preferred to do that on my terms, I knew it didn't work that way.

He still lived in the same red brick ranch-style house I'd been raised in for the first thirteen years of my life. With three modest-sized bedrooms and two bathrooms, it wasn't anything spectacular, but opening the front door, I was slapped right in the face with memories I'd shoved to the darker recesses of my mind. I hadn't thought about this house very much over the years, but I knew, without a doubt, if I was blindfolded and sent off on my own, I would still know every step of the place like the back of my hand.

I cleared my throat and shook my head to clear out the strange melancholy trying to grip hold of my throat, making it difficult to swallow.

"Hello?" I called out as I wiped my shoes on the doormat that read *Bless This Mess* before stepping across the threshold. I would have knocked, but the instant I raised my hand to do so, I recalled my father's booming voice always calling out "It's open" any time someone would stop by, a regular enough occurrence. In Pembrooke, you didn't need to lock your doors and, at least at Hershel Cavanaugh's house, everyone was welcome.

Just like it had been when I lived here, the walls of the entryway were covered in a collage of family photos in mismatched frames that had no particular order or theme. Hershel and Millicent's wedding photo stood out as the largest among all the rest, surrounded on all sides by pictures of me and my half-sister, Leighton, from infancy and beyond. Of course, there were more of her, seeing as she'd been around a lot longer, but I wasn't sure if it was my father or his wife who had made an effort to keep images of me in the mix.

Visitation never happened once I'd been pulled from my dad's home. According to Estelle, the back and forth was too much of an inconvenience. What with my private school, tutoring schedules, and all the extra-curricular activities she'd forced on me to ensure I remained out of her hair until I was needed, I never really had any free time to come back for holidays or summer vacations. Still, my high school and college graduation photos were hung with care among the rest of the family.

There were even a few images I knew had to have been printed out of magazines or online articles from interviews. And at the sight of them, that knot in my throat tried desperately to grow larger before I managed to swallow it down.

"Anyone home?" I called out, hoping the croak in my voice wasn't obvious to anyone but me. I heard noise coming from the direction of the kitchen at the back of the house, and a moment later, my dad and Millicent rounded the corner.

"There he is."

I had seen my father a few times since making the move back to Pembrooke, but the sight of him now still managed to catch me off guard. I got my height and most of my features from him, except for my hair color. Mine was a dark brown that bordered on black; his was much lighter. My broad shoulders and wide chest came from him as well, so to see him looking so thin he was damn near gaunt was like a sharp elbow to the solar plexus.

Growing up, I thought of my father as this larger-than-life character. He seemed powerful enough to handle anything. Thanks to the cancer treatments, that strength was gone. His skin was paler without that sunny bronze that came from working outdoors. His cheeks were sunken, dark purple half-moons colored the hollows beneath his eyes, and his once-strong shoulders were slumped. I knew he was going to be all right; he'd assured me of that when he first called to tell me he was sick. This cancer wasn't going to be a death sentence, but that poison they were pumping through him in order to kill it off was causing damage, and I hated seeing him in such a state.

Thoughts began to loop through my mind. *I should have tried harder to have a relationship. I should have been a better son. If only I wasn't such a cold, heartless bastard.*

The one thing that hadn't changed, though, was his smile. He'd always smiled like whatever brought it on was the best thing to ever happen to him, which was how he was looking at me. His blue eyes that matched my own were full of life and happiness at the sight of me.

"My boy," he crowed, throwing his arms open and waiting for me to walk into them for one of his signature back-slapping hugs. "Damn good to see you, son. Damn good."

I blinked away the sudden and unexpected burn from the backs of my eyes and lifted an arm to return his embrace with a much less enthusiastic pat. On top of the fact he felt much frailer than I recalled, I wasn't much of a hugger and stood tall after only a couple seconds, taking a step back to break the connection.

"Good to be here," I said, my flat tone revealing that statement to be a lie. Truth was, I would have rather been at home using these few hours to get more work done. It was never ending, after all.

I caught a look on Hershel's face when he pulled back, a puckered brow of confusion. "You smell like coffee, son. Is that . . . a new cologne or something?"

For the second time today, I had to beat back the desire to smirk. "Um, no. Had a spill in my car earlier, and the smell is still lingering," I answered as my mind darted back to that morning, to that stupid, suit-destroying cat—but mostly, to its radiant mahogany-haired owner.

I couldn't put my finger on what the hell had happened after she finally managed to pry that rabid animal's claws out of my shoulders, but that first sight of her twisted my stomach up like a sailor's rope and made my blood feel like a soda can that had just been shaken up. She was gorgeous, no two ways about it. Knock-you-on-your-ass-and-steal-your-ability-to-think gorgeous. Her features had been feminine and delicate, from her full, pink cupid's-bow lips to the slightly upturned tip of her nose. The very picture of sweetness as she blinked those wide, innocent eyes up at me, and something roared to life inside me at the very first smile she graced me with. This wild, possessive desire to take all that sweet and filthy it up.

She was tall for a woman, and one of my very first

thoughts was how I wanted to feel those long legs of hers wrapped around my head, her thighs squeezing so tight around my ears they blocked out all sound as I feasted on her sensitive pink flesh. I wondered what I'd find if I slid her panties down her legs. Would there be a tiny patch of curls the same russet brown as her hair, or would her skin be bare and glistening?

The intensity of those thoughts had slammed into me like a freight train, throwing me off balance, so I'd reacted the same way I always did when I thought my control was slipping—or worse, being stripped away from me. I lashed out.

Like the asshole I truly was.

But instead of getting emotional, she'd gotten pissed. It was impossible to miss. It was in her deep gray eyes, like thunderheads swirling and churning with a building storm. I knew right then and there I needed to get the hell away from her, because whatever had drawn me in from that very first glimpse only got stronger, stirring deep inside me and sending all the blood in my head straight to my dick.

This wasn't just any woman. She was the kind you took home to your parents. The kind you uprooted your entire life for. She was the kind of woman who could derail a man's carefully crafted world.

No fucking thanks. That had happened to me enough for two lifetimes. Never again.

Millicent came up next, shaking me from my thoughts of the stunning beauty with the dickhead cat. She may have been a tiny thing, but her embrace was even tighter than Hershel's.

I hadn't been sure what to expect when she and Hershel had started dating a couple years after my mother took off, but she'd never been anything but kind to me. Even after they had Leighton, I was never made to feel like the odd man out. That was part of the reason being forced to leave had been so jarring. I'd gone from being a member of a family unit to nearly complete isolation. I'd hated it at first, until I eventually came to appreciate being alone. That had become my normal. Now, as much as I remembered about my time here, I couldn't help but be a little unsettled. It was like stepping into a skin that didn't fit quite right because it belonged to a different person.

"Oh, look at you," she cooed, taking a step back to cup my cheek in her hand. "Even more handsome than I remember. So good to have you home."

I barely had time to brace against the impact of that word. *Home.* This place might have been that for me at one time, but it didn't feel like that anymore. Just like with my mother's house, this place felt more like a temporary stopover than my home. I wasn't sure I'd felt *at home* anywhere since I was thirteen. Even the big house on the mountain or the penthouse in Denver lacked that feeling. They were only the places where I caught a few hours of sleep between working.

"This is just a simple family dinner, son," my father said. "There was no need to dress up."

I looked down at the suit I'd put on after discarding my ruined one. "I didn't," I stated plainly.

They both blinked at me, and I didn't miss the look they shared before clearing their expressions and pasting the smiles back on their faces.

"Well, we're glad to have you back either way," Millicent shared. "Come on in. I've got potato salad in the fridge, some ranch-style beans, and your father's been smoking a brisket all day. Smells like heaven."

I followed them through the house to the kitchen, feeling like a stranger in the place I once called home. "Thank you for having me," I said stiffly, lifting the bottle of wine I'd picked up on the way here. "I wasn't sure what you drank, Millicent. I hope this is sufficient." I tried to make up for my lack of knowledge by purchasing the most expensive bottle the corner market had in its very limited stock.

A tug of discomfort tightened my chest at the realization that I didn't even know what my own stepmother preferred to drink. Shame crept up, and with it, my need to shut down grew deeper. It was going to be a miracle if I didn't come out of my skin by the end of the evening.

"Please, just Millie," she insisted, taking one of my hands in both of hers affectionately. "No need to be so formal. We're family, after all."

If only it were that easy.

Chapter Seven

Vaughn

They asked about work, about relationships and hobbies. Question after question in an attempt to get to know the person I was now, and all I could give them were stilted answers in return. I tried returning the sentiment and asking about their lives here in Pembrooke, but it came off more awkward than interested.

When the hell had I gotten so bad at small talk?

I could talk business with colleagues I knew the bare minimum about, discuss political affiliations or investments with people I had no interest in other than how we could potentially help scratch each other's backs. I could be whatever the situation called for, from brusque to intimidating, and, if the occasion arose where I felt the need to find a woman for the night to take the edge off, even charming. But when it came to my own flesh and blood, I couldn't find my footing.

Fortunately, I was eventually spared from the scrutiny by the arrival of Leighton. If the relationship with my father was murky, the connection with my half-sister was downright muddy. She'd only been three when I moved away, and since I hardly ever came back, we were practically strangers. But there was one thing I knew for certain when it came to Leighton.

She was a spoiled brat.

I wasn't sure if it was overcompensation on my father's part after I left, but the few times I'd been around over the years, I'd witnessed him cave to his little girl more times than I could count, giving in to whatever whim she'd had at the moment. I knew he spent money on her that he and Millicent didn't necessarily have, just because he couldn't bring himself to tell her no.

It was his tender heart that had him wrapped around Leighton's little finger, and from what I had gathered, the older she got, the better she was at manipulating that softness in him. I saw it first-hand when she waltzed into the dining room, twenty minutes late for our scheduled dinner, without so much as an apology for making everyone wait.

"I'm here," she singsonged as she breezed into the room. The man on her arm looked about as comfortable to be there as I was. His gaze darting between the three of us already sitting at the table, to the one and only available place setting remaining.

Millicent's cheeks flushed as she stood from her chair to receive a peck on her cheek from her daughter. I watched curiously as she tried and failed to keep her smile from looking brittle. "Leighton, I told you this was a *family* dinner. Your brother's home for the first time in years." She cast an apologetic look at the man before looking back at her daughter. "It was supposed to just be the four of us."

Leighton's bottom lip poked out in a ridiculous pout. She may have been ten years younger, but she still acted like a child. "But Barrett's important to me," she whined. "Dad understands. Right, Daddy?" She implemented a baby voice as she looked to our father and batted her eyelashes.

Hershel cleared his throat and tugged at his collar, clearly uncomfortable with being put between his wife and daughter. "Uh, well . . ." Leighton gave him big, sad doe-eyes that he fell for hook, line, and sinker. I could actually see him crumbling under her attention. "I'm sure it's fine with Vaughn, sweetheart," he told Millicent, earning a vicious glare from his wife. "No harm in letting Leighton's boyfriend stay. There's plenty of food."

Having gotten her way, Leighton bounced on the balls of her feet, clapping her hands together. "Thank you, Daddy," she said, all sugar and spice as she leaned down to place a smacking kiss on his cheek.

While Millicent moved into the kitchen for another place setting, my half-sister and her boyfriend took the two chairs across the table from me.

"Well, well. The prodigal son's finally returned," she said as she shook out her napkin and placed it daintily in her lap.

I narrowed my eyes, studying her closely in an attempt to find out what game she was playing. I might not have known her well, but on top of being a self-centered child, she got a real kick out of playing dramatic, immature games, and now that she had an audience by way of her boyfriend, I was sure she had something up her sleeve.

"How many years has it been since you've seen our father?" She tsked, shaking her head. "It's really sad that it took him getting sick for you to finally show up."

And there it was. She was in the mood to play the loving doting daughter while trying to make me feel like shit. Too bad I didn't have the feelings necessary for her act to have any effect.

"Leighton Angelica Cavanaugh!" Millicent jerked to

a stop just inside the dining room, her flabbergasted gaze on her daughter. "You take that back right now."

I sat back in my seat, propping my elbow on the arm of my chair and rubbing at my chin. "It's quite all right, Millie," I assured her before looking back at my half-sister. "Besides, I see the spoiled little princess never left."

Leighton sucked in an affronted gasp, shooting her eyes over to our father. "Daddy, say something! You're just going to let him talk to me like that?"

Hershel shifted uncomfortably in his chair. "The both of you behave yourselves now. This is supposed to be a happy occasion." He looked at me and smiled, then did the same to Leighton. "Both my kids are under one roof for the first time in way too long. What greater reason to celebrate?"

Displeased with not being the center of attention, Leighton shot me a look across the table before pasting a sugary smile on her face and looking back to Hershel.

"You know, speaking of reasons to celebrate, Barrett and I have some news. That's why I wanted him at dinner tonight." I took a lazy sip of wine as she brought their clasped hands up on the table, shifting them back and forth so the diamond on her ring finger would catch the light. "We're getting married!" she squealed so loud it made my molars grind together.

The wine Millicent had just sipped sprayed out of her mouth. "You're *what?*"

My father's complexion grew even paler. "You're engaged?"

"When did this happen?" Millicent demanded to know.

"I didn't realize you two were so serious," Hershel said, trying to cover his shock.

Leighton turned to give the silent Barrett an affectionate look that felt forced to me. "We're so excited, we just couldn't wait to tell the world. It's going out in the *Pembrooke Press* tomorrow, but we wanted you to be the first to know."

Millicent massaged her temples. "It's already going out in the local *paper?* How—that's—when in the world did this happen?"

If I had to guess, it was sometime between my father's diagnosis and the announcement that I was returning to town. Leighton had never done well with having the spotlight shifted off her, and judging by the sheen of sweat on her *fiancé's* upper lip, I was willing to bet he'd been strong-armed into an engagement before he was ready.

"So, it was a little sudden," Leighton answered with a petulant tone, confirming my suspicions. "But when you know, you know. Right, bunny?"

Bunny gave her a wobbly, unsure smile. "Uh, y-yeah. That's right."

Christ, my diva half-sister was marrying a spineless doormat. I could only pray they wouldn't procreate, because the last thing this world needed was a mix of those traits.

It was nothing for her to shake off her mother's very obvious disconcertment and grab onto the excitement, now that she was once more the center of attention. "Oh, I've been dreaming about this since I was a little girl," she cooed. "I want a *big* wedding, Daddy. Something grand. I want to be the talk of the whole town."

Millicent cleared her throat. "Leighton, honey. Maybe we should talk about this another time. After all, your father's been going through so much."

That pout came back, full force. "I know Daddy's sick. But that's why we should do this soon, don't you think?" She looked back at Hershel with wide eyes brimming with tears that were all for show. Reaching across the table, she put her hand on his and squeezed. "If you getting sick has taught me anything, it's that there's no time to waste. We need to grab our happiness with both hands, don't you think?"

I loved my father. I respected him. But damn, he was a sucker when it came to this woman. In light of her bullshit speech, his concerns melted away into a broad, happy smile. "You're so right, darlin'."

Millicent leaned forward, pressing her palms onto the table. "Hershel, honey, we can't afford some big, grand wedding."

Leighton's chin began to tremble, and I had to clench my hands into fists so tight the blunt ends of my nails dug into my palms to keep from calling her out. "But . . . th-this is all I've ever wanted," she claimed on a watery whisper. "It's my dream."

Goddamn her.

My teeth ground together so hard it was a miracle they didn't turn to dust. Because I knew what I was about to do. And, I was willing to bet, so did Leighton.

I couldn't stand the thought of my sick father stressing about money while he was fighting this battle, or my stepmother worrying about finding a way to keep everyone happy while trying to take care of her husband. I was an asshole, sure. But I wasn't cruel.

"I'll be happy to cover the cost of the wedding," I managed to grit out. I might have lost all respect for my half-sister for putting Hershel and Millicent through this, but the way my stepmother's shoulders sunk with relief and my father's chest rose on a deep breath, I knew I'd made the right call.

Even as I looked across the table at Leighton's snarky, victorious grin.

Because despite what she may think, to me, none of this was about her. This was all about repairing a relationship that had been damaged years ago, and if that meant shelling out some money, so be it. Lord knew I had plenty. And it wasn't as though I was saving for my own wedding.

Hell, this was probably the only one I'd be paying for.

Ignoring my half-sister's bitchiness, I kept my focus on Hershel. When his eyes met mine, the lines of tension that had been tightening around them was gone as he let his appreciation shine through, and I felt something shift in my chest.

It almost felt as if a chunk of the ice that had been encasing my heart for so long had chipped off. But that couldn't have been the case.

Right?

Chapter Eight

Jolie

The sun was already shining bright when I left my house that morning, heading for town to meet Ryan and Tarryn for brunch.

The bright, vivid blue of the sky and the pleasant temperature had brought people out in droves. They walked up and down the sidewalks of downtown Pembrooke, bouncing from shop to shop.

Taking advantage of the beautiful weather, I parked a few blocks down from Sinful Sweets Café and walked the rest of the way, returning waves and greetings from the people I passed and pausing occasionally to do a bit of window shopping. I spotted a pair of boots in one of my favorite boutiques and immediately fell in love.

Checking my watch, I noticed I still had some time before I had to meet my girls, so I pulled the door open, smiling at the happy tinkling of the bell above the door, and stepped into the shop. "Morning, Grace," I said, greeting the woman who ran the boutique.

I was so focused on the boots I was moving toward, as if being drawn to them by an invisible magnet, that I barely noticed the strange look she cast my way. However, it was there and gone so fast that I convinced myself it had to have been all in my head.

"Morning, Jolie. You here for something specific, or just browsing?"

"Something very specific," I answered as I reached the shoe display, snatching up the boot that had pulled me through the door. "Oh my God," I breathed as I twisted the coveted shoe from side to side, taking in all the beautiful detailing that had been stitched into the buttery soft leather. "These are even prettier up close. Grace, I'm pretty sure I'm in love."

The woman smiled brightly as she came over to join me. "Yeah, those are some sexy shoes, for sure. Just got them last week, and I'm already almost out of stock."

I clutched the boot to my chest and sucked in a dramatic breath. "Don't tell me that. Not when I've only just found them."

Grace shook her head good naturedly at my ridiculousness. "You're a seven and a half, right? I may have a pair or two left in your size. You want to try them on?"

Hell yeah, I did. "More than I want chocolate cake to have zero calories."

"Be right back."

She headed for the back of the shop, and I flipped the boot over, nearly swallowing my tongue at the price tag stuck to the sole. I placed the shoe back on the display and slowly backed away as two voices inside my head started arguing with each other.

One voice insisted that I deserved to treat myself every once in a while, that I worked hard and that those boots were my reward. Business was going well, and I'd managed to sock away a pretty decent savings. I could afford one little splurge.

The other voice, however, was arguing that the savings account was supposed to be for emergencies, not something as frivolous as a new pair of shoes. And honestly, did I really *need* them? It reminded me that, while I loved my cozy little house, it wasn't meant to be my forever home, that I was supposed to be saving up for something bigger, something I could raise a family in. And even though business was doing well at the moment, things could change in the blink of an eye, and I needed to be prepared.

The voice in favor of the boots sounded like college-aged Jolie, while the voice opposed sounded an awful lot like my reasonable parents.

I was still suffering through the internal struggle when the bell over the door tinkled again, and a voice like nails on a chalkboard spoke behind me, making my teeth clamp together as the little hairs on the back of my neck stood on end.

"Oh, those are so pretty! I just *have* to have them!"

Those two sentences were like a blast of frigid water right to my face as Leighton Cavanagh rounded the corner and rushed past me like I wasn't even standing there, snatching up the boot I'd been coveting.

She held it up like she was a character from *Lion King*, introducing the boot to the kingdom before turning her head in my direction. "Oh, Jolie, I didn't see you there," she said in a saccharine sweet voice that dripped with insincerity. "What do you think? Wouldn't these just look *so great* on me?"

The smile I gave her felt brittle and forced as I let out a non-committal hum. I didn't dislike Leighton Cavanaugh because she had practically started dating my ex a minute after we broke up—well, it wasn't *only* because of that.

It was also because she was a stuck-up, condescending . . . well, bitch. No point in mincing words. She was a spoiled brat who thought she deserved to have everything handed to her on a silver platter simply because she wanted it. From what I knew of her, she bounced from part-time job to part-time job, never lasting more than a couple months because working for a living just "wasn't her thing". Not when she had her parents to bail her out all the time.

I didn't know the Cavanaughs, only seeing them around town occasionally, but Hershel and Millie seemed like good people. It was like the apple had fallen into the back of a pickup and been driven clear across the country when it came to Leighton.

"You're in luck," Grace said, returning from the back with a shoebox in her hand. "There was one pair left in seven and a half."

"Ooh, that's my size!"

I darted past Leighton and reached out, snatching the box away from Grace before Leighton could get her grubby hands on my new boots. Because the moment she reached for them, my decision was made. Those shoes were mine. She already took my man. I'd be damned if I let her get my boots too. The woman had to learn she didn't get *everything* she wanted some time, right? And I was more than happy to teach her that lesson.

"Oh, sorry." I pulled my expression into a fake wince, like I felt bad for her. Not my fault she was five minutes behind me.

You snooze, you lose, babe.

"These are mine. I'm afraid you'll have to come back when Grace gets her next shipment in."

I couldn't help but smile snottily when Leighton's lips pulled into a sneer.

She grabbed hold of the other end of the box and tried tugging it out of my hands, but I tightened my grip. The only way she was getting that box was over my cold, dead body. "But, have you paid for them yet? If you haven't paid for them, they aren't yours."

I yanked the box back. "The only reason I haven't paid yet is because you won't get your greedy little hands off my box."

Grace looked between the two of us nervously, clutching her hands in front of her. "Um, i-if it matters, there's another shipment coming in next week."

"There, see?" I exclaimed cheerfully as I continued playing tug-of-war with the boot box. "You can get your pair next week. I'll be taking *mine* now, though."

"But I can't wait another week for these? I have very important events coming up."

I couldn't help but roll my eyes. She didn't even know the damn boots existed until a few minutes ago. "Looks like you'll have to find something else to wear."

She looked beseechingly at the clerk, like they were longtime friends. "Grace, I'm sure you understand. I have my *engagement party* coming up, and these boots would just look so perfect with my dress."

Tires squealed inside my brain at her declaration before my gaze cast down to her hands, still clutching my box. All the air inside my lungs wheezed out of me like a balloon being deflated. I could feel my cheeks growing hotter as I stared at the shiny diamond nestled on her ring finger and knew my face had to have been turning the color of cherry pie filling. It took a few seconds to realize it was happening because I was holding my breath.

"Oh, you haven't heard?" the she-devil asked demurely. God, I wanted to punch her in her stupid pageant-contest-perfect face. "Barrett and I are getting married." She released the box with her left hand and placed it on her chest. "It was in the paper this morning. I'm surprised you didn't see it."

You can't punch her out. You can't punch her out, I repeated over and over in my head.

"We're both just so happy. Over the moon, really."

I rethought my warning not to punch her out. I was friends with Eliza Prewitt, after all, and her father was the local sheriff. I was sure he wouldn't lock his daughter's friend up for assault . . . for long, at least.

It took everything in me not to react when all I wanted to do was reach out and snatch the silky-smooth blonde hair right out of her scalp. Instead, I ripped the box out of her hands and passed it over to Grace, the smile on my face feeling as fake as the Tofurkey my mother tried to pass off as the real thing last Thanksgiving—thanks, dad's crappy cholesterol.

I was determined to take the high road, damn it. Even if it killed me.

"Will you ring this up for me please? I'm in a bit of a hurry." Then I turned back to Leighton. "Congratulations. I hope you two will be very happy together."

What I really hoped was that they'd both fall in a pit of poisonous snakes . . . but high road and all.

"Oh, we will. Barrett said he couldn't wait to make me his wife."

My face was starting to feel like it was encased in plastic. "Yes, well, I'm glad you weren't bothered that the ring he'd given me was so much bigger. You know, some women can be so petty about things like that. It's nice to see you aren't one of them."

Welp, so much for the high road.

With my shopping bag in hand, I stormed through the doors of Sinful Sweets Café like a pissed-off tornado, hell bent on destruction. I didn't miss the curious eyes drilling into my skull from all sides, and could only assume it was because everyone had seen the announcement in the *Pembrooke Press*.

Ignoring the stares, I moved straight to the table Ryan and Tarryn were currently sitting at, the two of them leaned in close together like they were reading something.

"You won't believe what just happened," I stressed as I dropped my purse and the box containing my new boots in an empty chair across from them and collapsed dramatically into the one beside it.

They shot straight up at my arrival, hands fluttering frantically to slap closed the copy of the *Press* they were looking over, but they weren't fast enough.

"Oh, hey, babe," Tarryn greeted, her voice pitched way too high.

"You look great," Ryan added, then pointed to my shopping bag. "Whattaya got there?"

"A pair of the hottest boots in the world. But more on that later." I pointed to the paper Ryan was trying to slide off the table discreetly. "What were you guys looking at?"

"This? Oh, nothing." Tarryn folded the paper up as

small as she could. "We were just looking through the coupons. I'm thinking of becoming a coupon clipper. I saw this show on Netflix that got me interested. And you know how I love a good deal."

Tarryn would hate clipping coupons, she didn't have the patience for something like that. But I appreciated the lie all the same. It was good to know my girls were looking out.

I arched a brow at her. "You were looking at Barrett and Leighton's engagement announcement, weren't you?"

Their shoulders slumped at the same time, their frames deflated and twin looks of sympathy spread across their faces. I loved my friends to death, we were closer than any blood relation. But the pity radiating off them was enough to make me ragey.

"You've seen it already?" Ryan asked, her hand moving across the table like she was reaching out to soothe me until she caught the look of pure murder on my face. Wisely, she pulled back.

"I haven't, actually," I grumbled as I grabbed the empty coffee mug sitting on the table and proceeded to fill it, using the pot they'd already ordered before I arrived. I ripped open a sugar packet with more force than necessary, spilling half the contents onto the table before trying again. My spoon clanked loudly against the inside of the cup as I aggressively stirred in the cream and sugar. "I got the wonderful news up close and in person when she tried to steal my boots right out of my hands." A smile that felt downright vicious pulled at my face, making me look like a maniac, I was sure. "But I got the last pair in our size, so she can suck it."

Tarryn's hand made the journey across the table, coming down on the one I was still using to stir my coffee violently. "Okay, crazy. I think maybe you should take a second and breathe. Your smile has a real Penny-wise thing going on right now."

Ryan's brows pulled together in a worried frown. "She's right, honey. You look downright feral. I think you're actually scaring some people."

I toned down the killer-clown grin that was creasing my cheeks and picked up my coffee cup, taking that first fortifying sip. I swallowed down the caffeinated good-ness and let out a sigh, feeling a little saner with each passing second.

My friends gave me a much-needed minute to prop-erly collect myself after the bomb that had dropped on me earlier. I closed my eyes, counting to ten in my head and taking calming breaths until I felt stable once more.

"Okay, I'm better now," I assured them.

Their relief was palpable. Tarryn leaned forward,

propping her elbows on the table and cradling her chin in her hand. "Okay, so what happened?"

I recounted the whole scene with the boots from start to finish before pulling them out to show them to my friends.

"What a nasty little bitch," Ryan seethed after I shared all the nasty, underhanded things Leighton had said to me.

Tarryn nodded vigorously. "Agreed. She's the worst. But I love that you managed to still get the boots *and* insult her ring."

I chuckled, feeling pretty damn proud of myself for that as well.

Ryan studied me closely before asking, "So, you're okay about this? I mean, you aren't going to spiral again and spend the next two weeks drowning yourself in cookie dough ice cream until we have to pull you out of it with another intervention?"

Okay, so I may not have handled the breakup all that great the first time around. But that was a year ago, for crying out loud. "I'm fine," I assured them, feeling a twinge of guilt at the concern in their expressions. Alongside my parents, these two had been my rocks when the breakup first happened and the handful of months that followed. "I'm over Barrett, I swear." The relief I felt at the truth of that statement was a huge weight off my shoulders. The pain of loving him and losing him was gone. After seeing him for the kind of man he really was, it hadn't been hard for those feelings to shrivel up and die.

But my pride was something else altogether, and it was pride that had me up in arms over my ex being engaged to the woman he'd started seeing so shortly after our breakup. I prided myself on being a good person, and I didn't like wishing ill on people, but I would have been lying if I said I didn't hope the both of them got a terrible case of cystic acne the day before their wedding. But I'd keep that to myself.

Eliza appeared at the end of our table just then, dressed in a crisp white chef's coat with the name Sinful Sweets Café embroidered across the left side of her chest. "Hey, sweetie. How are you doing?"

I bit the side of my tongue to keep my snarky response at bay. Eliza Prewitt was a friend of mine, one of the sweetest people I'd ever known. She'd had it rough growing up, thanks to a shitty mother. But when her father fell for Chloe Delaney years ago, things started looking up for her. Chloe gave Eliza the mother figure she never had with her own, even expanding her bakery, Sinful Sweets, to include a dine-in café after Eliza completed culinary school.

Now she was married to her childhood best friend,

retired football star, Ethan Prewitt, living out the happily-ever-after she absolutely deserved, and the last thing she needed was for me to act like a jerk all because she was trying to be a good friend.

"I'm fine, really," I assured all three sets of eyes that were watching me way too closely. "I'm not heartbroken, and this isn't going to send me spiraling, I swear. It was just a bit of a shock, that's all. Now that I've had time to process, I'm over it."

Well, not *completely* over it, but enough that they didn't need to worry about me stepping in to exact some karmic retribution, since that stingy bitch was taking her sweet time doing it herself.

Eliza nodded proudly. "Good. You deserve so much better than that jerk."

"Exactly," Ryan agreed. "As far as I'm concerned, those two deserve each other."

Tarryn's hand came down on the table like she just had the most brilliant idea in the world. "You know what you need, Jo? You need to get back on the horse. Find another dude to dust the cobwebs off."

My brow crinkled and I choked on the sip of coffee I'd just taken, sputtering and spilling it down my chin. "Oh my God," I wheezed once I was able to pull in a full breath. "I don't have cobwebs, you asshole."

Eliza and Ryan just laughed.

"You know what I mean," Tarryn exclaimed with an eyeroll. "It's been a year. You need to get back out there, already. This may be a small town, but it's not lacking in hot men."

At the mention of hot men, why in the hell did my mind immediately go to that sexy-as-sin stranger who'd insulted me *and* my cat? I shook my mind clear of his gorgeous face and rock-hard body. It was one thing to be good-looking, but another entirely to be a raging prick.

No thank you.

"Amen to that." Eliza threw her hands up in agreement.

I jabbed my finger in her direction. "You hush. Women happily married to hot men don't have the right to chime in." She mimed zipping her lips and throwing away the key before I turned back to Tarryn. "And as far as getting back out there, I'll do that when I'm damn good and ready, and not a moment sooner."

I planted my feet and prepared to stand so I could go to the bathroom to clean up my little coffee spill, but as soon as I shoved my chair back, it collided with something behind me. Something—or should I say *someone*—who let out a grunt at the impact.

"Oh my God. I'm so sorr—" I started, spinning around to apologize to the person I'd just plowed into, only for my gaze to lock onto a pair of teal eyes ringed in copper.

"You," I let out on a surprised breath, almost as though my earlier thoughts had summoned him out of thin air.

"You have *got* to be kidding me," the man from the other day barked out as he looked down the front of his suit to take in the blooming coffee stain spreading across his once crisp white button-down.

Whoops.

Chapter Nine

Vaughn

This had to be some kind of cruel joke. Either that or I'd pissed off some higher power recently who was getting a real kick out of getting back at me via second-and-third-degree burns. At the rate things were going, I was going to need a skin graft soon.

I'd been so focused on taking that first sip of coffee—Sinful Sweets really did brew a superb cup of coffee—that I hadn't been paying adequate attention to the table I was passing, and the woman shoved her chair backward, plowing right into me, sending the coffee splattering down my front.

This was what I got for venturing into town again because I'd been too busy over the past few days to run out and replace my broken coffee maker at home. Never again. I was never leaving my house *again*.

"Oh my God. I'm so sorr—" The cat owner's lips parted on a quiet exhale as those dove gray eyes of hers went wide. "You."

"You have *got* to be kidding me," I gritted out, hunched forward and grasping the front of my shirt in an effort to keep the steaming hot fabric off my skin.

I could have sworn I heard her say, "Holy shit. Not again," under her breath as she whipped back around to her table and snatched up a wad of paper napkins. "I'm *really* sorry." She spoke at a rapid-fire pace as she dabbed and rubbed at the coffee stain on the front of my shirt that was finally cooling, but had rendered *another* shirt ruined. "I swear, I didn't do this on purpose."

A bolt of electricity shot through me at her touch, the current traveling beneath my skin and creating this strange pins-and-needles effect I'd only ever felt when a limb had fallen asleep. Thrown by the sensation, I grabbed her wrists to stop her, jerking when that simple touch caused a static shock I knew she felt by the way those expressive eyes of hers flared when they shot back to mine.

I dropped her wrists, breaking the connection, and did my best to shake off the disconcerting feeling. My brows climbed higher up my forehead. "You sure about that?" I meant it to be teasing, but that simple touch left me flustered. And judging by the way her brows slammed together in a frown, my tone was much more brusque than I meant for it to be.

She promptly stopped smearing the coffee stain, oblivious that she was only making it worse, and shot me a killing look. "Of course I'm sure. I'd never intentionally cause someone pain . . . or ruin a perfectly good cup of coffee, for that matter."

"Um, do you guys know each other?"

I looked at her companions. I didn't recognize the one who'd asked the question, but the other woman sitting beside her was the one who'd assisted with this lady's cat the day of our first encounter. She elbowed the blonde sitting next to her. "That's the guy I was telling you about. The one Smoosh climbed like a tree."

I fought back the curl in the corner of my mouth as I turned back to the woman who couldn't seem to stop physically assaulting me. "I take it *Smoosh* is your devil cat?"

"Yes," the blonde answered quickly at the same time Calamity Jane over there cried, "She's not a devil cat!"

Her friends did a terrible job of trying to mask their snickers, earning an evil glare from Calamity.

It hit me that I still didn't know this woman's name, which sat in my stomach like a lead ball for some reason, but the nickname I'd come up with in my head fit her to a tee.

With her focus on her friends for the briefest moment, my eyes traced every inch of her face, taking in the arch of her brows, the thick, dark lashes that lined her almond-shaped eyes. I warned it not to, but my gaze traveled to her mouth. Her lips were pursed unhappily, but there was still no missing how full and pink they were. I caught my mind wandering to how it would feel if I were to trace that indent on the top lip that made a perfect bow shape with my tongue.

Fucking hell. Get your shit together.

I blinked back the visions of leaning down and kissing this complete stranger as she turned back to me. Christ, my cheeks felt hot. Was I actually *blushing?* What the hell?

Never. Coming. Into. Town. *Again.*

"Smoosh is actually a very sweet cat. She just has this weird fear about her carrier. I'm sure if you got to know her, you'd like her."

"Doubt it," I returned. I was about as much a fan of cats as I was people, maybe less so. "And you'll have to excuse me for having no interest whatsoever. Between the two of you, I worry how much money I'll be flushing down the drain for replacement suits."

Her entire face crinkled, and damn if I didn't think

she looked adorable as hell, even while trying to look menacing. "You're just as much to blame as me or Smoosh."

My chin jerked back at her weak defense. "And how exactly do you figure that, Calamity?"

"I'm not a calamity," she bit out. "And who the hell even wears a suit on a freaking *Sunday*, for crying out loud? Haven't you ever heard of a day of rest?" She threw her hands in the air dramatically. "If you dressed like a normal person, that spilled coffee wouldn't be such a travesty."

A bubble of incredulous laughter spilled out of my mouth. I couldn't remember the last time I laughed, incredulous or not. "So it's my fault for wearing suits? That's your reasoning?"

"Yes," she continued snobbishly, even though we both knew she didn't have a leg to stand on. "That second cup of coffee had to be the universe's way of telling you to pull that stick out of your ass and lighten the hell up."

Calamity was a hazard to those around her, and a massive pain in my ass, yet, instead of being annoyed that I was standing in the middle of a crowded restaurant having a grade-school-level fight with this strange woman, I was entertained. I hadn't stopped once to consider how behind schedule the childish argument we were having was going to make me. Hell, in the past five minutes, I hadn't thought of work at all.

I couldn't remember the last time that had happened.

On that note. I couldn't remember the last time someone had talked to me the way Calamity just had. It was almost . . . refreshing. I usually garnered one of two reactions. If people knew who I was they'd fawn over me because of how much money I had or what I could possibly do for them. Or if they didn't, they found me intimidating because of how I came off and my lack of people skills. This woman didn't have the first clue who I was, but she sure as hell wasn't intimidated.

"Um, Jo . . ." her blonde-haired friend said, her gaze directed over our shoulders at something outside. "We've got a bogey incoming, and it seems to have locked on you as its target."

"What should we do?" the other friend asked. "You want us to block your path so you can sneak out the back?"

Calamity looked in the direction of her friends a second before the color faded from her cheeks. "Ah, shit," she hissed, all the fire that had been burning hot in her gaze only a second ago going out like a campfire that had been smothered with sand.

Curiosity tugged my attention toward the window her friends were looking through at the same time it pulled my brows into a frown. It took a few seconds for me to recognize the man heading right for the door as Leighton's fiancé, Bart. Or Barnett. Or Barney, I couldn't remember.

"*Shit, shit, shit, shit.* This is the last thing I need right now," she said in a panic, drawing my gaze back to her as she shuffled from foot to foot like she was seconds away from bolting.

Something uncomfortable and hot churned in my gut, leaving me unsettled. It made my skin itchy and my muscles tight. Jesus, what the hell was going on? "You know that guy?"

She puckered those sexy lips and blew a dramatic raspberry. "Yes, unfortunately. He's my ex."

That churning got even worse, making it feel like my intestines were tied in knots. My fists clenched involuntarily. I hadn't cared much for the guy when I had to suffer through that family dinner with Leighton and all her bullshit, but having Calamity call him her ex made me hate him on sight. He could have been the one to cure cancer or have dedicated his life to feeding the homeless and it still wouldn't have mattered. My dislike for him was solidified.

"Your ex?" My heart went from beating steadily to

grinding like something had been shoved into its gears. "You dated that guy?"

Why the hell did I keep asking, like the answer would somehow change? And why did it matter so damn much?"

"We were engaged, actually. He broke it off, and I found out today that he's engaged *again*. Only this time it's to the worst woman ever."

Maybe if Leighton and I had grown up together—and her personality was completely different from what it was now—I would have felt a flutter of brotherly loyalty. But we hadn't been raised under the same roof, and Leighton was who she was—specifically, the worst.

However, that wasn't what was sticking in my head just then.

"You were engaged to that guy?"

What she did with her eyes was a combination of a roll and a cross as she puffed her cheeks and blew out a self-deprecating raspberry. "Don't remind me, okay?"

The unsettling sensation that had been churning inside me started to calm at her response. "So you don't want him back?"

Again . . . why did I care?

There wasn't an answer to that question. I just knew I did. Which meant I needed to get the hell away from this woman as fast as possible. But instead of doing that, I ended up doing something so out of character I didn't recognize myself.

From the corner of my eye I could see Barney closing in, and instead of thinking, I just acted. "Don't stiffen up," I said in a low rumble of warning as I reached up and took her chin between my thumb and index finger, tilting her face upward.

Her dove gray eyes that revealed everything she was feeling went wide. "Wh-what are you doing?"

"Just . . . trust me. What's your name?"

"J-Jolie."

Jolie. It was unique. Beautiful. Fitting. Just like Calamity.

"Well, Jolie, remember what I just said." On that, I closed the distance between us and brought my lips down on hers. A live current shot through my veins instantly like I'd grabbed hold of a fallen powerline.

The sharp inhale she sucked in at the press of my lips against hers spurred me on, pumping through me and causing my free hand to come up and grip the swell of her hip. My eyes remained open, taking in the million different feelings that skittered across her expression in a single heartbeat like a spinning kaleidoscope of emotion. I sure as hell didn't expect the massive punch to the sternum at that first feel of her soft, pillowy lips, but when her eyelids fluttered closed, my fingers pressed deeper into her skin, absorbing the heat coming off her skin beneath her clothes.

"Jolie?"

At the sound of Barnaby's voice Jolie's eyes flew open and a growl worked its way up my throat at having her name fall from his mouth. A voice in the back of my head screamed that he didn't have the right to speak such a perfect name, but the tiny bit of rationality still lingering kept me from reaching out and punching him like I so desperately wanted to. It was as if one little kiss was enough to undo all my control and send me back to the most base, primitive version of myself.

She broke the kiss before I was ready, taking a step back, and stumbled over her own two feet. She would have hit the ground if my arm hadn't shot out and wrapped around her waist, yanking her against me. I should have gotten the hell out of the shop the moment she caused me to spill a second cup of coffee on myself. I should have turned and walked away instead of engaging in another argument. And I sure as hell shouldn't have kissed her. But what was done was done, and I couldn't seem to make my body listen to what my brain was trying to get across. In fact, when I felt her body tense beside mine, my arm tightened in anticipation of her trying to make a break for it.

Bartholomew's eyes bounced back and forth between us before settling on where my hand rested on her hip, intimately touching her like I had every right. His jaw hung open as he tried to wrap his head around what he was seeing.

"Do you two know each other?"

Jolie sputtered as she tried to form a response. "Uh, we . . ." That was all that came out.

I was suddenly very aware of the fact that the entire café had grown eerily quiet and Jolie and I seemed to be the center of attention. I could feel all those eyes drilling into my skin, sending an uncomfortable prickle down my spine, but I held fast to her and stood my ground.

"We're seeing each other."

Where the fuck had that come from?

I ignored the choking coughs coming from her friends at the table behind us. Jolie's poker face was terrible. *Something we'll have to work on,* a voice in the back of my head said before I could stop it.

This wasn't supposed to be a permanent thing. Hell, I wasn't sure *what* it was supposed to be. For the first time since I was thirteen, I'd acted without thought. Without a plan. It was a foreign concept for me. After having it taken from me far too often when I was younger, control was now something I required, and the last thing I felt in the situation I'd just created for myself was in control.

But with this calamitous woman pinned to my side, I felt anchored instead of adrift.

Strange.

"You're—you two—you guys are seeing each other?"

Jolie's mouth opened and closed over and over. Clearly, she wasn't going to be any help with this whole ruse.

"It's new." I opened my mouth and the lies just kept on coming. "We met the other week, not long after I arrived in town." I lifted my chin in a defiant gesture like I was silently daring him to object or call me on the bullshit I was spewing.

Proving, once again, he didn't have much in way of a spine, Bartleby blinked away his surprise and pinned a brittle smile on his face. "Small world, huh?"

Jolie spoke for the first time since our kiss, tilting her head to the side curiously. "How so?"

"I just mean I'm with Leighton, and now you're dating her brother? Talk about a coincidence."

I heard a string of muffled curses from the women behind us, but I was too focused on the one still tucked beneath my arm who was now staring at me with what appeared to be murder in her thundercloud gaze.

"Half-brother," I quickly amended. "And we aren't that close." Turning back to the douchebag, I explained, "Jolie and I haven't had the whole family talk yet. Like I said, it's new. Did you need something, Baxter?"

He blinked twice. "I-it's Barrett. And, um, well . . ." He fidgeted anxiously, finally taking notice of the attention our little trio had drawn and lowered his voice before continuing to speak directly to Jolie. "I saw you through the window and I just . . . wanted to say I was sorry, you know, for springing the whole engagement thing on you. I mean, I wanted to tell you personally, but you know Leighton." He let out an uneasy chuckle that made Jolie's shoulders stiff as a board. "Anyway. I'm sorry you had to see it in the paper instead of hearing it from me."

Christ, this dickhead wasn't only spineless. I wouldn't have been surprised if my sister had his nuts in a jar on her bedside table. Those two deserved each other, that was for damn sure.

"No problem," Jolie responded. Finally seeming to get with the program, her body began to loosen, and my heart beat heavily against my ribs when she sank deeper into my side. "I'd say it all worked out for the best." She tilted her head and rested it on my shoulder as she lifted a hand to place on my chest. Just like that, the saliva in my mouth dried up like I'd just sucked on a cotton ball. My Adam's apple bobbed on a thick swallow as my hold on Jolie tightened. She smelled like what I imagined sunshine might smell like—all citrus and sugar, and I couldn't help but lower my head to her hair and breath in deeply.

For fuck's sake. Now I was sniffing her?

His smile dropped a fraction. "Yeah, totally. For sure," he said, sounding like he didn't believe it for a second.

I shifted my attention back to the man in front of us, giving him a look that had sent better men than he scurrying out of boardrooms. "Well, it was good to see you again, Baxter. But I'm sure you have other things to do."

The muscles in his jaw ticked. "It's Barrett. And you're right. Leighton wants to do some wedding stuff today," he added pettily. "I was on my way to meet her."

I shooed him off with a wave of my hand. "Then by all means, don't keep her waiting."

I took immense pleasure at the sight of his cheeks turning a mottled red, but instead of saying anything to me, he looked back at Jolie. "See you around, Jo."

I watched as he finally made his way out of the café, waiting for the panic that usually accompanied my lack of control to slam into me like a Mack truck. But it didn't come.

Not even when Jolie turned to look up at me, her expression full of rebuke.

"You don't have any clue what you've just done."

I didn't, but even as I dug down deep, I couldn't find it in me to care.

Chapter Ten

Jolie

I let out a groan of annoyance as my cell started to vibrate across my desk. Even putting the damn thing on silent hadn't done me a bit of good. For how often it went off, it sounded like a jackhammer bouncing across the wooden surface.

At the sight of my mother's name popping up on the screen, I collapsed back in my cozy leather swivel chair with a huff. If I didn't answer, she was going to keep calling and calling. Hell, she'd probably go so far as to make my father call me, or worse, recruit Charlotte, which meant the rumors flying around town over the past eighteen hours would get back to my brother all the way in Hope Valley, and more likely than not, his head would explode.

For everyone's sake—including my own—it was best for me to answer.

Snatching up the phone, I swiped the screen to answer and brought it to my ear. "Hi, Mom," I greeted as I went back to my laptop and clicked on the track pad to save the work I had been trying to focus on all morning.

The photographs from the Bridezilla/Robot wedding were turning out better than I'd hoped, but I needed to make sure they were perfect before sending them off to Lexi.

"Is there a reason I had to hear from my friend Jean during our weekly Bunko game last night that my daughter has a new man in her life instead of hearing it from her?"

And there it was. The small-town grapevine was in full effect, putting Lorene Prescott in the mood to lay mother guilt on thicker than peanut butter on a slice of bread.

I let out a weary sigh, reaching up to pinch the bridge of my nose. "Mom, it's not what you think."

"Oh, well then how about you enlighten me, sweetheart, and tell me what it is?"

I opened my mouth to answer, only to come up short, because the truth was, I was still trying to wrap my brain around what had happened in the middle of Sinful Sweets Café the morning before.

One second I was fighting with that arrogant, pompous ass whose only facial expression was an intense frown, and the next, he was kissing and touching me in front of my ex and half the damn town like he had every right.

And the craziest thing about the whole scene—aside from the above-mentioned kissing and touching—I hadn't hated it. I mean, sure, the man was a grade-A jerk, but something about him was downright magnetic. I'd actually *liked* the way he held me. It made me feel protected, almost cherished. And I'd *really* liked that kiss.

In fact, I'd replayed that damn kiss more times than was healthy over the past several hours. I'd thought about how the man—I still didn't know his name—had used the perfect amount of firmness. I thought about how nice it felt to have someone else's lips brushing against my own for the first time since Barrett and I had started dating, and how much I missed making out with a man. Our sex life might not have been affected before Barrett dumped me, but I couldn't remember the last time we'd made out, kissed like we couldn't get enough of each other, like the only air we wanted to breathe was what came out of our partner's lungs.

I missed that. And all it took was a relatively chaste kiss with a complete stranger in the middle of a crowded restaurant to spark that craving back to life in a way I knew wasn't going to go away any time soon.

Damn him.

If I'd been smart, I would have hung around and tried to get the scoop on what the hell he'd thought he was doing, putting on that little show for my ex, but the way my body had lit up for him had freaked me out, and instead of handling the situation like an adult, I bolted out of Sinful Sweets like my ass was on fire. I'd needed to get away from all those prying eyes and mumbled whispers. Now people were talking. Rumors spread like wildfire, and I didn't even know the name of the guy who'd started it all.

The worst part was, I couldn't ask around, because everyone would know it had all been fake, and they'd probably think I'd orchestrated the whole thing because I was the pathetic woman who still wasn't over her ex, even though he'd clearly moved on.

Unless I wanted to be the laughing stock of Pembrooke, I had to save face. That was why, instead of telling my mother the truth, I found myself saying, "It's, well . . . it's still really new."

I squeezed my eyes closed and smacked my palm to my forehead at my lame response. But it was the best I could do in the moment.

"I can't believe you're seeing someone and didn't tell

me." I could see her in my mind's eye, shaking her head in disappointment as she sat at her kitchen island, flipping through one of her favorite cooking magazines. "You give one hundred percent of yourself, hoping you're raising your kids right, then something like this happens."

My face screwed up like I'd sucked on a lemon. "Okay, wow. That's a lot, even for you."

My mother's tinkling laughter carried through the line. "Had to see how far I could take it."

I tapped my fingernail on the top of the desk and pulled one of my feet up to rest in the seat of my chair. "And you've officially reached your max."

She blew out a breath and started over. "So, Vaughn Cavanagh, huh?" I heard he was back in town after all these years. Also heard he grew up real nice, but he was kind of . . . well, a jerk, honestly."

I sat up a little straighter, my curiosity officially piqued. "You know him?"

"No. Not him personally. I know his parents. Not well, but enough to remember him living here when he was a kid before his mother divorced his dad years ago. Vaughn lived with Hershel for a spell before moving away to live with his momma when he was in middle school. I don't think he's been back since."

That wasn't much information, but at least I'd gotten

a name. *Vaughn Cavanaugh.* It fit him somehow. It was classic and manly and pretentious all at the same time. Just like the man the name belonged to.

"Were you friends with his mother?"

She snorted through the line. "Estelle? Please." I could imagine her rolling her eyes. "That woman was as snooty as the day is long. Truth be told, I'm not sure she really had any friends. It's hard to get people to like you when you walk around acting like you're better than everyone. She had aspirations that went beyond this town. That's fine and all, but she was always high and mighty, looking down her nose at the rest of us."

I went from tapping to unconsciously scratching at the finish on the desk. "She sounds . . ."

"Awful, I know. And she was. Which is probably why people say her son's just as cold as she was. Probably got it from her."

My mind went back to how it felt to have his strong arm wrapped around me like a steel band holding me to him. He sure as hell didn't feel cold then. Or when he kissed me. In fact, I remember the heat pouring from his body was nearly hot enough to singe me. Even his cologne held a bit of heat. A scent like amber and spice clung to his skin, creating a warmth in my chest when I inhaled it.

I thought back to that first interaction in the middle

of the road outside my house and how I thought he'd been a complete asshole. He still gave off that vibe the day before, like he had no desire to be around anyone else. But then he'd seen my discomfort at the thought of running into Barrett, and he'd just acted. A man as cold and unfeeling as what my mother had described wouldn't do something like that for a complete stranger. Right?

I chewed on my bottom lip as I tried to form my thoughts into something that made sense. "Well, he's kind of stiff, and he's got a real hard-on for wearing suits, but, I don't know . . . there's something about him," I said, a bit taken aback by the fact that the words pouring past my lips weren't an act, but the god's honest truth. "I don't think he's as big a jerk as he leads people to believe."

"Well, of course not. Or my girl wouldn't be interested in him," my mother threw back, her words a reminder that Vaughn and I weren't actually dating. In fact, we weren't anything to each other.

"Yeah. For sure. Of course not."

"I'm glad you've put yourself out there again. Barrett wasn't worth your time, but I'd be lying if I said I wasn't worried when I heard he'd gotten engaged to someone else."

And that someone else just so happened to be my

new fake boyfriend's half-sister. How was that the world I was living in?

"You deserve to be happy, sweetie. That's all I want for you."

My stomach dropped to the floor while my heart lodged itself in my throat. "You know, I don't have to be in a relationship to be happy, right? I mean, I've got a lot of other good things in my life. My happiness isn't dependent upon a man."

"Oh, honey. Of course not. I know you don't *need* to be in a relationship to be happy. But I also know my girl is a romantic at heart. You watched *Pretty Woman* and that *How to Lose a Guy* movie so many times when you were younger, you could quote them from memory."

"That's because those are awesome movies," I defended, knowing in my gut she was right. I watched movies like that because I wanted a man to love me the way the heroes in those movies loved their women. I wanted the big grand gesture. I wanted to be the girl walking down the street that someone noticed and couldn't get out of his head.

Ugh.

"Anyway, whether this man is the one or not, I only want to make sure he treats you right. That nut-less bastard never deserved you."

"Mom!" I sputtered, my jaw dropping in shock at the way she spoke about my ex. She wasn't wrong, of course, but Lorene Prescott was known for being sweet as sugar.

"Do I lie?" she asked in that stern mother voice of hers.

I let out a sigh. "No," I relented. "You don't lie."

"Exactly. Now, I'll expect you to bring your new man to dinner this week. Jean from Bunko was all too happy to rub my face in my lack of knowledge, so I expect to be able to pay her back next game night."

My back shot straight, my foot falling back to the floor with a thud. "Uh. I-I don't know if that's such a good idea. I mean, we're still so new. I don't think we're at the meet the parent phase of things yet."

"Don't be silly. Any man who kisses you in public the way he did is more than ready to meet your mom and dad. I'll make my famous lasagna. Talk to him about it and get back to me."

"But, Mom—"

"Oh, gotta go! Doris from book club is calling on the other line. I need to let her know I'm well aware of my daughter's new boyfriend before that *Jean* gets to her. Talk soon, sweetheart. Love you!"

After blowing a quick kiss through the line, she hung

up, leaving me wondering how the hell I was going to track down my fake boyfriend and pay him back for screwing up my life.

Chapter Eleven

Vaughn

The room we were sitting in wasn't so much a room as it was a small curtained off section of the third floor, tucked back into a corner, but at least Hershel had privacy. And his own television that he could watch while he sat in a leather recliner that looked about as comfortable as a folding camp chair, getting poison pumped into his veins for the next three hours.

Some reality baking competition played at a low volume on the TV as my fingers flew over the keys on my laptop, using the spells where my father dozed off to get some work done. I hadn't realized just how much these chemo sessions took out of him. I'd spent the first hour after he'd been hooked up to the IV trying to swallow down the lump of cement that had formed in my throat at the sight of him in that goddamn chair, a blanket draped over his lap because he couldn't seem to stay warm as the drugs worked their way through his body.

It was hard to look at him. He just seemed so fragile.

"You know, you work too much."

My head came up, my eyes colliding with Hershel's. If I had a dollar for every time I heard that, my status as a millionaire would have been catapulted to billionaire by now.

I shook off the comment, knowing he hadn't meant anything by it. "Hey. Sorry." I quickly saved the draft of the email I'd been working on and folded the top of the laptop down. "I didn't mean to wake you."

He adjusted in the chair, letting out a frustrated grunt as he tried to get comfortable. "You didn't. It's impossible to conk out for too long. Damn chair is hard enough to make my ass fall asleep."

I slid the computer into my bag and started to stand. "Do you want me to get an extra pillow? Or maybe they have a more comfortable chair somewhere. Give me a minute and I'll take care of it." It would have given me something to do, to make me feel useful. I wasn't used to feeling helpless, but that was how I felt, sitting in my father's little room, watching him receive his treatment.

He chuckled and waved me back down into my own

uncomfortable chair. "Don't worry about it. I'm fine, really. You don't need to go harassing the nurses."

"Who said anything about harassing them?"

He grinned in a way that said he knew me better than that, despite all the years that had separated us. "The look on your face, for one."

I leaned back in the hard, plastic chair, bringing one ankle up and propping it over my knee as I arched a single brow.

"Not saying it to insult you, son. It's just who you are. You're intense, always have been. Even when you were a little kid."

"You mean cold." The words spilled out of their own accord. I hadn't realized I'd been thinking them until they were out there, unable to be pulled back.

My father shifted again, sitting up even straighter. "I meant what I said. Sure, intensity can sometimes be mistaken for being cold, but I know you, Vaughn. I know you aren't cold."

Unlike my mother.

I was sure he was thinking it just as I was. Because the only intense thing about Estelle Cavanaugh was her complete disdain for the human race.

I cleared my throat that suddenly felt dry and scratchy, reaching up to loosen the tie wrapped around my neck. "Yes, well, it doesn't really matter now, does it? My reputation is what it is, and I'm fine with that."

Or at least I had been.

The corners of his mouth curled upward. "What does your new girl think of your reputation?"

My brows slammed down in the center, forming a deep V. "My new girl—" I started, the confusion evident on my face, at least until I remembered the scene I'd caused in the middle of that crowded café the other day. "Oh, yes. My . . . girl." My tie suddenly felt like it was strangling me, but I couldn't reach up and adjust it again without giving away my discomfort. "She seems to like me just fine," I answered lamely.

I thought back to the fire that sparked in her gray eyes, that flash of anger before she hissed *"You don't have any clue what you've just done."* I was sure it said something not at all flattering about me that the fight in her gaze had made my dick thicken and my blood pump faster. At least until she bolted on me, running out of there like her ass was on fire. One spontaneous act in years, and it had backfired stupendously. I didn't even have her last name, for Christ's sake, and it wasn't like I could ask Bartleby for it without giving myself away.

"At least for the time being," I tacked on, because fake or not, I was sure whatever it was I felt between

Calamity and me would end the same way all my other acquaintances with women ended. Horribly.

It never failed that the woman I was spending time with would get tired of how much I worked or how withdrawn I was. I'd been called a workaholic, a robot, an emotionally stunted asshole, you name it. All because I refused to change myself or my lifestyle to better fit my companion. I couldn't really blame them, though. No matter how well things started, it always went down the same road. I'd explain that work came first. They'd claim to be okay with that, then, in a matter of weeks or months, they'd change their tune. They'd want me to prioritize them more, make them feel like they mattered, and when I'd explain—rather bluntly—that was never going to happen, it was as good as over.

I'd accepted that as my lot in life. For me, there was no work/life balance. There was only work. Intimate relationships were too unpredictable. Too volatile. I couldn't control them the way I could my job. At least there I had complete control.

"I'm glad you've found someone to spend your time with."

I shot him a bland smile, tugging at the French cuffs of my shirt to hide my discomfort with the turn the conversation had taken. "I have plenty of ways to fill my time."

"You have work," he contended.

"Yes. Work that's very important and time consuming," I said more defensively than I had intended. "And have you forgotten I'm here for *you*? Not some random relationship that most likely won't last more than a handful of weeks."

Hershel's features softened. "I'm going to be okay, son."

That lump in my throat was getting bigger by the second. "Yes, I'm aware," I said, my tone coming off bored and mildly irritated to mask how I was really feeling. Even though I'd heard as much straight from the oncologist's mouth, it was still hard to believe it. Really and truly believe it. Especially when I sat with him as the chemicals meant to save him ravaged his body. It was the first time I'd attended one of his chemo treatments, but I knew from Millicent what would come after.

He'd be violently ill, followed by a few days where he could do little more than sleep. Then, just as he seemed to be on the mend, it would be time for another course.

As if he sensed I needed to move off the current topic, he shifted gears. Unfortunately, what he'd decided to switch to wasn't any better.

"How is your mother doing?"

I gave him a skeptical look. "You really want to know?"

He lifted one gaunt shoulder in an easy shrug. "Of course. We might not be married anymore, but we shared a life together at one time. It would be nice to know she's doing well."

I took a few seconds to really study him, looking for any signs of insincerity, but there were none. He really meant it. He wanted her to do well. To be happy. The woman had ended their marriage in a way that could have only been described as cruel. Then, years later when he'd finally managed to move on, she reared her head in order to take his son away from him. Still, he only wanted the best for her. That much was clear.

"She's . . . Estelle. You know how it is. No one really knows how she's doing because she can't be bothered with silly things such as emotions."

His focus trailed off, moving to the window overlooking the parking lot, but I could tell by the way his gaze became cloudy that he was too lost in thought to notice what was happening outside this cold, sterile building.

"You know, I always hoped that one day she'd meet the person she was meant to be with. The person who fit her better than I could. It was clear from the very beginning we were just too different, but I never once regretted our years together, because they brought me you. I hate the thought that she's still alone."

I ignored the tightness in my chest at his heartfelt declaration. I was really off my game today. "I think she prefers it that way, honestly. She's never really been a fan of people." That was something she and I had in common.

He let out a breath and turned back to the television. "I suppose you're right," he said, his voice carrying a hint of sadness for the woman he'd once been married to.

The silence that descended on the room only lasted a minute before the chime of Hershel's cellphone filled the air. He reached for the phone sitting on the small table beside his chair and let out an exhausted breath before placing it back down without answering.

My brows went up when I saw Leighton's name flashing across the screen. "Everything all right?"

"Huh? Oh, yeah. It's fine," he answered, but the way he began massaging his temples told a different story. "It's only wedding stuff. You know your sister. She can be a bit temperamental."

That was a polite way of saying she was a selfish bitch. I could feel the muscle in my jaw clench as I ground my molars together, struggling to keep my irritation from show-ing. "She knows where you are right now, doesn't she? Is this really the time for her to be calling and dumping wedding stuff on your plate? Besides, she's been engaged all of five minutes. Why is everything so pressing all of a sudden?"

"She claims she doesn't want a long engagement. She has her heart set on hiring a certain event planning company, but she's having some trouble nailing them down, and it's causing her a bit of stress."

Stress that she was undoubtedly dumping on the shoulders of our sick father because she couldn't be bothered to think about someone other than herself.

"Dad, this really isn't something you should be worrying about right now. I know Leighton tends to act like these things are the end of the world, but she'll survive not getting the event planner she wants."

He let out another sigh, his entire frame slumping like the weight of the world had been dropped on his shoulders. "She's worried it'll end up affecting her big day. You know how women get about their weddings. I told her I'd talk to the planners, see if I could smooth things out and get them on board."

Of course he had. Because his heart was too goddamn big for his own good. Especially when it came to his daughter. I couldn't believe he was even thinking about something as insignificant as wedding planners at a time like this. His focus needed to be on getting better.

And Leighton needed a serious fucking wakeup call, that was for damn sure.

"You know what? I'll take care of it."

His head whipped around, his brows winging upward. I couldn't fault him for the skepticism in his expression, but if it meant taking some of the burden off of him, I'd suck it up and deal with something as stupid as a company that helped plan weddings for entitled brats.

"Vaughn, you don't have to—"

"I want to." The lie came out easy enough. After all, I'd been doing enough of it the past few days, I'd be a pro in no time. "You just focus on your health, and I'll take care of this issue."

And hopefully get through my half-sister's thick skull in the meantime. But I wouldn't hold my breath on that one.

Chapter Twelve

Vaughn

I pulled up in front of Three's a Charm Events and slid my car into park. Through the windshield I took in the building's façade, thinking that, yep, this was definitely the kind of place you'd expect a wedding planning company to be housed.

The shop looked like it had once been a carriage house before it was converted into a business. The board and batten siding had been painted white to offset the rustic cedar shingles under the eaves along the front of the building.

Two large concrete pots sat on either side of the entrance, each holding perfectly manicured topiaries. The window boxes were overflowing with brightly colored flowers, and to the right of the entrance was a trellis covered in some kind of climbing vine that was covered in deep purple flowers. The signage hanging from the middle eave read *Three's a Charm Events* in a dusky blush color, the script full of loops and swirls.

It looked like Disney had thrown up all over it. Like it had been pulled right out of a fairy tale and dropped in the middle of Pembrooke like Dorothy's house falling on that wicked witch in the *Wizard of Oz*. The only things missing were the birds and squirrels coming out to greet you with a fucking handshake and a song. From a business standpoint, I could respect it. It was smart, really, how feminine and . . . enchanting they'd gone with the esthetic. It called to every bride who pulled up in this gravel lot, telling them this was the place that could create literal fairy tales.

But as a person who refused to ever get married, my balls tried to burrow their way back into my body. I immediately regretted telling my father I'd handle getting these people on board for Leighton's wedding. A large part of me wanted the throw my G-Wagon into reverse and get the hell out of there. The urge to call Hershel and tell him I'd tried my best, but they wouldn't budge was strong, and I would have gladly done it if I didn't think he'd end up climbing into his truck one day after his chemotherapy treatment and drive his ass down here to try and take care of it himself.

That sealed my fate. I wasn't leaving until they

agreed to take Leighton on as a client. With a resigned sigh, I pressed the button on my dash to kill the engine and climbed out, traveling the few feet from my car to the door like I was walking toward my doom.

I was sure the soft, melodic chimes that rang out as soon as I pushed the door open were meant to be calming, but they set my teeth on edge. My eyes took in the small reception area as I made my way to the front desk. The walls were covered in framed black and white photos of different weddings the coordinators had worked on, and I had to admit, from a quick glance, I was impressed. Whoever the photographer was, they had real talent. Even in black and white, the energy of every photograph came through. It was no wonder these people were in high demand.

I would have rather had my molars pulled out with rusty pliers than ever get married, but even I had to admit from the pictures on the wall, they were damn good at their jobs.

"Hi. Can I help you?"

I pulled my attention from the photographs and turned to the cheerful, smiling redhead behind the front desk. I moved in her direction with purpose, ready to get this done so I could get the hell out of here and back to the work I'd been neglecting far too much lately.

"Yes. I need to see about scheduling a wedding with your event coordinators."

Her smile deflated a bit at my curt tone. "Oh, well, um . . . I'm sorry, sir. We're not taking any new clients at the moment, but I'd be more than happy to give you the number for another local company. They do good work; you have my word that you'll be happy with them."

I seriously doubted that, because if Leighton didn't get what she wanted, she made sure no one was happy. "That not going to work," I clipped. "It needs to be *this* company."

The woman's smile faded away completely, replaced by a look of uncertainty. It was a look I was more than familiar with since it was how most people I had to deal with looked at me. Trepidation mixed with the smallest hint of fear, like they weren't sure if I was going to make a scene or threaten their lives.

"I'm sorry, sir, but we're completely booked up for the next several months."

I felt my mouth pull into a tight line. Christ, if I didn't make this happen, there wasn't a doubt in my mind Hershel would step in, and this was the last thing he needed to worry about. Stiffening my spine, I squared my shoulders and lifted my chin, adopting my board-room voice.

"Unacceptable," I snapped loud enough to make the receptionist jolt. I brought my palms down on the credenza between us. "I need to speak with someone in charge. Now."

The woman's eyes grew glassy, and she sniffled right before scurrying from behind the counter with a muffled, "Just a moment, sir."

Once she was gone, I let my shoulders fall ever so slightly, the exhaustion that came simply from knowing Leighton already weighing on me. My attention turned back to the photos on the walls, and I moved closer, taking them all in. Each one was that of a bride and groom in different stages of wedding day bliss. Some were on the dance floor, surrounded by friends and family. Some were standing at the altar experiencing their first kiss as husband and wife. Each was a candid shot made to capture the authenticity of the moment.

Then I got to the picture hanging from a place of prominence right above the door. It too was in black and white like all the rest, the frame matching all the others. However, it wasn't of a newly married couple. In it, three women stood side by side, their arms thrown over each other's shoulders as they beamed at the camera.

I recognized the two on the outside immediately, but it was the woman in the middle, her smile even bigger and brighter than her friends, that made my stomach drop to my feet.

"Shit," I hissed as I moved closer to the picture, blinking like I somehow saw it wrong the first time, but every time I opened my eyes, Jolie's smiling face was staring back at me.

And just like that, I knew I was fucked.

Jolie

Our receptionist, Becca, scurried past my open office door, sniffling and batting at her cheeks as she rushed down the hallway.

"Whoa. Hey," I called out, jumping out of my chair and rounding my desk. I made it across the threshold and into the hall at the same time Tarryn peeked her head out of her office across from mine. Becca was standing in the doorway of Ryan's office a little farther down, her cheeks pink and eyes puffy.

"What's going on?" I asked as Tarryn and I closed in on them.

"Th-there's a guy up front. He—he's demanding to speak to someone in charge."

My skin prickled, the tiny hairs on my arms standing on end. I took a step closer to her, ready to go full-on Mama Bear if the situation called for it. "Did this guy do something to you?"

I wasn't sure what the hell he'd done to make Becca cry, but I was sure whatever it was, it was junk punch worthy, and I was more than happy to dole out his punishment. Becca was a constant ray of freaking sunshine, for crying out loud. Making her cry was like punching an entire litter of Yorkie puppies right in the face. Just plain wrong.

She shook her head, taking the tissue Ryan passed her way and dabbing under her eyes. "He was just rude. And super intimidating." My back snapped straight. "He came in saying he wanted to see about booking a wedding, but I told him we weren't taking on any new clients, just like you guys told me to say, and he got really bossy. Wouldn't take no for an answer and demanded to speak to one of you guys."

That was it. This guy had just sealed his fate. It was junk-punch o'clock, damn it.

I turned on my heel and started down the hall toward the small but cozy reception area that we'd spent countless hours designing and furnishing so it was absolutely perfect. I was ready to throw the hell down.

"Jolie, slow down," Ryan attempted to reason from behind me, her heels clicking on the tile floor as she and Tarryn raced to catch up to me. She'd always been the more diplomatic out of the group. That gut punch she'd given Daniel Boyd in the third grade had been a one-off. Most of the time she was the levelheaded one, the one who thought things through and planned before taking—or not taking—action. Unless you hurt someone she loved. Then she went feral. To this day, Barrett still didn't know she was the one who keyed the words *Dickless Wonder* into both sides of his car *and* the hood before slashing his tires. He'd hurt me, so she'd gone full Carrie Underwood on his ass.

"Let's just take a moment and think this through," Tarryn attempted.

I reached the reception area before either of them could catch me, mouth opened in preparation for ripping this dude a new asshole, but before I could get the words out, I spotted the man in question and screeched to a halt at the sight of Vaughn in the reception area, staring up at the photo of Ryan, Tarryn, and me outside the office building the day we opened Three's a Charm.

My girls stumbled into my back at my abrupt stop, and I knew by the muttered curses from each of them they recognized him only a second after I did.

"*You*," I said on a growl. Vaughn whipped around, those aquamarine eyes of his flashing with something I was too fired up to put a finger on the moment they landed on me. "You made my receptionist cry, asshole."

His hands came up in surrender. "Jolie—"

"Becca," I called out over my shoulder without taking my eyes off the man standing only a few feet away. "Will you please go get me a cup of coffee from the break room? Fill it all the way to the top." My eyelids narrowed viciously. "And heat it up in the microwave for forty-five seconds. I want to make sure it's *really* hot."

"Becca, do not do that," Ryan said in that strict boss voice of hers. "I think we're all more than capable of handling this like adults."

She could speak for herself, because I wasn't really feeling very adult at the moment. I crossed my arms over my chest and tried to melt the skin off his perfectly chiseled face with my eyes. Was I overreacting? Possibly. A little. But this guy had come in here, throwing his weight around like it was his right, and made my friend cry. And that was *after* taking liberties in front of the entire town and throwing the life I'd been trying to piece back together into a meat grinder and pulverizing it beyond recognition.

There was also a slight possibility that part of my irrationality stemmed from the fact that I'd been suffering from some rather inconvenient sexual frustration since that kiss. I didn't know up from down, and when I was thrown off balance, I tended to act before thinking. It wasn't the best character trait to have, but at least I was aware and owned it.

I just hadn't done anything to actually fix it.

Vaughn hadn't taken those unique eyes off me since I stepped into the reception area, and I would have been lying if I said that being under his intense scrutiny wasn't a little disconcerting. He just had this . . . energy about him, all the time. Tarryn would call it big-dick energy, and for the first time in my life, I understood what that meant, because this man reeked of BDE.

"May I speak to you?" he asked in that hard tone that seemed to be his default. He cast a furtive glance at my girls before returning those oxidized copper eyes to me and adding, "Alone?"

I opened my mouth to tell him anything he had to say to me, he could say in front of my partners, but Ryan got there first. "Why don't you take him back to your office?"

My jaw dropped in affront as I turned to look back at

her like she'd just lost her damn mind, but I read her expression loud and clear, and it said *don't screw with me or I'll make you pay.*

"Fine," I said with a childish pout, turning my glare back on Vaughn. "Come on." Then I stomped down the hallway without waiting to see if he was keeping up.

Chapter Thirteen

I realized just what a huge mistake I had made when I shut the door to my office behind Vaughn, sealing us in together.

I should have taken him out into the parking lot for this conversation, not closed myself in a room where just turning around would have me bumping into those linebacker shoulders of his. It wasn't like it was a very big office in the first place, but having him in the space made it feel like a shoebox. A shoebox that suddenly smelled strongly of his amber and spice scent. God, why did he have to smell so damn good? It was probably going to take forever to get that smell out of here.

I moved around my desk, putting some space between us, and plopped down into my chair before waving for him to take one of the small fluffy white upholstered chairs sitting across from me. Like most everything else in the Three's a Charm building, my office was designed to cater to our clientele, meaning everything was soft and feminine and downright pretty.

As soon as Vaughn sat down, I had to bite my lip to keep from laughing at how ridiculous he looked. Even all that BDE he was swaggering around with was no match for tufted velvet. He shifted his considerable bulk in an attempt to get comfortable. When that proved to be impossible, he shot me a withering look. "Really? You couldn't have sprung for full-sized furniture? You had to get these hobbit chairs?"

I rocked back in the white leather executive chair, bracing my elbows on the arms and steepling my fingers together. "You aren't exactly our target demographic here." The skin around my eyes tightened as I narrowed them into a vicious glare. "We cater more toward the bride. You know, the woman who most likely doesn't know her fiancé is running around kissing complete strangers?"

His chin came up, his eyes pinning me in place. "What?"

"You came in demanding that we help you plan your wedding. That's what Becca said before you ran her off. You know, the sweet receptionist you made cry? Still not over that, by the way."

His top lip curled up, exposing a row of straight pearly white teeth. "Trust me, there is no woman. I know this may come off as an insult given your line of work, but I have absolutely no intention of marrying. Ever."

My face pinched up. "Then who—" I stopped and sucked in a jagged gasp. "You did *not* come here demanding that we coordinate the wedding of your sister to *my ex-fiancé!*"

"In my defense, I didn't know it was your company at the time."

I shot out of my chair, bracing my palms on the top of my desk. "Nope. Nuh-uh. Absolutely not. You may as well just go now."

Vaughn closed his eyes and pinched the bridge of his nose, slowly blowing out a breath like he was silently counting to ten. When he finally opened his eyes again, that impassive mask of his was back in place. "Would you please sit down so we can talk like two adults?"

If people didn't stop telling me to behave like an adult, I was going to start throwing shit. "You have a lot of nerve, you know that? I can't believe—"

"I'm not going to ask you to plan Leighton's wedding, alright?" He pushed an irritated gust of breath past his lips. "Believe it or not, I'm not *that* big of an asshole. I didn't come here for Leighton anyway. I came for my father."

Something moved over his face, a flash of emotion I might have missed if I hadn't been paying close enough attention. It was there and gone from one blink of an eye to the next, but the impact of that one little blip was strong enough to steal the breath from my lungs, it was so profound.

I collapsed back into my chair, the fight draining out of me. "I don't understand. For your father?"

A vein in his neck throbbed, his Adam's apple bobbing prominently on a thick swallow. "He's sick. That's why I temporarily relocated to Pembrooke in the first place. But Leighton . . ." He reached up to rub at his temple. "She seems to forget he's undergoing treatment for cancer. Or maybe she doesn't consider it since it's not about her. Either way, he's spoiled her since the moment she was born, and when she called him, crying that she couldn't get an appointment with the most popular wedding coordinators in the area, he was going to try to handle it himself. I couldn't let him do that. Not when he needs to focus on himself."

My chest expanded on such a deep breath, it was a wonder I didn't pop a lung. A lump the size of a golf ball had taken up residence in my throat, and I had to work overtime to swallow it down. "I-I'm sorry about your dad," I said quietly. "I didn't know."

He gave his head a resounding shake. "I wouldn't expect you to. And it's fine. He's going to be okay. Eventually."

"But it's still hard. I get it."

His head came up, his eyes narrowing on me like I'd spoken aloud what he was thinking. His expression shifted again, turning hard all of a sudden, as if he was angry at himself for showing even the slightest bit of vulnerability. If it were possible, he grew grumpier.

"Anyway, that's all beside the point." He paused, reaching up to tug at the collar of his dress shirt. This one was the palest blue that really made that rim of copper on the outside of his irises stand out. The man really did have a hard-on for his suits, but I had to admit, he could wear the hell out of them, that was for damn sure. He cleared his throat, almost seeming nervous. "We should probably talk about the . . . you know."

I swiveled my chair from side to side as I scrutinized the man sitting in front of me, looking ridiculous in a chair that was two sizes too small for him. My brows rose toward my hairline. "You mean how you dropped a bomb on my life by kissing me in front of half the town and told my ex we were dating?"

Those notches between his brows deepened with his frown. "Excuse me for doing you a favor."

I let out a bark of exasperated laughter, my eyes widening. "I never asked you to do that! I'm perfectly capable of handling my ex on my own, thank you very much."

He tucked his tongue into the inside of his cheek, giving me a dubious look that prodded at my insides. "Really? Because you looked like you were two seconds away from running out of that building like your ass was on fire." He let out a scoffing laugh. "That would have shown him, wouldn't it?"

I tried my hardest to mask the wince his words caused, but I must not have been fast enough, because instead of looking like he'd just scored a point, his expression fell like he'd just accidentally kicked one of those adorable puppies that are tiny enough to fit into a tea cup.

"I'm—" The muscle in his jaw ticked as his nostrils flared on a sharp exhale. "Sorry," he gritted out like that one word left a bitter taste in his mouth. "I shouldn't have said that. It was unnecessarily rude."

"Is that supposed to mean all the other times you've been an asshole to me have been necessary?"

He reached up to massage at the center of his forehead like I was the most vexing person he'd ever met, and I would have been lying if I said I didn't get a little thrill out of that. "Look, I'm not . . . very comfortable with apologies."

I snorted. "Really? You hide it so well."

The hard look he shot me probably would have sent most other people running. But for some strange reason, I found it thrilling. "Why did you do it?" I asked. That question had needled at me for days now. "It's clear you don't like me, so why bother trying to help me out?"

"I don't . . . *not* like you," he said, his voice low and rusty, and that admission rendered me momentarily speechless. "I can acknowledge that our first couple of encounters weren't ideal, but I don't dislike you. I *do*, however dislike your ex." His expression turned to granite. "Very much."

"What? Don't like the thought of him with your precious little sister?" I hadn't meant to say that, but I especially hadn't meant for my snide tone to give away my true feelings of Leighton Cavanagh.

I'd expected Vaughn to get offended, expected that he was another person in her life that spoiled her and turned her into the vapid little brat she had become, so it shocked the hell out of me when he scoffed, shaking his head on an emotionless laugh. "Please. I wouldn't exactly call us close. And as far as I can tell, the two of them were made for each other."

It was a wonder the bottom of my jaw didn't slam into the top of my desk from falling open so fast. Catching the surprise on my face, one corner of Vaughn's mouth curled upward ever so slightly in a cocky smirk. It was the closest I'd seen him come to smiling—probably the closest the stoic man would ever get. For crying out loud, he was so emotionally stunted that his attempt at apologizing had been cringe-inducing. He looked like he would have preferred to gargle glass than force those words out.

"Caught you off guard with that, didn't I?"

I wiped the surprise off of my face and replaced it with a flat, bored expression. "If it's not because you're worried about your sister, why don't you like Barrett?" I probably should have let it go, but my curiosity was well and truly piqued, and the question would bug me until I finally caved and asked anyway.

"Because from what little I know about the man, he's a spinless, sacless doormat who is all too happy to lay down at my half-sister's feet so she can step all over him," he answered with raw honesty. I also didn't miss the way he stressed the word *half* while describing his connection with Leighton, like it was important to him that I understood the distinction.

"He won't admit it, but I'm almost positive he ended our engagement and broke up with me for her."

My eyes widened and my hand came up to cover my mouth as soon as the last word of that sentence escaped, like I could possibly pull them back, unsay them somehow. I wasn't sure what the hell had possessed me to reveal something so personal to this man. That was the first time I'd spoken the words out loud. I hadn't even been able to bring myself to admit that ugly truth to Tarryn or Ryan. I'd been sitting on it for the past year, letting the shame that belief caused fester inside me.

I shook my head, suddenly feeling far too vulnerable. "I-I don't know why the hell I told you that. Please, just forget I said anything."

Vaughn's ticking jaw and furrowed brow were the only outward signs the man felt something besides boredom. "I'm afraid I won't be able to forget it, Calamity. Knowing that makes me glad I acted so impulsively that day at the café." My throat went dry and the air in the room grew thick and humid all of a sudden. "And you should know, I don't act impulsively. Ever."

Uh-oh. I did *not* want to like this guy.

Just like that, his big dick energy returned and he didn't look so ridiculous in that little chair any longer.

"That's the second time you've called me that." His head canted to the side in confusion. "Calamity," I explained. "Gotta say, city slicker, I'm not sure if I should be flattered to rate high enough that you'd bestow a nickname on me, or insulted at the meaning behind it."

"Don't be insulted." Those words came out as an order in that gruff voice of his, sending sparks of electricity through most of my body's erogenous zones. What the hell was that all about? I shook off the odd, unexpected attraction suddenly trying to stir at my insides, stomping it out like I would a spider that crossed my path.

I wasn't sure how to feel or respond, so I decided to go with my default setting: snarky. "You can't order me to not be insulted."

Challenge sparkled in those eyes of his, lighting a fire deep in my belly. "I can when the name isn't meant to be an insult. And I'm pretty sure you already knew that."

I sat back in my chair, staring across at him inquisitively and, dare I say, with more interest than I should feel toward the brother of my enemy. "I had a feeling, but you know what they say when you assume."

"It makes you an asshole."

I let out a bubble of astonished laughter at his unexpected joke. If you had asked me a week ago if this man had a sense of humor, I would have bet money the answer was no. But I saw it right then, and I actually appreciated the dry, detached way in which he delivered it more than if he'd added a smile or a laugh of his own to the end of it.

"I'm starting to think there's more to the man beneath those stuffy suits than I originally thought. I think you may actually be full of surprises, Vaughn."

He sat back in that man-splay that I always found sexy. You know what I'm talking about. The one where the guy spreads his legs wide while propping an elbow on the arm of his chair and cradling his chin in an almost lazy fashion. It screamed confidence and sex. And it shouldn't have worked for a guy sitting in a teeny velvet girly chair, but *damn*, it did.

"Ready for another one?"

I actually wasn't sure, but I felt the need to at least fake the same level of confidence this guy was exuding, so I pasted a bored expression on my face and waved my hand as if to say *out with it already. I am a very important person, I don't have all day.*

"I think we should keep up the ruse we started back in that café."

I choked on my own saliva. So much for playing it cool. "You *what?*"

"Remember what you said to me after I told Beelzebub we were together? You said I didn't have a clue what I'd just done. By your cryptic warning and the fact my father has already asked about you, I take it word is already spreading all over town."

I stifled a laugh by biting the inside of my lip. "First of all, his name is Barrett, but I'm sure you already knew that." He waved me off dismissively. "And second . . . Yep. That particular bit of gossip spread faster than the Black Plague. I already got the obligatory guilt call from my mother who demanded I bring you to dinner. I've decided to handle the situation like any responsible adult would."

He lifted one dark, sculpted brow. "By burying your head in the sand and pretending it didn't happen?"

"You know, for a fake boyfriend, you're surprisingly astute."

"See? I already know you better than Beany Baby ever did. So what do you say?"

I rocked back and forth in my chair as the two of us watched each other in silence, the atmosphere swirling around us getting thicker with a kind of tension I couldn't bring myself to put a name to but that left my skin tingling all the same.

Something told me saying yes to this man was akin to making a deal with the devil, but the intrigue was too great to ignore. I felt like a kid who had to reach out and touch the burner on the stove to see for myself if it was hot, despite my mother's warnings. "I say . . . okay. Let's do this."

He unfolded himself from that ridiculous chair, stretching to his full height, which had to be a few inches over six feet. As I followed suit and stood up, I couldn't help but notice that the top of my head would barely reach his chin. Given that I was five seven and was rocking high heels, that was impressive as hell.

I rounded the desk and moved to the door. I twisted the knob and pulled it open, sucking in a lungful of fresh, unelectrified air.

His eyes locked with mine as he met me in the open doorway, stopping right in front of me. He stood so close his knuckles brushed against the front of my blouse as he buttoned his jacket, sending a zing through my blood. I pulled in a broken breath as I tipped my head back to look into those intoxicating eyes.

He was all I could see, all I could smell. The heat from his skin was wrapping me up like a warm blanket. "So when do you want to get started?"

"Uh . . . what?"

He did that barely-there smirk again, and damn if it wasn't sexy as hell. "We should probably meet up somewhere private to go over our stories, right? I'm not sure if you're aware of this, but you have a terrible poker face."

Indignation pinched my face into a scowl. "I have an

excellent poker face, thank you very much." Just as soon as the sentence came out of my mouth, I jolted back in shock when his fingers came up to caress my jawline.

"I rest my case," he said arrogantly. "No one is going to buy this if you flinch every time I touch you."

I couldn't stop my lips from forming a pout. "No fair. I wasn't prepared. If I'd known you were going to touch me, I wouldn't have flinched."

He arched a brow, communicating I'd proven his point without having to say a damn word.

"Fine." I huffed out a breath and rolled my eyes. "Dinner at my place tomorrow night." I moved to my desk and scrawled my address and cell number onto a bright pink sticky note. Tearing it off, I passed it to him, an electric current traveling up my arm at the brush of his fingers against mine when he took the slip of paper from me.

"See you tomorrow, Calamity. Try not to spill coffee on any poor, unexpecting men in the meantime."

I crossed my arms over my chest and smirked. "I make no promises. Hey, Vaughn?" I called when he turned to leave, bringing him up short. "What are the odds of your father showing up here in the next few days?"

The flare of his nostrils was answer enough. Still, he said, "Too high, but I'll do what I can to prevent it."

Something tugged at my chest, not only for Vaughn, but for his sick father as well. A man who only wanted to give his daughter her heart's desire.

"We'll do the wedding."

The infinitesimal widening of his eyes was his only giveaway. "You don't have to—"

"For your father. To spare him the grief." And for Vaughn, who was stuck in the middle. But something told me he wouldn't appreciate hearing that, so I left it unspoken.

He arched that sexy brow again. "You're sure?"

I waved him off and blew out a raspberry. "Please. I'm a professional, thank you very much. I've totally got this." I lifted a single shoulder in a shrug. "And if I don't, they'll never be able to point the sabotage back at me."

I could see the humor in his gaze. "Tomorrow, Jolie."

"Tomorrow, City Slicker. And don't forget to apologize to Becca on your way out."

I closed the door on his unhappy growl, waiting until I heard his footsteps leading away before I started laughing.

Chapter Fourteen

Jolie

I wasn't sure why I felt so nervous, but as I stood in the center of my living room, turning a slow circle to inspect everything, I couldn't ignore the way my heart banged around inside my chest like a pinball.

I'd had what I called low-grade anxiety all day long at the thought of Vaughn coming to my house so we could discuss this fake relationship we'd agreed to. It had been a test for my sanity having him in my office the day before. The thought of him being in my home made my skin tingle and my blood pump too fast. Those red cells were shooting through my veins like the cars at the Indy 500. Tarryn and Ryan hadn't missed it either, and those jerks had gotten a real kick out of teasing me mercilessly. They knew the truth about my and Vaughn's little stratagem, but they'd been sworn to secrecy, and I trusted they would take the truth to their graves. That didn't mean they weren't going to give me hell about my *new boyfriend* in the meantime.

I'd raced home from work an hour early so I had enough time to get dinner started, then spent the better part of the evening cleaning my house from top to bottom until I could see my reflection in every surface.

The lasagna was done, the garlic bread was warming in the oven and filling the house with the most incredible smells, and I'd mixed up a fresh salad that was waiting in the fridge to be pulled out. I'd even stopped off at Sinful Sweets for some of Chloe's delicious mini chocolate tarts for dessert.

I couldn't tell you why I'd pulled out all the stops the way I had, I hadn't been able to stop myself. But as the minutes ticked closer to the time Vaughn was set to arrive, I started to question everything. What if he didn't like pasta or had some kind of gluten or dairy allergy? What if the candles I lit simply because I loved candles made the whole vibe feel too romantic? What if he took one look at my house and thought *small and unimpressive?*

Smoosh came traipsing in, plopping down on her furry ass and staring at me with those judgmental yellow eyes.

"Don't look at me like that," I scolded. "I would have done all of this for any guest I had coming over."

She blinked. We both knew I was lying. For the most part, my house stayed pretty clean, and every Sunday I scrubbed and dusted and mopped. But if it had been my parents or friends coming over, I would have already been dressed in my pajamas, having lost my bra the moment I walked through the door, and the stack of mail that had been sitting on my kitchen island still would have been there, along with last night's dishes that had been "soaking" in the sink all day.

I narrowed my eyes at my critical cat. "Please. Like you have any right to judge me. You clean your private parts right out in the open for everyone to see."

As if to prove she didn't give a single shit, she hiked her back leg straight in the air and started bathing herself, her kitty way of giving me the middle finger, I was sure.

"Stop that. And you better be on your best behavior tonight. You didn't exactly make us look good last time. I've tried talking you up, but he's still skeptical, so I expect you to put your best foot forward."

I must have gotten through to her, really made her feel guilty, because she stood up and moved closer, arching her back and rubbing herself against my legs as she made a figure eight between my feet, purring like she was the most loving, docile feline in all the world. Bending down, I scooped her into my arms and lifted her up, snuggling her into my chest.

"I can't stay mad at you when you get all cute like that. Who's Mommy's wittle smoosh face, huh? Are you my wittle smoosh face?"

Just then the doorbell rang, sending a shockwave through me like the earth had moved beneath my feet. I closed my eyes and pulled in a breath through my nose, counting to ten to get my pulse under control. This was ridiculous. I usually only felt like this when I was getting ready for a first date, and that couldn't have been further from the case tonight. This wasn't a date. This was . . . a strategy session. There was no reason for me to be such a massive jumble of nerves.

The bell rang again, jolting me back into reality and telling me I'd been standing frozen for too long.

"Be right there," I called out, bending to put Smoosh back on the floor. I headed toward the door, brushing at the front of my shirt to get rid of the cat hair. I'd opted for casual tonight, changing into a pair of loose-fitting jeans that were cropped at the ankle and had a frayed hem. I paired it with a gray scoop-neck tank with a drawing of a sunrise that I half tucked at the front. I'd decided to go barefoot so it didn't seem I was trying too hard—counting myself lucky I'd gotten a pedicure earlier in the week—but had refreshed my makeup and hair as soon as I got home.

With one last deep, cleansing breath, I grabbed hold of the knob, pulled the door open, and got my first glimpse of Vaughn Cavanaugh standing on my front porch. And it was enough to make my mouth drier than the Sahara.

Once again, he was in a suit—today's was black with a white button-down beneath. He'd forgone a tie, leaving the collar unbuttoned just enough to give me the smallest peek of that divot at the base of his throat between his clavicles. I never thought of that spot on a man as sexy. Until right then.

His suit jacket was brushed back so he could put his hands in the pockets of his slacks, putting his trim waist on display, and if I cocked my head to the side and squinted, I was certain I could see the outline of ab muscles beneath the fabric of his shirt.

"Are you going to invite me in or am I going to have to stand here all night while you leer at me?"

That sure as hell snapped me out of it. I lifted my eyes to his face. His lips were in a flat line, but I saw the humor dancing in his gaze and glared. "I wasn't leering, jackass. I was wondering if you owned any kind of clothing other than suits. Be honest, you sleep in them too, don't you?"

"Of course not. I sleep in pajamas that have a suit screen printed on the front. Kind of like those tuxedo T-shirts."

My lips spread into a smile as a snort of laughter rattled up my throat. "You're ridiculous," I said with a good-natured shake of my head. "Come on in. You're right on time. Dinner is ready."

He stepped across the threshold, and I didn't miss the way his head turned from side to side, taking everything in as he slipped the jacket off his arms and folded it over the back of my couch. "It smells good in here."

I rolled my eyes. "You don't have to sound so surprised about it. Not to brag or anything, but I'm a pretty decent cook. My mom made sure of that."

I thought I caught a hint of interest in his eyes as he looked at me. "She taught you to cook?"

"Yep. Starting as soon as I was old enough to reach the stove. I helped her with dinner most nights. I'm not good enough to open my own restaurant or anything, but I know my way around a kitchen well enough that I'm not stuck eating the same five meals every week or living on takeout." I led him into the kitchen and grabbed the oven mitt I'd discarded earlier so I could take the garlic bread out of the oven. "I hope you like lasagna. I didn't think about asking if you have any food allergies. Sorry about that."

"No allergies. And I like lasagna just fine."

I looked over my shoulder and smiled as I used a bread knife to slice the flaky bread into symmetrical slices, only to have the air squeezed out of my lungs when I caught his eyes lingering on my ass before they flicked up to my face. He was checking me out. No doubt about it. I whipped back around quickly, hoping he didn't notice that my cheeks were most likely the color of raspberry filling as I transferred the bread into a pretty little basket I found at one of the stands at the local farmer's market a couple years back.

He stepped closer, coming up beside me. "Is there anything I can help with?"

I cleared the frog out of my throat, ducking my head as I worked to shield my burning cheeks from view. "Um, y-yeah." I pointed at the stack of plates and silverware I'd pulled out earlier. "If you could set the table and put the lasagna on the hot pad I placed in the middle that would be great."

I felt his arm brush against my back as he moved past me, despite having plenty of room in the kitchen to prevent that, and had to bite down on my bottom lip to keep from smiling. While he moved into the dining area, I rushed to the fridge and yanked it open, sticking my overheated face into the cold box in the hope of cooling my skin down before I gave myself away.

"Get it together," I whispered to myself. "He's just some guy, and this *isn't* a real date."

"Anything else I can do?"

I let out a squeak at the sound of his voice, jumping in fright and banging my elbow on the shelf holding my coffee creamer and milk. "Ow, damn it!"

"You okay?"

I shook my arm out and pasted on a smile as I grabbed the salad bowl and turned around. "Yep. I'm great. Just getting the salad." My gaze darted away from his, but not before I caught the arch in his brow that told me he knew I was full of shit. "Would you mind grabbing the bread?"

With the basket in hand, he followed me into the dining area right off the living room. I'd already set out a bottle of wine and wineglasses, as well as water before he arrived. "If you don't want wine or water, I've got beer and iced tea."

"Wine is fine. Thank you."

We sat down, silence descending on us as we plated our food. It was starting to feel awkward when Vaughn surprised me by cutting the tension and asking, "That demon cat of yours isn't going to attack me again, is it?"

I shot him a murderous look. "Smoosh isn't a demon

cat. And no, she's in a pretty good mood today, so I'd say you're safe."

He added a helping of salad to his plate before doing the same to mine without me having to ask. The move certainly didn't make my heart flutter. Not one damn bit.

Chapter Fifteen

Jolie

I kept telling myself my skin didn't tingle with awareness of his close proximity, but the voice in the back of my head was cackling and calling me a dirty liar. At some point, he'd cuffed the sleeves of his shirt, putting his forearms on display, and it was proving very difficult to keep from drooling at the sight of the thick, corded muscles that ran from his wrists to his elbows. What was worse was how his bicep strained every time he bent his arm to take a drink, testing the tensile strength of the seams, or how his throat worked on a swallow. When the hell did a man's throat become a turn-on? Had I really been out of the game that long?

"Its temperament is probably due to the fact you named it Smoosh. What in the world possessed you to do that?" he asked, snapping me out of my ogling.

I let out a laugh, unable to find it in myself to be insulted. I knew it was a ridiculous name for a cat, but it worked, so I went with it. "First of all, *it* is actually a *she*. And what possessed me was her face," I answered as I grabbed a slice of garlic bread and passed the basket to Vaughn. "She has the cutest little smoosh face."

"Hmm. Must have missed that when she was trying to claw me to death and smother me at the same time."

"She was having a particularly bad day," I defended. "Anyway, I kept calling her smoosh face, so I just decided to make it her name."

"Poor cat," he muttered drily before forking off a corner of his lasagna and popping it into his mouth.

I waited, trying not to hold my breath as he chewed slowly and swallowed. Finally, when he remained silent and blank-faced for too long, I couldn't take it any longer. "Well? What do you think?"

He sipped his water with that damn arched brow. "Think of what?"

I groaned with exasperation. "You're the worst. You know that?"

"It's good," he finally said, putting me out of my misery with that barely-there curl of his mouth that was there and gone so fast I wasn't sure it could even be classified as a smirk. I wasn't sure I'd ever get used to how close to the vest Vaughn played his cards. It was intriguing and frustrating all at the same time. "If I haven't said it already, thank you for cooking."

"You haven't, and you're welcome. It really wasn't any trouble." That was a lie, of course. I'd spent the few hours before he arrived running around like a chicken with its head cut off, but he didn't need to know that. "I've always enjoyed cooking for other people. It's one of my love languages."

He lifted his brows. "Love languages?"

I chewed the bite I'd just taken, looking at him curiously as I forced it down. "Yeah. You know, love languages?" He shook his head like he still didn't understand. My chin jerked back in bewilderment. "You've seriously never heard of love languages?"

"Continuing to say it won't suddenly make me understand," he said with a bland look.

I rolled my eyes. "They're basically how you express your love to people. I like showing them they're important by feeding them, taking care of them."

He sipped at his wine. "Ah."

A beat of silence passed between us as I waited for more.

"What about you? What's your love language?"

He crunched into the garlic bread and lifted his wide, rounded shoulder in a shrug. "I don't think I have any. I don't like people enough to have a language that conveys caring."

I choked on the sip of wine I'd just taken. "You don't like people?"

"Not particularly, no." He said that with the same level of detachment a person might announce the weather. Like it was nothing at all. "Huh. Would you look at that? It's raining outside." The end.

"That's—" I shook my head, trying to wrap my brain around that. "Vaughn, you can't claim you don't like people like that, like some blanket statement that encompasses everyone. I mean, there has to be at least a few people you like, right?"

He wiped his mouth on the cloth napkin I'd set out earlier—yes, I went so far as to pull out the fancy cloth napkins I never used because they were a pain in the ass to wash. "There are people I tolerate, but I'm a very busy man. Every day of my life is on a rigid schedule. Without it, things would fall into chaos. I've found most people tend to mess with that schedule or create chaos on their own for the hell of it, so I've chosen not to bother wasting my time."

"But—what about your parents? Or your sister? I mean, they're your blood. Wasn't it basically engrained in you from birth to love them?"

He arched a brow and pointed the tines of his fork in

my direction. "Ah, but you see, I never said anything about love. Love and like are two very different things. Of course I love my family. But Leighton is the perfect example of loving someone without liking them. I think she's a self-centered, dramatic brat who cares too much for herself and not nearly enough for those around her. Those are qualities I don't like one bit."

"So what you're basically saying is you're only tolerating me?" I clarified, raising my brows in a silent challenge. I was silently daring him to say he didn't like me while sitting in my home and eating the food I'd taken the time to buy and cook for him.

He paused mid-chew, as though the question actually threw him off. "I think . . . you may be the exception," he said, wonder coating his words, like he only then realized he liked me. And why in the hell did I find that flattering? I should have been insulted, not experiencing a swarm of butterflies taking flight in my belly.

"Wow. Uh . . . thanks?"

"Believe me, I'm as surprised by that as you are," he said grudgingly, and for some reason, the tone of his voice made my head fall back on a deep, muscle-clenching belly laugh.

I wiped at my cheeks with the backs of my hands once I finally managed to get ahold of myself, noticing that Vaughn was watching me with an intensity that made my heart flip-flop in my chest.

"You have a very nice laugh," he stated plainly.

I poked at the inside of my cheek with my tongue to temper my smile. "Thank you. I guess it's a good thing you like me since everyone in Pembrooke thinks we're in a romantic relationship, huh?"

His eyes drilled into me like they were seeing deeper than anyone had ever bothered to look before. "I guess you're right."

I cleared my throat, looking down at my plate and using my fork to move things around as I tried to calm my rapidly fluttering pulse. There was something about this man I couldn't put my finger on. He claimed not to like most people. He didn't have the usual sense of humor. He seemed stiff and unflinchingly rigid. But my gut was telling me there was more to him. He claimed to be an asshole, and for all intents and purposes, he appeared to try and live up to that self-imposed reputation. However, I was beginning to think it was a mask he wore to keep people at a distance.

The truth was, I didn't think he was nearly as rude and unfeeling as he led people to believe. "Speaking of which, if we're going to make this work, we probably need to know about each other, don't you think?"

He finished chewing his bite, sitting back in his chair

and wiping his mouth before placing his napkin on the table beside his empty plate. After a sip of wine, he sat back in that man-spread that was even more potent thanks to the cuffed sleeves and exposed throat.

God, I really needed to get a grip.

"Sounds reasonable. What do you want to know?"

I turned my chair to face him, crossing one leg over the other as I sipped my wine, keeping it in hand for easy access. "Well, I guess for starters, how old are you?"

"Thirty-eight." I choked on the sip I'd just taken. "That surprises you?" he asked, curiosity and humor in those words.

I wiped at my mouth with the back of my wrist like a freaking lady. "Um, *yeah*! You look like you're thirty-three, maybe thirty-four, tops." I flopped back with a pout. "It really isn't fair how easy you guys have it. You age gracefully, you can pee standing up, and you lose weight faster than we do."

His eyes widened, his brows inching toward his hairline. "I'm . . . sorry?"

"As you should be," I grumped.

He shook his head and his lips curled a teensy bit higher than they had before. It was enough of a smirk for me to realize I wasn't sure I'd survive it if this man let out a full-blown smile. "What about you? How old are you?"

"I turn twenty-nine at the beginning of next month."

He nodded. "Good to know. If we're still putting on this charade then, you'll need to provide me with a list of things you'd like for your birthday."

I was about to take another sip of wine when my stomach cramped at his comment. Placing the glass on the table. I tried not to question how it was possible I'd somehow managed to forget this was fake in the past thirty seconds, and why the reminder made me feel a little nauseated all of a sudden.

I did my best to shake the sludge-y, unwelcomed discomfort off. I barely knew this man. It was ridiculous to be upset.

"Oh, that's—Vaughn, that's really not necessary. But thank you."

"We'll cross that bridge if or when we get to it." I was sure we'd never reach that bridge. He reached for the wine bottle, re-filling his glass and topping mine off—again, without having to be asked. It was when he did those kinds of things I struggled to see him as the callous asshole he claimed to be.

"You said your mom taught you to cook. Are you two close?"

The tension in my shoulders loosened up at the shift in subject matter, and I visibly brightened at the thought of my mother. "Very," I answered. "I'm actually close to both my parents. And my older brother, even though he doesn't live here anymore, which bums me out more often than not."

He tucked his chin into his hand as he regarded me, his index finger absently stroking across his bottom lip. I tried to ignore the tingle that started beneath my skin, but it was impossible.

"Where does he live now?" I got the feeling he wasn't asking because he was digging for information for our ruse, but because he was really interested in knowing, and I was suddenly hit with a disconcerting thought.

Fake dating Vaughn Cavanagh might not be as easy as I originally thought. Because I was kind of starting to like the guy.

Chapter Sixteen

Vaughn

J olie spent the next half hour telling me all about her brother, Dalton, his wife, and the baby they had on the way. The whole time she spoke, her cheeks were tugged up in the brightest smile I'd seen her wear. Seeing the happiness on her face when she spoke about her family made my chest squeeze. She really was breathtakingly beautiful, and that smile only magnified her beauty.

The color in her cheeks rose to a pretty petal pink as she curled her lips between her teeth and bit down. "I'm sorry. I can't believe I've been talking about myself for so long. I'll stop now," she said with a hint of embarrassment.

"No don't. I like hearing you talk." The admission spilled past my lips without any input from my brain, causing her eyes to widen. "About your family, I mean," I added quickly, suddenly feeling heat spread beneath my collar. That iron grip I had on my control at all times tended to waver whenever I was in her presence, but instead of being agitated by it, I was . . . enthralled.

Everything about Jolie intrigued me. From the one-sided conversation I heard her having with her cat before I knocked earlier, to the flashes of shyness, to the brash, almost impudent threats she made when I hurt her friend's feelings. Everything about her grabbed my attention and refused to let go. This woman affected me in a way no person had before. "You're very passionate. It's nice to see."

It was more than nice. I wanted to know more. I wanted to know *everything* there was to know about her. That had certainly never happened before. I hadn't been lying earlier when I told her I liked her—as surprising as that revelation had been. And the more time I spent in her presence, the more there was to like.

She smiled sweetly, leaning forward to prop her elbow on the table and cradle her chin in her hand. "What about you? Are you close with your family?"

That question made my mouth dry and my throat tight. I took a sip of water, having moved away from the wine after my second glass since I had to drive, hoping it would ease the gritty sandpaper feeling in my throat.

Usually I didn't mind sharing the truth about my relationship with my family. It was what it was, as far as I was concerned, and I honestly never really cared what anyone thought about that. Until Jolie.

"I'm in Pembrooke in the hopes of repairing my relationship with my father," I admitted. It was the second time in as many days I opened up to this woman in a way I hadn't expected to.

Her expression softened, her free hand coming across the expanse of table between us to rest on top of mine. That simple touch bolstered me somehow, placing me on more solid footing.

"Things between us have been strained since I was young."

"How young?" she asked gently, not trying to push so much as help guide me to where she sensed I was going.

"Thirteen. I was actually born here, believe it or not. This is where I spent my childhood."

She tucked her tongue into her cheek, making it stick out as she momentarily cast her gaze away from me, that brief flitter of shyness returning. "I have a confession to make," she said, catching me off guard. "I don't want you to think I was gossiping behind your back or anything, but when my mom heard I was seeing someone, she called me, and I might have kind of asked about you. Just a little bit," she added quickly, holding her index finger and thumb a few centimeters apart. I'd lost count of how many times I'd nearly smiled so far this evening. If there was anyone who could make me do it, it was probably Jolie Prescott.

"Anyway, apparently my mom knew your mom and, well . . ."

My humor dried up quickly. "I can only imagine what your mother would have to say about mine."

Jolie's eyes flashed with panic. "She wasn't rude, I promise. It's just that—"

"My mother makes the glacier that sank the Titanic come off warm and cuddly. Is that about right?"

The giggle she let out reminded me of soft bells or windchimes before she quickly slapped her hand over her mouth to silence it. "I'm sorry. I didn't mean to laugh."

"No, it's fine," I assured her, once again fighting back a grin of my own. I didn't understand how it was possible she could make me want to smile when I was discussing Estelle Cavanaugh, but it went to show how full of surprises she really was. "It's the truth, anyway. My mother has never been very, well, motherly. Getting pregnant was an accident. When she divorced my father, she gave me a choice who I wanted to stay with. Even back then I understood the differences between her and my dad. I knew she preferred to be unincumbered while he thrived when he had people to take care of. His love language, as I you called it."

"So you chose to stay with your dad," she surmised in a quiet voice, those brilliant gray eyes of hers shining with something I wasn't quite ready to identify yet.

"He needed me more," I answered, forcing casualness into my voice while the truth of it made my stomach feel like it was being tied into a million knots.

Jolie's chest expanded on a deep breath, her gaze growing scrutinizing. "You know, you aren't nearly as cold and uncaring as you try to make people believe."

I cleared the gravel from my throat and took a huge gulp of water, wishing I hadn't reached my limit on alcohol before this part of the evening. "Yes, well, that's your opinion. Anyway, for the next year it was only the two of us. My mother moved away, and the only times I heard from her were the occasional phone calls every couple years on birthdays or Christmases. Hershel met my stepmother Millicent when I was eight. They were married by the time I was nine and got pregnant pretty soon after that. I was ten when Leighton was born."

"Was that hard for you? Having your dad meet someone and get married again?"

I shook my head, watching the clear liquid coat the sides of my glass as I twisted it in a circle. "No, not really.

Millicent has always been very kind. She behaved as though she were an extension of our family as opposed to the two of them starting a whole new one and me being a castoff from a previous life. Though, my mother has a completely different take on it." I met her gaze, seeing the curiosity lingering there, but to her credit she remained quiet, letting me get the story out on my own.

"I never understood her issue with my father meeting Millicent. I still don't, honestly. She made it clear she didn't want to be married to him anymore and she hated this town, but she liked to tell me I wasn't really a part of their family unit, that no matter how hard any of us tried, I would never truly fit in because I'd always be a reminder to the both of them of a failed past."

Jolie shocked me out of my glum memories by snorting loudly, and when I blinked back into the present, her faced was scrunched up in what I could only describe as righteous indignation. "No offense, Vaughn, but your mom sounds like the literal worst."

A burst of stupefied laughter exploded from my throat, clearly shocking Jolie as much as it did me. The noise I let out felt as foreign as it sounded, like the muscles specifically used for laughter had atrophied from disuse.

As if sensing I was so caught off guard I wasn't sure

how to continue, Jolie put me out of my misery and moved the conversation forward. "If you chose to live with your father how is it that you left Pembrooke when you were thirteen?"

"Again, that was Estelle. She decided my time spent with my father had made me soft. It was her opinion that I would be better off living with her. Hershel tried his hardest to convince her to let me stay, but she had more money and better lawyers. He had a family to take care of and couldn't afford to fight her."

"God, Vaughn. I'm so sorry." Her hand came down on mine once more, her delicate fingers squeezing gently, but that simple touch was enough to send an electric shock up my arm and through my chest. I wanted to turn my hand over, to thread our fingers together, which was bizarre for many reasons, starting with the fact that I barely knew this woman and ending on the realization that I'd never held hands with a woman in my life.

"It's okay, really. I should actually be thankful. I'm as successful as I am today because of her pushing me, so I can't really complain."

"Yes, you can," she demanded, her grip on my hand growing even tighter. "You absolutely *can* complain, because what happened to you wasn't fair. She didn't take what you wanted into consideration. She was bitter and selfish, and you're the one who paid the price for that. I'm really sorry to say this, but I *really* don't like your mother. Not one damn bit. And if I have any say in the matter, I'd rather not meet her while we're doing this whole . . . thing because I don't think I can be nice."

Fuck holding her hand. I was suddenly swamped with the desire to pull her into my lap and fuse my mouth with hers. It was a base need so strong I felt like a caveman, void of all logic and common sense. A need that didn't fit into my carefully crafted and controlled life. One word was pulsing in my head in time with my heartbeat: *Want.*

"You don't have to worry about that, it's a moot point. She's made it abundantly clear she has no desire to ever set foot in Pembrooke again."

It was an opinion, until very recently, I'd shared with her.

"And the whole town wept with gratitude," she muttered dryly.

Christ, she was cute. It was getting more and more difficult to keep the growing attraction I felt for her tamped down.

Just then, a blur of gray and white darted into the dining room so fast I didn't have time to brace against another attack. Before I knew it, the ball of demonic fur posing as a house pet leapt onto my lap. My entire body locked tight with dreaded expectation as the cat braced its back legs on my lap and walked its front paws up my chest.

I'd pressed my back into the chair so hard it was a wonder the wood didn't fuse with my spine. "What's it doing?" I gritted out of the corner of my mouth, not wanting to break eye contact and risk missing a sneak attack.

Jolie laughed. A full-on, stomach-aching kind of laugh that came from the deepest part of her belly. She held her middle as her head fell back, cackling at my expense as my balls drew up into my stomach in fear.

"Glad you find this amusing," I grumbled as the cat on my lap let out a purr so loud it could have rattled the glass in the house. Then, to my utter bewilderment, it began to rub its head across my jaw.

"She likes you," Jolie finally said after the longest minute of my life, in which I worried for the safety not only of my suit but the skin beneath. "She's snuggling. You should feel very lucky, because she doesn't do this with just anyone. She's a bit . . . choosey. Usually you have to work for her affection."

"Yes, well, as delighted as I am that she's decided to like me after our last encounter, I think we might be better off enjoying each other from afar."

Jolie rose from her chair with a playful roll of her

eyes. She picked the cat up by her middle and removed her from my lap, snuggling the thing against her chest. "All right, you grump. I'll save you and your precious suit from a vicious attack of cat hair. Let me put her in my room."

Once she left, I looked down. My top lip curled up at layers of cat hair that were sticking to my shirt and slacks. I'd be lucky if the drycleaner in this town could get it all out. Lord knew it would be a pain in the ass to get out of my car.

A week ago that might have been enough to send me on a rant, but all I felt in that moment was minor agitation that my allergies were likely to be activated in a few minutes.

She returned a minute later, just as I was standing from my seat and dusting fruitlessly at my clothes, trying to get the cat hair off. "Here. I brought you a lint roller. Didn't think you'd appreciate tracking cat hair into your car," she said as though she'd read my earlier thoughts.

That tightness in my throat returned at her thoughtful gesture. "Um, thank you." I took the roller from her hand and started swiping it down my front as she reached up to pluck at strands of cat hair near my collar.

The room suddenly felt half the size it had been a minute ago. That sunshine scent of hers enveloped me like an embrace, tugging at my chest and causing my dick to swell uncomfortably beneath my slacks. As much fun as I was having, and as badly as I would have preferred to stay, I knew it was best we call it a night. I needed to get back on solid footing, and I couldn't if she was there, invading every one of my senses until nothing else mattered.

"It's getting late," I managed to choke out, the words harder to say than I had anticipated. Summoning up all the control I'd let slip through my fingers since arriving, I forced my body to move, bending to pick up my empty plate and stacking it on top of Jolie's so I could carry them into the kitchen. She grabbed our glasses, following after me.

"You don't have to do that," she insisted when I started rinsing. When I didn't stop, she placed her hand on my forearm to halt my progress. "Really, you don't have to." She smiled but I couldn't help but notice it didn't reach those glittering gray orbs I was quickly becoming obsessed with. "I'm kind of particular about my dishes. I'll take care of this. You said it yourself, it's getting late."

At her last sentence, a need for self-preservation that had been driving me less than a handful of minutes ago faded into oblivion, leaving behind a rancid, sticky coating of shame. Being an asshole had never bothered me in the past. It was something that had always come naturally, a defense mechanism from my childhood that was so engrained in me now it was practically woven into the fabric of my personality. However, for the first time since I was a kid, I wished that wasn't the case, because I felt like I'd hurt her somehow, and I *hated* that feeling.

Unfortunately, there was no way to take it back.

With a stunted shake of my head, I dried my hands on the towel she handed me, the air filling with awkward tension as we watched each other silently. My feet felt like they were stuck in some sludgy mess that made walking difficult as I headed for the front door, grabbing my jacket from where it was draped over her couch on the way.

"Thank you." I had to clear my throat to rid it of the thickness that made those two words come out far more gruffly than I'd intended. "For dinner. It was really good."

She flared her eyes dramatically before smiling a true smile, and I refused to think about the way that made my chest feel like a ton of bricks had been lifted right off it.

"Wow. I'm pretty sure that 'really good' for you is the equivalent of a five-star review on Yelp."

I rolled my eyes at her teasing, the corner of my

mouth trembling once more with the need to grin. "All right, smartass. I'll see you later. Try to stay out of trouble, would you?"

Her grin turned downright cheeky. "I make no such promise." Then she shocked the hell out of me by popping onto her tiptoes and pressing a lingering kiss to my cheek, close enough to my mouth that I felt the brush of her lips against the very edge of my own. My heart was beating like I'd run the hundred-meter dash by the time she lowered herself back down. "Drive safe. I guess we'll talk soon?"

Unable to form words, I nodded before turning on my heel and heading for my car. By the time I climbed inside and started it up, my dick was like granite, standing so hard I could feel my pulse in it.

There wasn't a doubt in my mind that I was well and truly fucked, because if a kiss on the goddamn cheek was enough to guarantee I was going to have to fuck my own fist as soon as I got home, faking something more with Jolie Prescott was going to destroy my sanity.

Chapter Seventeen

Jolie

The nervous energy that had been buzzing beneath my skin like a million tiny bumblebees grew more intense as soon as I made the turn the GPS indicated, pulling up in front of Vaughn's house.

It had been two days since our dinner, and while we'd texted fairly regularly, we hadn't seen each other since that night. It had been a bit of a blessing and a curse. My world had been feeling a little lopsided since he walked out my door, and the truth was, I really only had myself to blame. I never should have kissed him. It was only supposed to have been a mild, friendly kiss on the cheek that meant nothing at all. But at the very last second, my body had acted of its own accord, shifting direction so that I got a bit of his lips as well.

On the surface it had been totally innocent, but it had left my insides feeling like they were on fire. That low simmer deep in my belly only grew stronger as each day passed. I was grateful for the short break from him, desperate to get things back to center. However, that night seemed to have awakened something in me. My body was more aware than ever that it had been a long, lonely year since I'd been touched. I'd gone nearly three hundred sixty-five days without sex, my only release coming from an inanimate battery-powered object, and now it was all I could think about. Every time I closed my eyes to give in to my body's baser needs, it was Vaughn's face that popped into my head.

How was it that, even when he was being grumpy as hell, I still found him a million times more attractive than any other man I laid eyes on? In fact, there was something about that ever-present scowl of his that turned me on more than usual.

I'd spent the past two days telling myself that avoiding him was for the best, yet every time my phone pinged, excitement coursed through me, shoving my stomach into my throat. It was the very same sensation I got every time I rode a rollercoaster. That mixture of thrill and fear that created something heady and addictive. The few times it wasn't him on the other end of the message, my heart sank with disappointment.

I told myself not to read into it, no matter how *date-like* that dinner at my place felt, it hadn't been real. In fact, the only reason I was sitting in my car in front of his house instead of at my own after a long, tiring day at work, was because we both agreed we needed to put in a little face time in town. The gossip on us hadn't died down one bit, but when Ryan had returned from a coffee run earlier that morning, she informed me she overheard some people talking, and they seemed to be of the opinion that Vaughn and I had already broken up since we hadn't been seen together since that morning at the café.

As much as I hated lying, I hated the idea of Barrett and Leighton laughing behind my back—or worse, *pitying* me—even more. So there I was, sitting in front of what I imagined a ski chalet in the French Alps might look like. Lush and expensive as hell. Also breathtakingly beautiful.

I'd known about this development since it was built a few years back, but despite Pembrooke being a small town, this was the first time I'd ever ventured there. Most of the residents were vacationers, people who only came to Wyoming a few months out of the year and didn't really mingle with the townsfolk. That wasn't too uncommon around these parts. Our winters were beautiful. Autumns too. They brought people from all around the country.

I shifted into Park and shut my car off. Instead of getting out, I leaned forward, hugging my steering wheel to get a better look through the windshield. "Whoa," I breathed, taking in the beautiful house, the façade a perfect combination of stone, glass, and wood. I seriously needed to google Vaughn. He'd casually mentioned his wealth a time or two, but I never really thought much of it. Apparently my definition of wealthy was vastly different from his.

One of the large wooden double doors at the very front swung open while I was in the middle of drooling, and the grump in question stepped out, arching a questioning brow in my direction. He was wearing navy slacks, a white button-down—rocking the forearm porn with the cuffed sleeves again—and camel-colored dress shoes that matched his leather belt perfectly. The tie was missing again, and if I had to guess, this was the closest he ever got to casual.

His hands had been tucked into his pockets, but as I sat rooted in my driver's seat, he slowly pulled one out, bringing his cellphone up to his ear. A second later, my own began to ring.

He spoke as soon as I swiped the screen and brought it up to listen. "Are you going to sit there all night like a creepy weirdo, or do you plan on actually coming in?"

"I'm not sure I can. I might get my middle-class on everything."

I smiled as I watched him roll his eyes, his face wearing that same grouchy, flat expression he favored. I was quickly coming to discover that it was a mask he wore to keep people at a distance. I just didn't know why. I'd learned that if you wanted to get to the heart of what he was *really* feeling, you had to look at his eyes. He was good at masking them as well, but things tended to creep in if you paid close enough attention. "Always such a smartass. Just get in here."

He disconnected before I could say anything else, turning around and disappearing inside the house without a backward glance. I quickly climbed from my car and skip-walked toward the door to catch up, closing it behind me and stuttering to a stop right inside the entryway.

"Jeez," I breathed as I took in the tallest ceilings I'd ever seen, the stunning chandelier that cast a golden glow on the stunning moldings and rich dark wood accents, and the breathtaking view from the windows I could see from where I stood. It appeared most of the back wall was crystal clear glass, providing a panorama of beauty. "What a view," I breathed, moving on autopilot past a curved staircase to the second level and into the living room for a better look at the valley, the trees, and the jagged peaks beyond.

Farther below, the property overlooked the sprawling lake that, come summer, would be packed with tourists and townies alike. The boardwalk was *the* hotspot in Pembrooke in the summertime, thanks to the carnival rides, games, and booths. In a few months, you'd be able to see people sunbathing down on the shore or splashing in the cool water from the very spot I was currently standing in.

I felt Vaughn come up beside me but I couldn't make myself look away. "The realtor said the view was a huge selling point for this place."

"I can see that," I said, my voice filled with awe. I forced my gaze to the man at my side, finding he was looking at me instead of the view. "You don't agree?"

He shrugged indifferently. "I don't really notice it. When I'm here, I'm either working or sleeping."

That made my chest hurt. From what little he told me about his mother the other night, it wasn't hard to see she played a large part in why Vaughn was so closed off. I was sure there was a lot more to the story that I hadn't gotten, and maybe I never would, but the very least I could do in our short time together was try and help him lower that wall he had built around himself in order to keep the world at bay. I knew his time in Pembrooke was temporary, but I wanted him to experience all the wonderful things this place had to offer. It truly was my favorite place on this big spinning rock. I wanted to give him the same feeling of peace and happiness this town gave me before he left.

"You said you lived here until you were thirteen, right?" He nodded. "Then you knew this town pretty well, right? What were some of your favorite things about it?"

Those stunning eyes of his trailed off, growing a little unfocused like he was trying to pull up a memory. "I don't know," he finally answered. "To be honest, I kind of blocked a lot of that time out."

A tiny piece of my heart chipped off at his admission. A lump of emotion rose up in my throat. I was more determined than ever to give him good memories of this place to take with him when he left.

"Okay, look out there and tell me what you see."

His chest rose and fell on a long, slow breath as he considered what lay outside the windows. His shoulders went up in a shrug. "I don't know," he said, his tone sounding almost agitated at how he struggled to answer. "Trees, water, mountains." His top lip slowly curled up as he continued. "Germs. Pollen. Ticks, most likely."

I jabbed my elbow into his ribs with a roll of my eyes.

"Take yourself out of the mindset of a rigid adult with a stick up his ass." He twisted his neck to glower at me, and I smiled brightly in response. "Do you want to know what I see when I look out?"

Something in his expression shifted. His face remained hard, but his scowl faded, replaced with an ardency that sent a thrill through my blood stream and settled into a fizz in my belly. "Yes." His voice was gruff and deep, serious, as though it were crucial for him to know what I saw when I looked out his living room window.

I shook myself out of the potent haze he'd drawn me into and faced the wall of glass once more, blinking the view beyond back into focus. "I see . . ." I cleared the frog from my throat. "I see the lake where I spent every summer with my family before my brother left to join the military. He used to throw me over his shoulder and run down that dock right there." I pointed out the lake. "I'd laugh hysterically as he launched himself off the very end, still holding on to me. We'd sink like stones for a moment before kicking up to the surface."

I felt my lips curve upward at the memory of Dalton. I could still hear my mother's scolding voice calling out that he needed to be more careful before my father would wrap his arm around her shoulders and assure her it was all going to be okay, that my big brother would never let harm come to me. "It never mattered how hot the day was, the water always felt perfect. And see there?" I shifted my finger, pointing at the stationary Ferris wheel on the boardwalk that would come to life in a matter of weeks once the schools let out for the summer. "I had my very first kiss at the top of that Ferris wheel when I was thirteen. It was"—I let out a quiet chuckle—"terrible and *way* too wet, but I can still remember how I felt when we reached the bottom and climbed off. It may sound ridiculous, but I got off that ride feeling like I'd just shed the skin of a child and was all grown up. It didn't take long to realize that couldn't have been further from the truth, but it's still a fun memory."

The two lines between Vaughn's brows carved deep into his skin. "Where is this terrible kisser now? Did you date him after that?"

I let out a thoughtful hum as I tried to recall. "Bobby Mahoney? I think he and his family moved to Coeur d'Alene some time in high school. And as far as dating, no way. I ran off that Ferris wheel like my ass was on fire, looking for Ryan so I could tell her all about my miserable first kiss."

He let out an unhappy grunt, shoving his hands back into his pockets as he turned back to the glass. "Bet he's still a shit kisser," he muttered under his breath.

I let out a bubble of laughter at his sudden surliness. "Careful now," I said teasingly. "You almost sound jealous."

Those grooves between his eyes sank deeper into his skin, probably deep enough to touch bone, for crying out loud, but he didn't utter a word, causing my humor to dry up instantly. This man kept me off balance in a way I'd never experienced before. It was as disconcerting as it was exciting, but the voice in the back of my head kept reminding me that it wasn't *real*. I needed to do better about listening.

I ripped my gaze away from those intense eyes. "Anyway, that's what I see when I look at this view."

"I like seeing this place through your eyes," he stated, those words sending a shockwave through my system.

I pulled in a deep breath, silently willing my pulse to return to a normal rhythm. "I—thank you."

I sensed him moving closer only a second before his amber and spice scent wafted all around me, creating a need deep inside to lean forward and drag my nose along that thick cord in his neck to see where the smell originated.

I needed to get out of here before I did something incredibly stupid. Like climb my fake boyfriend like a redwood.

Public. We needed a public place. Not just to keep

up pretenses, but to keep me from making a fool of myself. "You ready?" I asked, forcing myself to turn away from the view outside and start toward the door. "I don't know about you, but I'm starving."

"Wait." I pulled up short at that one word, turning to look at the towering man over my shoulder. He raised a single eyebrow, the closest Vaughn came to a teasing expression. "You aren't going to give me shit about wearing a suit?"

I looked him up and down, making sure to keep just how attractive I found him to be off my face. "I tease you because it's fun," I answered. "Not because I expect you to change. I want you to be comfortable, that's all that matters. And if dressing like that makes you comfortable, go for it."

That brow dropped, his lips parted on an exhale, and something moved across his features so fast I couldn't keep up. But none of that mattered. Because it wasn't real, and I'd do well to remember that.

Chapter Eighteen

Vaughn

The silence that had enveloped the cab of my G-Wagon the whole way to dinner was thick and muggy, making it difficult to breathe. I knew I was to blame for the discomfort surrounding us, but I couldn't seem to get my mind to stop spinning long enough to engage in something as fucking simple as small talk. It was ridiculous. I felt every time Jolie's gaze drifted my way, the apprehension swirling around the atmosphere. I knew I should try to put her at ease, but I couldn't manage to speak past the sandpaper suddenly coating my tongue.

I hadn't been able to stop replaying Jolie's words in my head since we left my house.

I want you to be comfortable, that's all that matters.

I couldn't stop hearing them. She'd said it so easily,

without a moment's thought. As if that type of kindness was an instinct. Something she did every day. And knowing her, it was. It was nothing for her to give me something like that. But to me it was *everything*. And I was struggling to process the storm swirling around inside me.

I couldn't remember the last time someone had put my own comfort first. My mother certainly hadn't. In fact, she'd spent most of my upbringing forcing me into a mold she deemed appropriate. The few women I dated all wanted me to be different. Less rigid, more fun. I was so used to them trying to change me and shape me into a version of myself that they preferred over the one I had shown them, that I'd decided a long time ago romantic relationships weren't worth the time and headspace required to make them function.

Jolie had never once made me feel like she wished I was different. Sure, she called me on my shit, and rightfully so, but unlike the women from my past, she actually understood my sense of humor—as minimal and dry as it might have been. Not only that, but she seemed to enjoy it. She was the type of woman who didn't hold back. She gave as good as she got. Hell, in most cases, she gave even better.

I located a spot on the street outside The Drunken

Moose and moved through the process of parallel parking on autopilot.

I shifted into Park and hit the button to kill the engine, but before I could open my door, Jolie's hand extended across the console, her fingers wrapping around my forearm to stop me. "Hey," she said softly. "Are you okay?"

"Fine," I clipped, giving her a curt nod. "Wait there. I'll get your door." I used the few moments it took for me to round the hood of my car to focus on my breathing and attempt to return my heart rate to a normal pace. Not that it did me any damn good. The instant I yanked her door open, that sweet citrus scent of hers smacked me in the face. It was like being hit with a beam of sunshine even though the sky was painted with the darkening colors of twilight.

"Hold on just a second." Instead of climbing out, she held firm in her seat, her eyes drilling into the side of my head. "Vaughn, look at me." I blinked, willing my mask of indifference back into place when I finally lifted my gaze to hers. "We don't have to do this," she said, taking me by surprise. "I know you aren't big on people, and that's totally fine with me. If this is uncomfortable for you we can just leave." The air squeezed out of my lungs like a wet towel being wrung out. How the hell was it possible that this woman I had only just met knew me better than anyone else in my life? Christ, she couldn't possibly be real.

"Honestly. I'm not all that hungry," she insisted, and I very well might have believed her if her stomach hadn't chosen that very moment to let out a growl loud enough to call her a liar.

Something shifted inside my chest. A chunk of that ice that had been encased around my heart for years broke off, leaving a gaping hole wide enough for those inconvenient, bothersome emotions I'd cut off long ago to creep in.

"Can I touch you?" The question fell out of my mouth fast, the desperation mixed into those words impossible to mask.

Jolie's chin jerked back in bewilderment at my question. "What?"

The desire to feel her beneath my hands was growing more intense by the second until it was basically all I could think about.

I did my best to temper the storm building inside me, spinning around like a tornado before I spoke again, but I knew it didn't do any good. "Can I touch you?" I repeated past the sand storm in my throat.

God, please say yes, I pleaded silently with whatever higher power was listening.

"For . . . appearances. People will expect it, right? I

just . . . wanted to ask if it was all right. To touch you, you know, how I would if we were really dating." The bullshit excuse of putting on a show left a sour, rancid taste in my mouth, like I'd just eaten bad sushi.

I didn't date. Though, even if I did, I had never been a fan of public displays. That was one of the many complaints from the women in my past. But none of that mattered when it came to Jolie. I was becoming less and less rational the longer I spent in her company. I didn't feel like myself. Or . . . maybe this was who I was supposed to be all along and I hadn't realized it until now. I wasn't sure. That uncertainty was enough to knock me off balance, but for some reason, being near Jolie helped to center me. She was something I could hold tight to in order to stay afloat.

I thought I saw a flash of disappointment in her stormy eyes, but it disappeared in a blink, there and gone so fast I had to have been imagining it. "O-okay. Yeah. Um, sure." She blinked, her gaze bouncing from the hand I extended her way to my eyes. "You can touch me." Her voice came out softly, almost a whisper, and the sound of those words spoken in her sweet, melodic voice made my dick twitch before growing thick.

She rested her hand gently in mine, the delicate size and softness of her palm a contrast to my own. A static charge lit up beneath my skin, making my heart slam against my ribs so hard I was surprised Jolie couldn't hear it pounding away.

I could feel my pulse in my temples as I slowly worked my fingers through hers, interlacing them together. When I lifted my head, shifting my focus back on her, Jolie was looking dazedly at our connected hands. My fingers tensed around hers, drawing her attention back to me. "Is this okay?"

I waited with bated breath for her to answer; I didn't want to let go. In fact, I wanted even more. I wanted to pull her against me, throw my arm over her shoulder and hold her tight to see if she fit against me as perfectly as her hand fit in mine. It was an inclination I'd never experienced before. I usually thrived on being alone. I preferred distance from most people.

But the better I got to know Jolie, the closer I wanted to keep her. To the point I was starting to worry what I was going to do when the time finally came for me to leave.

Jolie

. . .

I wasn't sure what had changed in the time we left Vaughn's house to now, but something had caused the man to get so lost in his own head I wasn't sure he was aware I was right there beside him. His frown was deeper, his lips were pulled into a thin pinched line. The skin around his eyes had tightened with his pensive expression.

I thought that maybe the man I'd gotten to know since that dinner at my house was finally coming back to me when he'd asked if he could touch me, but as we walked hand and hand toward the restaurant, I could feel him retreating again. That wouldn't do.

We were only feet from the entrance of The Drunken Moose when I dug my heels in and refused to take another step, yanking on his arm to get him to turn around and face me.

That furrow between his brow deepened even more when he turned to look back at me. "Jolie? Everything okay?"

I didn't know whether or not what I was about to do was the right thing, but I was following my gut. Vaughn Cavanagh wasn't exactly the easiest man to know, but I felt like I was getting there. Slowly, sure, but getting there all the same.

"No. It's not okay."

His hand was still locked firmly with mine, our

fingers tangled together in a way that felt almost . . . intimate. He took two steps back toward me, closing the distance between us, his eyes glittering with concern. "What's wrong? Are you sick? Do you need—"

"You're insufferable," I blurted.

He rocked back on his heel, his chin jerking back and his eyes widening in surprise at my outburst. "What?"

"You heard me," I said, all bravado and bluster. As I took in his bewilderment, I couldn't help but question what I was doing. *Jeez, why the hell was my heart suddenly beating so fast?* But it was too late to turn back now. "You're insufferable. And you can be kind of bossy. You know that? And—" I struggled to think up another insult. If this had been a week ago, I would have thrown his grumpiness in his face, maybe the cold exterior he wore for everyone else, but I knew better now. My mind raced but I couldn't come up with a single negative. The more time I spent with Vaughn, I discovered the more there was to like about him, so I made something up on the fly. "You're too tall."

"I'm . . . too *tall?*"

I lifted my chin haughtily. "That's right. You're too damn tall. I get a crick in my neck having to tip my head back to look at you." I was full of shit, of course. I actually loved that he was so much taller than I was. "Now you do me."

He shook his head in confusion. "What—"

"This is us, Vaughn. I tell you that you're an insufferable jerk, and you tell me I'm a smartass who has a psychotic cat. You call me Calamity and I call you City Slicker." I waved my hand back and forth in the space between us. "We give each other shit. That's our thing. We don't get all awkward and quiet with each other; we argue because we're both hard-headed and because we're damn good at it. And I don't think I'm out of line when I say I think we both kind of enjoy it. I'm willing to bet I'm the first person in a long time to give you a run for your money."

The vise that had been squeezing tighter and tighter around my chest released when his expression cleared and the corner of his mouth trembled with one of his suppressed grins. Every time I saw that tremor the determination I felt to finally pull a real smile from him grew. I'd get him one day, damn it! I was determined.

"You *are* a smartass," he finally said a few seconds later, and as crazy as it was, hearing him say those words made my lips curl into a cheek-splitting smile. Because it meant he was back. "Your cat is a menace and you're a danger to anyone in a thirty-foot radius who might be holding a cup of coffee."

I let out a giggle. "Not anyone. Just you. I'm pretty sure I'm only a vessel for karma. It's a role I take very seriously."

He rolled his eyes, nearly causing my knees to buckle at the outward show of emotion. As badly as I wanted to mention it, I kept my mouth shut, not wanting to risk that wall of his slamming back up when it appeared I had finally gotten him to start lowering it.

"Come on, Calamity. Let's get you fed before that monster in your stomach tries to bust free."

With giddiness fizzing in my belly like a shaken bottle of champagne, I let Vaughn lead me by the hand into the restaurant, so focused on how nice it felt to have his fingers wrapped around mine that I didn't even notice everyone staring.

Chapter Nineteen

Jolie

The woman behind the hostess stand at the front of The Drunken Moose looked up from whatever she was writing on as we made our way in her direction. The professional smile she already had pinned in place morphed into one of appreciation as her gaze slowly raked over Vaughn's tall frame.

I couldn't fault her for looking. The man was gorgeous, no two ways about it. But the way her eyelids grew heavy as she batted her lashes at my fake boyfriend caused something territorial to spark to life deep inside of me. I had never been a jealous person, so the fire slithering though my veins left me more than a little unsettled.

"Table for two," Vaughn said in his signature monotone. A frisson of pleasure moved through me when I looked up and saw he was too busy scanning the inside of the restaurant to pay a lick of attention to the woman standing in front of us. I couldn't stop the victorious Cheshire Cat smile that stretched across my face at the flash of disappointment that swept over her features before she shook it off.

The Drunken Moose was split into two halves, one side for the bar crowd, the other for the diners coming in to enjoy a sit-down meal. As the hostess led us to the dine-in side, Vaughn placed his hand on the small of my back, sending sparks shooting up my spine like a fire-cracker whizzing into the sky.

I had given him permission to touch me when he asked because I wanted him to. I *really* wanted him to. Probably more than was healthy. I hadn't expected my entire body to light up like the sky when the clock struck midnight on New Year's Eve. It was so bad that when I felt his thumb rubbing gentle circles through my clothes, my knees turned to gelatin, threatening to give out. Luckily, they held out until we made it to the booth the hostess indicated with a sweep of her hand.

I slid into the bench facing the front of the building, expecting Vaughn to take the one across from me, but he surprised me by coming around to my side of the table and slipping in beside me, scooting close enough for me to feel his body heat before executing that man-spread that caused his outer thigh to press flush against mine.

Heat rose up my chest and neck, and I knew without having to check that my skin was turning an obvious shade of red. As much as I tried denying it to myself, I had dressed for this evening's fake date with Vaughn at the very front of my mind. The high-waisted, flowy summer skirt, chunky belt, and strappy sandals made me feel cute and feminine, but when I matched them with a fitted, white strapless body suit, I felt like I'd gone from good-girl-next-door cute to downright sexy. The tight material molded to my body and hugged my curves, giving my boobs just the right amount of boost. It was cut low enough to give a hint of cleavage without being tasteless and put my collarbones and neck on full display. However, with the furious blush currently heating my skin from the inside out, I was starting to regret my choice of top. It was damn near impossible to hide my body's reaction to the man sitting *right* beside me.

I licked my dry lips, my fingers fidgeting with the menu the hostess had placed in front of me as I kept sneaking sideways glances at Vaughn's strong profile. He wore a look of concentration as he scanned his own menu, and for the first time, I noticed his usually impeccably-shaven jaw was covered in a hint of a five-o'clock shadow I'd never seen him sport before, like he hadn't bothered to shave that morning. That stubble provided a ruggedness that, mixed with his typical GQ, moneyed style, took him from smoldering to forest-fire level hot.

"Um . . . i-is this how you'd sit with a real girlfriend?" I asked in a hushed voice.

His brows scrunched together as he lowered the menu onto the table and turned to look at me, shifting in a way that brought him even closer. He lifted his arm closest to me, stretching it across the back of the booth in a way that made me feel completely surrounded. And I would have been a bold-faced liar if I said I didn't enjoy the hell out of it. "Is this a problem?"

I shook my head vigorously, sending my hair swishing across my bare shoulders. "No, not at all." His brows rose at the eagerness in my voice. I cleared my throat and tried again, hoping not to give too much away this time. "I just mean, people will totally buy this . . . you sitting close like this. Makes it look real." I smiled to disguise the way my chest constricted painfully at the reminder that this was all for show.

From so close, I could see the way Vaughn's pupils expanded, swallowing up that unique teal blue as it spread closer to the band of copper at the edge of his iris. His spicy scent invaded my senses as he leaned in closer. When he spoke, his voice was a low, deep baritone that vibrated through my chest, sending goosebumps up my arms. "And what about this?" The hand that had been braced on the table only a moment ago lifted and tucked a lock of hair behind my ear. However, instead of dropping it once the task was complete, the tips of his fingers continued along my jaw and the sensitive cord of my neck before tracing over my shoulder. "Would something like this be okay?"

My throat worked overtime to swallow the wad of cotton that had suddenly formed. "Y-yeah," I stuttered, my pulse thrumming wildly as I bobbed my head in a dazed nod. "Yup. T-totally. Perfectly okay with me."

"And what about this?" Without breaking contact, he trailed those same fingers across my clavicle from one side to the other, stopping on my pulse point just long enough to feel how it was beating at the pace of a hummingbird's wings.

My eyelids fluttered on a blink as I slicked my tongue across my bottom lip before pulling it between my teeth and biting down.

His gaze darkened even more as they traveled down to my mouth and locked on it.

Oh my god, he's about to kiss me, my brain screamed before adding, *please*, please, *let him kiss me!*

I wasn't sure when he'd inched closer—or maybe it had been me that had closed the rest of that miniscule distance. Either way, there was barely enough room for sunlight between us now.

My chest rose and fell as my breathing accelerated. He was all I could see, his own ragged breaths all I could hear. He surrounded me completely, taking over everything, and in that moment, I couldn't find it in me to care. It felt like something really big was about to take place and I was simply along for the ride. However, before anything could happen, the sound of a clearing throat burst our little bubble like a pin being stuck into a balloon.

I jolted back into the present, the haze that Vaughn had sucked me into clearing up like the sun burning off a dense fog. I blinked, bringing everything back into focus, and found Eliza standing with her husband, Ethan, at the very end of our table, tucked into the crook of his arm.

"Sorry to interrupt," she said, but the knowing grin on her face said otherwise. The little shit wasn't sorry at all, and I was seriously starting to question our friendship.

The side of me that hadn't been laid in *far* too long and was desperate to know how it felt to kiss Vaughn Cavanaugh when he finally lost grip on his control wanted to tell that clam jammer to get lost so I could get back to what was maybe, possibly about to happen before her interruption.

"Vaughn Cavanagh," Ethan said, a smile of familiarity tugging at his lips. "Man, I thought that was you. It's been a while."

My gaze bounced between the two of them before settling on Vaughn, watching as the furrow of confusion on his forehead slowly smoothed out as recognition took over. "Well, I'll be damned. Ethan Prewitt."

Ethan let out an abbreviated laugh. "Wasn't sure you'd remember me. It's good to see you." He held out his hand. I felt Vaughn's body tense at the gesture and unconsciously reached out to place my hand on his forearm in a show of comfort. I hadn't given any thought to the action or expected anything to come of it, but then he turned to give me a brief look, and the stark appreciation I saw swimming in his hypnotic eyes rendered me speechless before he pushed out of the booth to greet the man from his past.

What was supposed to start as a handshake morphed into one of those dude hugs, complete with clasped hands and back slapping when Ethan used his hold on Vaughn to pull him into his chest. The discomfort etched into his features wasn't outright obvious, but I'd gotten familiar enough with the man to catch the slight tightening around his eyes and mouth. Curling my lips between my teeth, I bit down to keep from outright laughing at his discomfort as I slid out of the booth to greet my friends.

I gave Eliza a hug, shooting her a quick narrow-eyed look when she giggled in my ear before shifting to Ethan and getting a kiss on the cheek. The manners my mother had instilled in me since birth wouldn't allow me to be rude. "Hey guys. It's good to see you." As soon as I pulled away from Ethan, Vaughn's arm shot out, wrapping around my waist from behind and yanking me back into him. The hold was unexpected and possessive. And so damn hot it sent a bolt of heat to my core. The way his large hand spread out over my belly, pressing deep, made my breaths short and choppy as my most intimate muscles clenched and my nipples tightened into stiff peaks.

"Are you just getting here or heading out?"

Please say heading out. Please say heading out.

Eliza's grin turned downright wicked. "Actually, we're just getting here. It looks like you guys haven't ordered yet. How about we turn this into a little double date?"

Well that settled it, I was going to have to commit murder. It was a shame. I really liked Eliza.

I was sure my attempt at a smile made me look like a lunatic as my back molars ground together. "Sure," I offered too brightly, causing Ethan's confused gaze to bounce back and forth between me and his wife like he was watching a tennis match.

He opened his mouth like he wanted to object at the same time the tips of Vaughn's fingers dug further into my belly, creating a whoosh deep in my core, but Eliza was already sliding her way into the booth that had been vacant since Vaughn and I sat down.

"Great," she chirped happily. "This'll be so much fun."

Ethan followed after her hesitantly, and I turned to the man clutching me. My eyes must have projected the question I wanted to ask, because he gave me a single abbreviated nod before releasing me so I could return to the seat I'd vacated. Just like he had the first time, he scooted until there was no space between us, but this time, instead of placing his arm across the back of the bench seat, he made no pretenses about hooking it over my shoulders as he returned to the study of his menu.

Across the table Eliza shot me a giddy grin, holding two thumbs up over the edge of the table. My stomach sank at her approval. It didn't sit well with me, lying to her, but I did my best to shake it off. Fortunately—or *un*fortunately, depending on how I looked at it—my focus was stolen away from the guilt churning my insides when Vaughn began sliding his fingers up and down my arm from shoulder to elbow, over and over. Goosebumps pebbled my skin and a zing shot from my nipples straight between my thighs at the featherlight touch.

I cleared my throat and tried my best to be discreet as I shifted in my seat, clenching my legs together against the ache that had formed there. It was a gentle caress, for crying out loud. There was no reason for my panties to be as wet as they already were.

Even though my brain was shorting out, I was still with it enough to notice that our table had grown quiet, and not in the comfortable way it would have been if it were just Vaughn and me. "So, uh . . . h-how do you two know each other?" I asked, looking between Ethan and Vaughn.

The tension melted away as Ethan spoke up. "We grew up on the same block." He chuckled and shook his head good-naturedly. "Used to run around getting into all kinds of trouble. Remember that one summer when we found that squirrel out in the woods behind your place?"

I shot a glance Vaughn's way and could practically see the wheels churning in his head as the memories started piecing together.

"That's right." His mouth started to hook upward, and I held my breath as I waited to see if he might actually smile, but he caught himself before it got that far and reined it back in. "You thought you could talk your grandmother into letting you keep it as a pet, only she screamed bloody murder when you walked through the door with it and you ended up dropping it."

Ethan's laugh was unrestrained and carefree, and I couldn't help but wish Vaughn was able to do the same, to let go long enough to . . . be happy. Truly, unreservedly *happy*. Because the better I got to know him, the more I realized he deserved it.

"What happened to the squirrel?" Eliza asked, as interested to see how the story played out as I was.

"Didn't it take something like, two hours for us to catch that squirrel?" Vaughn asked, his voice sounding lighter than I'd ever heard it before as he recalled the past. Almost on the verge of laughter. Something about hearing that made my own chest feel lighter, and the smile I hadn't realized I was wearing stretched even bigger.

"Yeah, it did. She grounded me for a week for that stunt. Didn't let me keep the damn thing, either."

At the sound of my giggle, Vaughn's head turned, his gaze catching mine before sliding down to my smiling mouth. Those ocean eyes of his darkened, his nostrils flaring on an exhale. Before I knew what was happening, his hand came up, his index finger and thumb cradling the tip of my chin and tilting my face up so he could press his lips to mine. It wasn't a kiss, really. More of a brush of his lips as our breaths tripped over each other's. Back and forth, back and forth, but it was still enough to cause stars to burst behind the backs of my eyelids once they fluttered closed. Still enough to make my belly flip like an Olympic gymnast and my skin to grow tight everywhere.

My chest rattled on a stuttered inhale, and it felt like it took an eternity for my eyes to peel open once Vaughn broke that tender kiss. It took a moment for my fuzzy vision to clear so I could see him clearly, but once I could, it was as if I were seeing him in a whole new light.

"Oh my god. You guys are so freaking cute."

My body jerked as the busy restaurant full of people faded back into focus. Until Eliza had spoken, I'd forgotten all about our new dinner companions. I buried my face in the crook of Vaughn's neck on a groan, my face heating up to the color of a stop sign.

His arm wrapped around my waist, pulling me so close to his side I was practically in his lap, but with his heat enveloping me and his smell filling my lungs stronger than it ever had before, the embarrassment I'd been feeling a moment ago quickly melted away.

"All right, baby," Ethan said in a warning tone that was mixed liberally with humor. "Stop trying to embarrass her already. She looks like she's about to melt into the booth's vinyl covering."

Vaughn's arm moved, but before I had a chance to miss the hold he'd had on me, his large, rough palm slid onto my leg beneath the table, a good few inches above my knee. His fingers curled around my inner thigh in a hold that made my inner muscles tighten and my lower belly hollow out.

His hand clenched, the tips of his fingers digging into my flesh in a way that made the apex of my thighs wet and achy, desperate for him to slide his grip just a little higher.

"My girl's made of tougher stuff than that," he said, the meaning of words throwing me off kilter just as much as the affection I heard laced within them. "Isn't that right, Calamity?"

I curled my lips inward to temper the ridiculously giddy smile that wanted to break free as I nodded. "I'd have to be to put up with you, City Slicker."

That earned me another corner lip tremble, and I nearly swooned on the spot. A voice in the back of my head was screaming at me to slow my roll. That I needed to get my head out of the clouds and remember what this really was before I ended up getting hurt. Only, I was afraid I was already too far gone to care.

Chapter Twenty

Vaughn

It was official, the tenuous hold I'd had on my control—as well as my sanity—was gone. Completely. I lost it somewhere between the impromptu double date with Ethan and his wife and that goddamn smile Jolie had given me after Ethan shared that story from our childhood. The one that made it impossible not to kiss her in the middle of a busy restaurant.

I couldn't keep a level head when she looked at me like that, those gray eyes lighting up and sparkling in a way I knew I would never get enough of. The whole evening had been one hit after another to that wall of ice that had formed in my chest years ago, making it impossible for anything else to fit inside. Now half that wall was lying in a crumbling heap, leaving me exposed and raw.

After that brush of our lips, I hadn't been able to keep my hands off her. The need to touch her had formed into this visceral thing that refused to be ignored. Like an itch deep beneath my skin that I couldn't seem to locate no matter how hard I tried. And from the way she'd squirmed beneath my hand when I had it resting on her thigh, shifting ever so slightly like she was trying to get it to slip higher, I knew she was feeling the same way.

Hell, I could still feel the heat of her arousal coming from between her legs, and as I drove my car through town on the way back to my house, it was taking everything I had not to reach over and slip my palm beneath her skirt to see if she was as wet for me as I was hard for her.

I was surprised to find I'd actually enjoyed sharing our dinner with another couple. I liked watching Jolie interact with her friend. The affection they had for one another was clear, and I was glad she had that. I had even enjoyed catching up with Ethan. The more stories from our past he regaled the women with, the more I was able to recall those earlier years when I'd lived in Pembrooke. It was as if the dam had broken and the memories came flooding back. Happy memories. Even cherished ones I'd completely forgotten about.

But as the evening progressed, it started to get harder and harder to concentrate on what everyone was talking about, what with all the blood in my body having centralized in my dick, and all. I had never been so hard in all my life. My balls felt like lead weights, full and heavy, and my dick ached from being so goddamn close to Jolie yet still not close enough. It had been that way since we sat down in that booth and had gotten progressively worse as the minutes ticked by, turning into hours. I knew the only way I was going to be able to stop that pain was by sinking so deep inside her that neither one of us would be able to tell where I ended and she began.

When dinner had finally come to an end, I'd been startled by the disappointment that felt like it had left a gaping hole in my chest. I wasn't ready for the night to end because it meant there was no reason to keep up the charade. As soon as I helped Jolie into the passenger seat of my car, any reason I had for touching her had disappeared. The closer we got to my house, the wider that chasm in my chest grew.

The white-knuckle grip I had on my steering wheel had caused my fingers to go numb. I couldn't remember the last time I wanted someone so badly that they took up every single inch of space in my head. It felt like a wild animal was clawing at my insides, desperately digging away to try and get to her.

"That was a lot of fun tonight." Her soft voice filled the cab of my Mercedes, reaching my ears and brushing against my skin like a physical touch. I grunted in response, the storm raging inside me making it impossible to form coherent sentences.

I saw her turn to look in my direction from the corner of my eye, her beautiful face marred with concern. "I'm sorry I let them join us. I should have said something. Eliza can be a little pushy when she's excited—"

"It's fine," I grunted, those two words scraping against my throat on the way out.

"It doesn't seem fine. You sound like you're mad."

"I'm not mad." I just couldn't fucking think of anything beyond pulling my car over, yanking her into my lap, and fucking her until this persistent buzzing beneath my skin *finally* went away.

"I don't believe you. If you're mad, just say so."

"I said I'm not mad," I all but shouted. Christ, I was a mess, yelling at this woman I was well and truly obsessed with because I didn't have the first clue how to actually communicate.

"Fine," she murmured under her breath, the defeat I could hear in her voice making my insides feel like they'd been tossed into a blender and set on puree. She twisted to face the windshield, her arms crossed over her chest in a protective manner that ripped my chest apart.

I was such an asshole. Why couldn't I just be normal, for fuck's sake?

My throat was so tight it felt like I was slowly suffocating, and that sensation only got worse as I turned into my neighborhood. I tried to swallow to make room for the words that needed to be said, but every time I opened my mouth the vise around my lungs twisted, wrenching even tighter. "Jolie," I managed to croak as I turned the wheel and guided the car into my driveway, coasting to a stop near my front door. "I'm . . ."

"You're what?" she prodded.

"I'm . . ." I tried again, in vain.

Her derisive scoff slammed into me with all the force of a Mack truck. "Forget it," she clipped, reaching over and unbuckling her seatbelt. My head whipped around just as she reached for the handle and shoved the door open. "Have a good night, Vaughn."

Panic had me in a chokehold as she climbed out of my car and started toward hers. My body reacted without any input from my brain as I threw myself out of the driver's side and rushed around the hood, moving faster than I ever had before. "Jolie, wait."

"It's late and I'm tired," she called, lifting a hand in a

wave over her shoulder without stopping. "See you around."

"Goddamn it," I ground out. "Will you stop being so stubborn for two fucking seconds?"

That did the trick. She whipped around so fast her hair and skirt swished around her. "Why?" she demanded, throwing her arms wide. "So you can keep acting like a dick? No thanks. I've filled my quota for taking your bullshit."

"That's not—" I came to a stop two feet in front of her, frantic breaths sawing painfully in and out of my lungs. "I'm sorry, okay?" I finally managed to get the words out, but I was terrified they were too late. Rubbing at the back of my neck, I began to pace, unable to keep still thanks to the adrenaline that had been dumped into my bloodstream. "That's what I was trying to say. I'm sorry. I know I was being an asshole. I just ..."

She planted her hands on her hips, her eyes narrowed into slits, the gray flashing with fire in the landscaping lights all around us. I wasn't sure what was more beautiful: when she was smiling up at me like I'd just made her the happiest she'd been in a long time, or when she was like this, ready to go toe to toe, refusing to take my shit because she knew she deserved better. "You just *what*, Vaughn?"

"I don't know what the hell I'm doing around you!" I

raked a hand through my hair in frustration as I shouted my admission. "My entire life is based on control. I don't do well without it, Jolie. But you . . . you make me so fucking crazy."

Her head jerked back on a gasp. "So you're saying this is *my* fault?"

"No. I'm not—" I forced myself to stop. Closing my eyes, I pinched the bridge of my nose while I concentrated on my breathing, counting to ten in my head. "That's not what I'm trying to do. Christ, I'm fucking this all up. That's what you do to me. You make me lose control. You make me . . . *want*. You make me need and crave. That's not something that's ever happened to me. I don't want someone to the point of insanity, and I sure as hell don't need anyone. I've made sure of that. But I don't know how to be around you and not touch you, not *taste* you. Not want you in every single way."

Her lips were parted, her skin flushed the prettiest rosy pink as her chest rose and fell. I couldn't miss the way her panted breaths caused her tits to strain against the material of her top. Those plump, round globes had been driving me out of my mind all night long. I'd wanted nothing more than to lean in and trace my tongue along her neck, over the swells of those perfect tits before dipping into that valley between to see if she tasted as sweet as I had been imagining since I first laid eyes on her.

"Then why don't you?"

My mouth had been opened, poised to say . . . I wasn't quite sure. But at her question, the words floated out of my head like a puff of smoke being caught on a breeze. "What?"

"Why don't you touch me?" Her words were still spoken in that demanding tone, her frustration evident in the way she stomped one sandaled foot, in how her fists were clenched at her sides, making her look sexy and adorable all at the same time. "Why haven't you kissed me?"

"I—have."

"No," she barked, her brows heavy over her eyes. "Not really. Not like you mean it."

My throat felt thick, my balls heavy. My dick was actively trying to punch its way through my slacks to get to her. I could feel my pulse throbbing in my temple. Hope and shock were warring inside me, unable to trust that I heard her correctly. "I-is that something you want?"

"*Yes!*" She threw her head back and shouted her answer at the sky, her arms coming up at her sides in agitation. "Damn it, Vaughn! I want you to *kiss me.*"

Something inside me snapped. There wasn't a

chance of holding myself back after hearing her say that. Any rationality I might have had a second earlier was gone. I was no better than a caveman as I lunged forward, gripping her head on both sides and twisting my fingers in her hair as our mouths crashed together. Jolie's fingers tangled in the front of my shirt, her nails digging into the skin beneath as she brought herself up on her toes to get closer.

Releasing her hair with one hand, I trailed it down her back and lower, gripping her ass and yanking her harder against me as I used my other hand on her head to tilt her to the perfect angle, forcing her lips apart with my own so I could slick my tongue into her sweet mouth.

I quickly swallowed down her whimper, letting out a low, deep growl as I drove my tongue into her mouth the way I wanted to thrust my cock between her thighs. Jolie's leg came up, hooking over my hip so her sex was lined up with the steel rod beneath my fly. She circled her hips as our mouths continued to devour each other's, and the heat I could feel coming from her pussy was enough to make me see stars.

"Fuck, Jolie. I can't stop," I panted as her head fell back, giving me perfect access to her delicate neck. I dragged my teeth along the sensitive cord before licking my way back up and pulling her earlobe between my teeth. "I can't stop. I'm dying for you."

Her breasts heaved against my chest, her delicate fingers gripping my hair as she held my face against her neck. I licked and sucked and bit, relishing the little noises each one pulled past her swollen pink lips. "Then don't. God, please don't stop."

Fisting her hair, I yanked her head farther back, forcing her back to arch and presenting her tits perfectly for my tongue. I did what I'd been praying to do, dragging my lips against the silky flesh before leaning lower and nipping through her top at one of her tight, puckered nipples.

"Touch me, baby. Please. *Please*, God. I need you to touch me." I was no longer above begging. I wasn't above anything if it meant getting even closer to her.

Before I knew what was happening, her leg dropped and her palms landed on my chest, pushing me back and forcing me to release her from the iron grip I'd had on her.

"Wha—"

"You wanted me to touch you," she breathed, dragging her hands down my front as she slicked her tongue across her bottom lip. "But I want to taste you."

Then she nearly ended me when she lowered to her knees in front of me.

Chapter Twenty-One

Vaughn

My brain was as useless as a circuit board that had just been dunked into a kiddie pool after that kiss. And what a fucking kiss it was. She blew all the other kisses I'd ever had out of the water. It was so damn good there was no longer room in my brain to recall any of them. She'd banished them all from memory, leaving room only for her.

My tongue was thick in my mouth and my lungs felt tight, unable to pull in a full breath as I watched the most beautiful woman I'd ever laid eyes on reach up and undo my belt, letting both ends fall to the side before attacking the button of my slacks with trembling fingers. I sucked a sharp hiss through my teeth when her knuckles grazed my cock, my release already on a hair trigger from that kiss alone.

Those big eyes came up, and for the first time, I noticed the way her pupils had expanded, eclipsing all color and leaving only black. "Sensitive?" she asked, all wide-eyed innocent as she pulled her bottom lip between her teeth and bit down almost nervously.

"It's agony." I gritted my teeth so hard the muscle in my cheek ticked. "I want you so bad I'm in physical pain. I'm afraid if I get your hands or mouth on my dick I won't last thirty seconds, but I'll be damned if I want it to stop. If you stop it just might kill me."

"Then I won't stop," she whispered, undoing me with the need she felt for me reflected in her eyes. "I promise."

My exhale was choppy as I stared rapt as she undid the button and lowered the zipper of my slacks. My cock throbbed violently as her fingers wrapped around the waistband of my boxer briefs and pulled downward. The relief I felt at having my erection free was nearly enough to bring tears to my eyes, but that sensation was quickly replaced with fireworks exploding inside my skull when Jolie wrapped her palm around the base and dragged it up experimentally, wrenching a grunt from the deepest confines of my chest.

My teeth clamped down on the inside of my cheek hard enough to draw blood, but it was the only way to keep from coming on the spot. It took a second for the haze to clear from in front of my vision, but once it did and I could see Jolie clearly, she was staring at my erection with a look of wonder on her face that made me want to yank her up and find the nearest flat surface to lay her out on so I could plunge inside her. It was only by sheer will and determination that I was able to hold myself back.

I had never been this horny in my life. Not even as a teenager who just discovered the wonders of beating off. I loved and loathed the sight of Jolie on her knees before me in equal measure. Loved it because of what was about to happen, but at the same time, every fiber of my being rebelled against the thought that the rough, unforgiving ground beneath her might be causing her pain. The thought of her hurting had my chest hollowing out, but before my mind could travel too far down that road, she parted her sweet pink lips and dragged her tongue along the underside of my cock, ripping a curse from my throat and nearly causing me to go blind.

I didn't realize I'd rocked back on my heels until Jolie reached around, steadying me by gripping onto my rear end with both hands as she slid the first few inches of me into her hot, wet mouth.

"Oh fuck. Holy *fuck!*" I locked my knees to keep

from going over and wrapped my fist around Jolie's hair, pulling it away from her face so I could see how her cheeks hollowed out and her lips plumped as she worked me over. "Heaven, baby. Your mouth is heaven. You have no idea what you're doing to me."

She blinked, bringing her gaze up to mine from beneath the fan of her lashes as she bobbed up and down my length, slicking my cock with her saliva. I could tell from the dazed look on her face and the way she squirmed, clenching her thighs together beneath her skirt, that she was getting turned on from sucking me off. She was doing everything to make this the best head I'd ever received, twisting her wrist at the base before pumping it upward to meet her mouth on each downward glide of her lips, steadily taking me deeper until the very tip bumped the back of her throat.

"Does fucking me with your mouth turn you on? I bet your pretty pussy is dripping wet right now. It is, isn't it, baby?" I panted, unable to remove my gaze from her face. She nodded her head, a whimper working up her throat and vibrating across the head of my shaft. "Do you have any idea how beautiful you look with your lips stretched around me like this? You're so good at sucking me off, doing such a good job, baby. *Christ*, you're so beautiful."

Her pace picked up at my praise, causing my balls to

draw up, but I didn't want to come like this. Not down her throat. The first time I came, I wanted to be as deep inside her as I could possibly get.

Reaching down, I grabbed Jolie beneath her arms and yanked her up, sealing my mouth with hers and swallowing down her yelp of surprise. Her feet dangled off the ground, forcing her to loop those long, lithe legs around my waist. I moved unseeing, refusing to break our kiss as I stumbled across the driveway, moving until her back hit one of the stone columns that anchored the roof over the walkway. Her mouth tore from mine on a cry, momentarily freezing me in place.

Taking her chin between my fingers, I brought her face back to mine, staring into her eyes as I asked, "Did I hurt you?"

"N-no," she breathed, shaking her head frantically. "More."

I bent my knees on a growl, fitting myself perfectly between her thighs and driving my hips upward, rocking against her hard. Her ankles locked against the small of my back, her head falling back on a moan as her fingernails dug into my shoulders.

"You like that?" I grunted, the heat from her cunt coming through the layers of her clothing and making me impossibly harder. "Does it feel good when I drag my cock across your pussy, Jolie?"

"So good, Vaughn. *So* good."

Hearing her say my name in that low, throaty tone that dripped with sex undid me. In that moment I knew there wasn't anything I wouldn't give her. My cock, my house. Hell, if she asked, I'd sign over every single dime in my bank account. That was how deep she'd burrowed beneath my skin. It was a terrifying realization, but I was too far gone to care.

Her hips began to circle, sliding her sopping wet center against my bare dick. Reaching up, I grabbed hold of the neckline of her top and yanked it down, exposing her breasts to the cool night air. Her nipples were a dusky pink, puckered so tightly they looked painful. "Please, *please*, Vaughn."

My mouth watered at the sight of her tits and the sound of her desperation. "Please what, Jolie?"

"*Please*," she pleaded. "I need . . ."

"You need me to suck on these perfect tits? Is that what you need? For me to lick and suck and bite these nipples until your pussy is so soaked for me I can slide my fat cock inside without hurting you?"

"*Yes*."

I did exactly that, leaning forward and sealing my mouth around one nipple and pulling hard as my hips continued to pump up against her. The needy sounds pouring from her mouth grew louder and more frantic as

I sucked those turgid peaks over and over, scraping them with my teeth as she rode me through her clothes.

Her hands grasped my hair and yanked my face up to hers. "Need you," she gasped against my lips, her pupils blown and her eyes unseeing. She was high on her craving. Good. Maybe now she would understand what I had been feeling for weeks. "Need you so bad, Vaughn."

I couldn't possibly go another second without feeling her hot, snug channel wrap around me. I wasn't sure I'd survive if I couldn't have her. "Can I be rough with you?" The words spilled out of my mouth before I could think, but I couldn't bring myself to regret them. "Give you whatever you want, baby. Any way you want it, I swear, but I'm losing my goddamn mind."

"*God* yes," she cried out, her head thrashing from side to side. "Be rough, please. I want to feel you tomorrow, and the next day."

Something primal roared to life inside me. "Tell me you trust me. That you know I would rather cut my own arm off than hurt you."

My words seemed to sober her a bit. She blinked, bringing her gaze back into focus. "O-of course I know that." Her hand came up to cup my cheek and I couldn't help but lean into her touch. "I trust you, Vaughn. I know you would never hurt me."

My head fell into the crook of her neck, the relief at having her trust flaying me wide open. Jolie's lips brushed the shell of my ear, the warm puffs of her breath sliding down the collar of my shirt and tickling my neck. "But I want you to fuck me like I'm your worst enemy. I *need* it."

I grabbed her by the backs of her knees on a vicious snarl, dropping her feet back on the ground before taking her by the waist and spinning her around so fast it had to have made her dizzy.

"Hands on the column," I gritted out, digging my fingers into her hips and yanking them back so she was forced to bend at the waist and brace her palms on the rough stone. My pulse beat frantically at seeing her stretched out and ready for me, my heart pounding in my ears. One single word echoed in my head. *Mine, mine, mine.* Over and over until it matched the rapid pace of my heart.

Sliding my hands down the backs of her thighs, I grabbed the hem of her skirt and yanked it up over her ass, bunching it around her waist. I let out a string of curses at the sight before me. Pure, perfection.

"Jesus, what is this?" I asked, running the tip of my index finger beneath the material that cut high on her hip and trailing it down where it dipped between the round cheeks of her delectable ass. It was a thong, but they weren't panties. More like a bathing suit with how it connected to her top.

"B-body suit," she stuttered as I dragged the tip of my finger through her cheeks and lower, sliding it through her hot, wet slit. "I-it, um . . . it unsnaps."

I could see that from my perfect vantage point. "No panties underneath either?" I *tsked*. "You're secretly naughty, aren't you?"

"I—I think I might be." She just kept getting more and more perfect.

Lifting my hand, I pulled in a breath as deep as I possibly could before bringing it back down against her ass cheek with a resounding slap. Her gasp cracked through the air like a gunshot, her wide eyes meeting mine when she jerked her head around to look over her shoulder at me. "That okay?" I asked, palming the spot I'd just slapped in slow, soothing circles.

Her tongue came out to wet her lips. "Y-yes. Again."

I spanked her again, this time on the other side. Her creamy skin bloomed red with my hand prints, and the sight of them was like waving a cape in front of a bull. I spanked her two more times, each one a little harder than the last, but not nearly hard enough to hurt her. By the time I finished, beads of precum were dripping from the tip of my cock, and when I cupped her sex, I felt how drenched that little spanking had made her.

I couldn't take it for one more fucking second. I had to be inside her. My need for her was so bad I couldn't remember how the hell I'd existed before meeting her. I quickly unsnapped her bodysuit, revealing her pussy to me for the first time, and it was just as beautiful as I knew it would be, all pink and wet and puffy, practically begging me to fuck it better than any other man had before.

The thought of another man having been there before me made me growl as I yanked my wallet from my back pocket and ripped out the condom I had inside. I tore it open with my teeth, my desperation for Jolie causing my hands to shake to the point I almost fumbled the ring of latex before I finally managed to slide it into place.

Bending forward, I traced the shell of her ear with my tongue before warning, "Hold on, baby. This is going to be hard and fast. I need you so bad."

Lining the head of my shaft up with her opening, I gripped both her hips in my hands and drove in on one quick, brutal thrust that made us both cry out. The moment I bottomed out, her walls clamped down like the hottest, silkiest glove. She fit me even more perfectly than I could have expected.

"Okay?" I asked, trailing my hand up her spine. I wanted to rail into her with every ounce of strength I had, but the need to make sure she was okay overrode everything else. I couldn't hurt her. I *couldn't*. It would torture me for the rest of my miserable life if I did something that caused her pain.

"So good," she whimpered, rising up on the tips of her toes and pushing herself back to get more. *Fucking perfect for me.* "So full."

"Can you still take it rough? You're so tight, and I'm not exactly small."

"You're huge." The breathy moan and the words she said were fucking great for my ego. "But I want it all. Keep going. Fuck me as hard as you can."

It was like a gun went off at the starting line, and I took off, pulling nearly all the way out and powering back in. It felt so good I shouted into the night air, unable to help myself as Jolie's sobs of pleasure started coming faster, with each drive of my hips. The noises she made mingled with the sound of bare flesh slapping together as I fucked her with everything I had, a sweat breaking out across my forehead and trickling down my spine.

It had never been this good before, and I knew with an absolute certainty that I felt all the way down in my bones that it would *never* be this good with anyone else. I hadn't even come yet and she'd already ruined me for all other women.

If I were being honest, she'd ruined me the moment I

climbed out of my car, covered in coffee and itching for a fight, and that scared the living hell out of me. But I couldn't make myself stop. My self-control had turned to dust.

With each forward plunge of my hips, she drove herself back, forcing me deeper, harder. But it wasn't enough. I still couldn't seem to get *deep enough*. I needed to dig myself beneath this woman's skin. I needed to make her as crazy as she made me. Her eager little moans drove me on, making it impossible to slow down.

Her neck gave out and her head fell forward, giving me a view of the way her fingers were digging into the stone column, and I couldn't stand the sight of it. It looked like it hurt, and I couldn't stand for that. Reaching around her front, I palmed her breast and pulled her up, drawing her back against my chest as I poured everything I had into fucking her so good she'd never forget me.

"Oh God!" she cried, clenching her teeth to trap the scream that worked up her throat. The new angle took me even deeper, made her pussy ripple and pulse around me.

My balls drew up tight to my body, the throb in them growing worse by the second. I wasn't sure how much longer I could hold out, but there was no way I was coming before her.

"Get there, baby. Please, I need you to get there."

"I-I'm so close. Harder."

Christ, I felt like a jackhammer pounding into her. I was actually worried I was doing damage to both our molars with how hard I was drilling into her, but if it was what she wanted, who was I to deny her?

I picked up the pace and tugged at her nipple, and that was enough to send a fresh wave of arousal through her, making her even wetter. She coated my cock so beautifully that I wished we were in front of a mirror so I could see the effect of what I did to her.

I pulled her skirt up higher, finding her swollen clit and began rubbing circles.

"Yes, Vaughn. *Yes.* I'm so close."

"Tell me, beautiful," I rasped into her ear, begging, as I silently chanted *don't come, don't come, don't come* in my head. "Tell me what else you need to get there."

"I want you to . . . b-bite me. Please?"

That quiet, uncertain *please* did it. How she said it like she wasn't sure if that was something normal to ask for, to want, made me determined to give it to her. So I did. My teeth sank into that cord that stretched from her neck to her shoulder, and just like that, she went off.

I probably should have covered her mouth to muffle her scream, but I wanted to hear it. I wanted to experience every single part of driving this woman over the edge. She came and came, rippling around me and squeezing so tight I didn't have any choice but to blow. My balls emptied on a blissfully agonized shout as I buried my face in Jolie's neck and inhaled her sunny scent—now mixed with hot, dirty sex.

We both collapsed forward, but before she could faceplant into that pillar, I wrapped my arm around her waist and kept her flush against me as I braced my other hand on the column, using what little strength I had left to hold us both up.

It felt like it took a lifetime for me to finally come back down to earth. My hearing returned first, our rapid breaths mingling with the sounds of the night: crickets and an owl hooting somewhere in the distance.

I'd lost all control and had just fucked Jolie brutally right out in the open for anyone to see. Last I knew, all the houses surrounding mine had been empty, but that had been days ago. What if someone had come up for a long weekend or something?

I'd lost myself completely in this woman, too consumed with her to think about anything else.

My dick slipped out of Jolie as I took a step back, yanking my pants up and tucking myself away before scrubbing my hands over my face.

"Vaughn?"

I hated the uncertainty in Jolie's voice more than I hated the loss of control I'd experienced with her. I turned around to face her, seeing that she's pulled her top up to cover herself and righted her skirt. I wanted to wipe the worry off her beautiful face. But I was back to that same bumbling, fuck-it-all-up-and-burn-it-down Vaughn that I'd been when we first pulled into the driveway. Once again, I didn't know what the hell I was doing. Other than ruining everything.

I needed a moment to think. I needed to screw my head on straight, but I couldn't do that with her around. I just felt . . . too much. I needed a reprieve. That was all.

"Are you okay to drive home or do you need me to take you?"

Jesus! Did I really just fucking say that?

She rocked back on her heel, her face pulling into a wince that gutted me before she schooled her features. "I'm fine to drive myself, thanks." Her tone was void of all emotion. The sound of it made me want to claw at my own ears, but I felt frozen in place.

The two of us stood in some sort of silent standoff, neither of us saying a word, and after a solid minute, Jolie let out a pained scoff and shook her head in disappointment. I couldn't get my feet to come unglued as she turned on her heel and stomped to her car. I couldn't get my lungs or voice to work either. All I could do was stand there, slowly suffocating in my own stupidity as she muttered, "This was such a huge mistake," before climbing into her car and taking off without a single look back.

Taking a crucial component to my very survival with her as she left.

Chapter Twenty-Two

Jolie

The sun was starting to peek through the slats of my blinds as I lay on my back, staring up at the rotating blades of my ceiling fan and stewing in a silent rage. I hadn't gotten more than an hour of sleep after storming away from Vaughn's house the night before. My body was primed and aching for more after the best sex I *ever* had, but the kindling of my temper had been smoldering since I climbed into my car and sped away, and it was taking everything I had to keep it from spreading into a blazing forest fire.

I really had to cake the concealer on to hide the circles under my eyes from lack of sleep—as well as the bite mark on my neck, but I wasn't going to think about that. I'd never in my life been so pissed off while simultaneously aroused to the point that I could feel my pulse between my legs. It was messing with my head. It also hurt a hell of a lot more than I wanted to admit to myself.

I dressed for work, putting extra effort into my appearance in the hopes that if I felt pretty, maybe my mood would improve. The summer dress fluttered around my legs as I walked, the gentle swish of the fabric against my skin bringing to mind how Vaughn's hands felt on me the night before and eliciting a riot of goose-bumps across my flesh.

Smoosh sat on the kitchen counter, flicking her tail back and forth and watching me with her typical bored expression as I poured coffee into a travel mug. "What?" I clipped, slamming the cup onto the counter with a huff when the feel of her silent judgment finally became too much. "Stop looking at me like that. I know what you're thinking." Other than I was certifiable for having actual conversations with my cat. "You think I put out too soon, and he's not going to bother with the cow because he's already had the milk for free." I let out an indignant snort and rolled my eyes. "Well, joke's on you, because all I wanted was the milk too."

Well, sort of. It wasn't as if I wanted him to get down on his knees and declare his undying love and devotion to me or anything. I liked the guy, and the sex was out of this world. I would have been lying if I said I didn't want more of that. But it wasn't like I expected him to wife me up or anything because we slept together. But it would have been nice if he'd at least waited until the tremors from the orgasm he'd given me had subsided before kicking me to the curb.

Heaving out a sigh, I grabbed my favorite bottle of creamer from the fridge and doctored my coffee, doing my best to ignore Smoosh's beady little gaze. "I don't care about Vaughn *at all*," I grumbled. "He wants to hit it and quit it, that's totally cool with me." I cut a glare in Smoosh's direction just as she canted her head to the side. "I am not lying," I insisted sharply when she lifted her paw and began licking it lazily, like the action was her silent way of calling me on my bullshit. "Whatever. I don't need your attitude." I quickly screwed the lid on my travel mug and grabbed my purse off the counter before jabbing an accusatory finger at my cat. "You'd do well to remember who feeds you before you start criticizing."

For crying out loud, I was losing my mind.

Before I could continue arguing with an animal that most likely couldn't understand a word I was saying, I stormed out the door and headed to work. I'd been hoping for a quiet day where I could close myself in my office and work on editing photos in peace and quiet, but I knew as soon as I walked through the doors of Three's a Charm that I wasn't going to be that lucky.

"Oh my God. You had sex."

I rocked back on a heel at Ryan's declaration. My eyes flared wide, and I proceeded to choke as the sip of coffee I had just taken went into my lungs. Tarryn rushed over to pound on my back until I was able to breathe again.

"I didn't—that's not—how could you possibly know that?" I managed to sputter as I sucked in a huge lungful of air.

"You're glowing," she stated plainly before letting out a laugh and shaking her head. "Nah, I'm just kidding." She pointed at my neck and explained, "You didn't cover up that hickey nearly as well as you thought and there's beard burn on your jaw and down your neck. At the very least you got a little frisky, and considering your dry spell, I took a shot that you wouldn't be able to stop at just a bit of necking."

I slapped my hand over the spot where I'd begged Vaughn to bite me as my face turned as red as a stop light. "I don't want to talk about it," I grumbled as I hitched my purse high on my shoulder and moved through the reception area toward my office. The click of my friends' heels on the tile floor behind me told me they weren't going to settle for my brush-off.

"Uh-uh, no way," Tarryn exclaimed, wagging her finger in the air as she and Ryan moved into my office, taking the chairs across from my desk. As they made themselves comfortable, I couldn't help but recall how ridiculous Vaughn had looked sitting in the chair Ryan was currently lounged in, and at the thought of him, my mood soured like month-old expired milk. "You get laid for the first time in a *year*, and you think you can get away with not telling your two bestest besties all about it? I don't think so, babe. I told you guys all about that weekend in Jackson Hole with that street artist. You owe me."

I held up my index finger. "First off, he was a criminal, Tarryn, not a street artist. He went around spray painting penises on buildings and stop signs, for crying out loud." She waved me off with a scoff. "Second, all I did was ask you how your weekend had been. You're the one who went into *elaborate* detail. I begged you to stop."

"She has a point," Ryan commiserated, giving Tarryn a stern look. "You do tend to overshare. But it's just one of the many . . . unique things that makes you who you are."

Tarryn's eyes rolled dramatically as she let out a huff. "Fine, whatever. You don't have to give us the details, but at least give us something." Her expression morphed into excitement as she bounced in her chair. "Like, was it that super sex grump you're fake boyfriending up?"

My blush gave me away, of course. It also didn't help matters that the two women sitting across from me knew me better than anyone else in the world. "We had a date last night—a *fake* date," I quickly amended. "Just so people would quit speculating. Things got . . . a little out of hand afterward."

Ryan's brows pinched together. "Out of hand how? He didn't do anything you didn't want, did he?" She let out a little growl. "So help me, if he did, there are far too many places in these mountains to dispose of a body. I'll make damn sure he's never found."

I appreciated Ryan's protective streak, even if it was a little psychotic at times. "No," I said with a shake of my head. "It was nothing like that. The da—*fake* date actually went really well. I had a lot of fun."

Tarryn's shoulders went up in a shrug. "Then what's the problem?"

I heaved out a gust of air, the tension that had been pressing deep into my temples all morning long growing more intense. "We kind of got into an argument on the way back to his place afterward. He got all quiet and monosyllabic, and I took it personally."

Ryan's head tilted to the side in confusion. "But . . .

isn't that how he always is? He has a reputation for being kind of an asshole."

"People don't really know him," I snapped defensively, the instinct to defend him too strong to ignore. "He's not the easiest person to know, but there's a lot more to him than most people realize."

The two of them shared a look, silently communicating something they were purposely keeping me out of.

"Anyway, things got a little heated, and he ended up admitting he was attracted to me."

"And that's a good thing?" Ryan hedged, uncertain where my story was going.

"Yes. I mean, I guess." I collapsed back into my chair with a heavy sigh. "We ended up losing control and going after each other right there in his driveway. It was . . ." I didn't even have words to properly describe how amazing, earth-moving, skull-exploding, out-of-this-galaxy incredible the sex had been. "I'm pretty sure he's ruined me for all other men," I admitted on a grumble.

Tarryn leaned back in her chair, letting out a long, low whistle. "Right there in the driveway? Damn girl." A wicked smile stretched across her face. "When you decide to get back up on the horse, you really go all out. Do Ryan and I need to start putting together bail money for when you get arrested for indecent exposure?"

I crumpled up a bright pink Post-It and threw it at her head as she giggled. "It just happened. It's not like we planned it. You know no one lives up in that community this time of year. That's where all the snow bunnies buy their vacation homes."

She waggled her eyebrows. "So what you're telling me is he has a magic dick *and* he's loaded? If I were you, I'd drop the *fake* off the front of *boyfriend* quick, fast, and in a hurry."

Ryan reached over and smacked her in the arm. "Will you be serious for one second?"

"Ow! All right." Tarryn pouted as she rubbed at the sore spot on her arm. "I was trying to lighten things up."

"Go on, sweetie," Ryan said with a wave of her hand. "We're listening."

"There really isn't much more to tell. He admitted he was attracted to me and we had sex. Really good sex. Then, the second it was over, he asked if I was good to get myself home."

The affronted gasp Tarryn pulled in was so big it threatened to suck all the oxygen out of the room. "He did *not*!"

I nodded. "I'd barely had a chance to put my boobs back in my top and he was basically telling me to kick rocks."

Ryan held up her hands and gave her head a shake. "I'm sorry, and you claim this guy *isn't* an asshole?"

"It's . . . complicated." As hard as I tried not to, I could still remember the look on his face when I looked back in my rearview mirror. The pain that had been carved deep into his features as he stood frozen in place, watching me drive away. He looked like I'd ripped off a piece of him and taken it with me as I left. Agonized with longing. The need he'd fucked me with had still been etched into every tense line and muscle of his frame, and seeing that only made me angrier. It had been obvious he didn't want to let me go. So why had he? "I don't know how else to describe it. He's different with me. Last night wasn't . . ." I shook my head trying to gather my thoughts. "I don't think he'd ever hurt me, not on purpose."

I could see the understanding in my friends' eyes, but their concern for me was even greater. "I get it," Ryan started. "And you know we'll support you in whatever you decide you want, but is this really something you want?"

"It was just sex," I insisted, but the words sounded empty, even to my own ears.

"It wasn't, though," Tarryn said, calling me on my lie. "You really like this guy."

Ryan gave me a sympathetic smile. "Like I said, we'll

support you no matter what. All we're saying is that it sounds like this guy comes with some serious baggage. You may want to consider that before getting any deeper."

I hadn't thought it was possible to feel any worse than I had when I first got here. I understood where Ryan and Tarryn were coming from, and I knew they only wanted the best for me, but their words sank deep down to the bottom of my stomach, leaving me feeling strangely hollow. It wasn't as though I didn't already know everything they were pointing out. Vaughn Cavanaugh was the most intense, complicated, infuriating man I'd ever met, no two ways about it. But I *knew* there was so much more to him than what he let people see. And I couldn't shake the niggling sense that he was someone worth getting to know, no matter how hard he fought it.

However, I would have been lying if I said the situation with Barrett hadn't left me battle-scarred and bruised, and after how Vaughn had treated me the night before, the need to protect myself was beating at my insides.

Honestly, I didn't know what the hell I was doing. But before I could try to figure it out, Becca's head popped around the edge of my opened office door, her knuckles tapping against the door frame. "Sorry to interrupt. Jolie, there's somewhere here to see you."

I tried my best to ignore the butterflies springing to life and taking flight in my belly, mentally stomping out the hope that it was Vaughn showing up to grovel for being a world-class jackass and beg my forgiveness.

Ryan twisted in her seat. "Is it a client? If so, I can handle the meeting."

Becca shook her head, her expression almost nervous. "Um, well . . . sort of."

Before I could ask who it was or what was wrong, my ex materialized in my doorway, smiling in my direction like we were long lost friends. "Hey, JoJo."

Son of a bitch. This was the *last* thing I needed.

Chapter Twenty-Three

Vaughn

With my hands tucked in the pockets of my pressed slacks, I stood at the large picture windows in my living room, staring out at the views I hadn't bothered to really take in until just then. As I watched the waters of the lake gently lap at the shoreline below, I recalled what Jolie had shared about seeing the town through the happy memories it had given her.

Thanks to Ethan, all those memories I'd kept locked up for years were flowing freely. Not only the ones he'd reminded me of, but *all* of them. It had been a shock to my system to remember how much I'd enjoyed those years I had lived here—especially the ones after my mother had left and it had been just my father and me. But with Jolie sitting there beside me, a buoy that kept me from sinking under, I had been able to wade through the shock and come out the other side.

Now I stared through the glass, remembering exactly how pleasant the water had felt as I dove beneath the surface in a competition with my dad to see who could reach the bottom fastest. I remembered the sheer joy I felt when I beat him every single time. Once Millicent entered the picture, she'd stand on the shoreline and cheer happily for each of my wins. Looking on it as an adult, I know he lost on purpose, but back then, those wins had filled me with so much pride I'd walk around with a puffed-out chest for the rest of the day.

I was seeing this town through new eyes, and it was all thanks to Jolie.

On that thought, I clenched my jaw and curled my hands into fists inside my pockets as I remembered how badly I'd screwed up the night before. I hadn't expected it to be so . . . damn . . . *good*. I knew the moment I slid inside her I was done for. Jolie had wrecked me completely. *Obliterated* me, and that had fucked with my head to the point that I'd ruined everything. I would have given anything to have someone I could call and talk my situation over with, but I had never been someone to offer a shoulder to lean on, let alone needed one myself. That realization sank to the pit of my stomach like a lead weight being dropped into the ocean. For the first time in my life, my solitude wasn't a comfort. It was lonely.

On a heavy sigh, I pulled my cell out of my pocket and scrolled through my contacts, noticing that most of the names stored in the device were business associates or contacts I kept on the hook for future endeavors. That had never bothered me before, but as I thumbed through, looking for one number in particular, I started to feel like something was missing. Was this really the life I wanted, something so closed off and limited? What was in store for me as I got older? Would I be one of those sad, pathetic old men whose work meant so much that I died alone at my desk? Would there be anyone to mourn me at my funeral?

Christ, when did my chest get so tight? I was either having a heart attack or those pesky little panic attacks had returned . . . the one I used to get after Estelle ripped me away from the only home I'd ever known.

Massaging the ache at the center of my chest, I tapped the screen to engage the call and brought the phone to my ear. Two rings later, my father's voice filled my ear.

"Vaughn?"

"Yeah. Hey, Dad. It's me."

His chuckled carried through the line. "I know that,

son. Your name popped up. I'm just a little surprised you're calling."

I was starting to regret my decision to call. "Is now a bad time? I can let you go—"

"No!" he practically shouted into the phone. "No, no. Now's a perfect time. I'm not doing anything."

My insides twisted up at my father's rushed words and the panic in his voice at the idea of me hanging up. I'd done that. Despite coming back to Pembrooke for him, he still felt uncertain about where our relationship stood. That was my fault, and as I stared out that window, I made a silent promise to him that I would fix the rift between us once and for all.

I swallowed audibly, trying to ease the sudden tightness in my throat. "Uh, so . . . h-how are you? Are you doing okay?"

Squeezing my eyes closed and scrunching my face, I reached up and banged my forehead with the side of my fist as a beat of tense silence passed between us. I didn't want to think about the fact that things with my own father were so strained that something as normal as a phone call was painfully awkward.

"I'm good," he finally answered after a few restless beats of my heart. "Real good, actually. Next week is my last chemo treatment and the docs are optimistic." For the first time in the hours that had passed since Jolie drove away from me, I felt something other than self-loathing. The tremor in the corner of my mouth returned, indicating a barely-there grin straining at my lips.

"Really? That's fantastic news," I said, the sincerity in those words coming through loud and clear. I hadn't realized a weight had been pressing down on my chest since the moment Hershel called me with his diagnosis until that very moment, when it finally lifted off and the worry I'd been carrying with me for months began to fade. He was going to be okay. The relief that came with that knowledge made my chest constrict and my eyes burn. "I'm happy to take you to that last appointment if you want."

My father cleared his throat before speaking, his voice sounding raspier than usual as he said, "Appreciate that, son. I know you have a lot on your plate with work and all, so that offer means a lot. Matter of fact, you being here at all means a lot. I don't know if I've said it before, but I'm grateful that you picked up and came back here for me."

I inhaled deeply through my nose and swallowed down the massive lump of emotion that had formed in my throat. "Yeah, of course," I insisted, knowing in that very moment that, if I'd been given the same options a million times over, I would have made the same choice every single time. The disdain I'd held for this town for so long was gone. Without my mother's influence, I was seeing things clearly for the first time in a very long time. The only reason I'd insisted I would never return to this place was because of Estelle. The only reason I convinced myself I hated it was because I let her venom sink into me. As shameful as it was to think I'd let her sway my mind, I knew better now. "We should do something after. As a way to celebrate," I suggested. "And maybe stick up a metaphorical middle finger to cancer."

Hershel's rich, happy chuckle filled my ear, creating a warmth inside me that bloomed and started to spread all throughout me. "That sounds perfect. And whatever we decide to do, maybe you can bring your girl along. Millie and I are dying to meet her."

That bloom shriveled up and some of the weight that had lifted came crashing right back down on me. "Yeah, I'm not so sure that's going to happen." I shocked myself with that admission.

"Oh . . ." There was a heavy pause that followed my confession, and I could only imagine what my father must have been thinking. "Do, uh . . . do you want to talk about it?"

My mouth opened and the words started spilling out without coercion. "I really fucked things up, and I'm not sure I can fix them."

I was met with a thoughtful hum that, for some reason, prompted me to spill the truth. Well, most of it, anyway. I shared the events of the night before, leaving out the sex as well as the fact that the whole relationship was fake. Not because I was worried what he'd think or say to that last bit of information, but because the feelings I had for Jolie churning inside me like a hurricane building steam were the furthest thing from fake. I laid it all out for him, how I got inside my own head, how I clammed up and turned into an asshole as usual, and ended up pushing her away.

I hadn't intended to share even half of that, but once I finished, the breath whooshed from my lungs on a gust of relief. I finally understood why people shared so openly with one another. Just the act of getting all of that off my chest was freeing. Cathartic.

At least that was how I was feeling until Hershel spoke. "Yep. I'd say you screwed the pooch big time, son."

I could see my expression go flat in the reflection off the gleaming glass in front of me. "Thanks a lot," I deadpanned.

He chuckled at my misery. "You messed up, no use sugar-coating that, but I wouldn't be having so much fun pulling your leg if I didn't think it was something you could bounce back from." That helped to ease the sting, but only a little. "Look, son, you were bound to screw up at some point, and it's pretty much a guarantee you'll do it again. You're a man, and we're prone to shoving a foot in our mouth more often than most of us are willing to admit. Lord knows I'd had to do my fair share of groveling. But Millie's always forgiven me. You know why?"

"Why?" I genuinely wanted to know. *Needed* to know.

"Because every single one of those apologies was sincere. Because I still do my very best to this day to learn from my mistakes. Because she knows from my actions that I don't take her for granted, even though I tend to piss her off."

Pinching the bridge of my nose to fight back the headache that was starting to stab behind my eyeballs, I let out a heavy exhale and asked, "What would you do if you were me? How would you fix it?"

"You go to your girl with your tail tucked between your legs, and you really and truly mean it; if she's the one for you, son, she'll forgive you."

"You make it sound so easy."

He let out a bark of laughter. "Hell no. You kidding? Relationships are hard as hell. You got two people with two different personalities that have to find a way to blend their lives together while doing such things as sharing the same bathroom. It's a wonder fifty percent of marriages end in divorce instead of homicide. But it's worth it. You care about this girl, you'll find a way to fix it. I have faith in you."

That bloom came back to life. "Thanks, Dad."

"Any time, son. I'm glad you called me with this, and . . . I hope you know there isn't anything you can't come to me with."

I was starting to see that, and it made that wall of ice in my chest melt even more.

Chapter Twenty-Four

Jolie

I could actually feel my heartbeat behind my left eyeball. That had to have been the start of a migraine, right? Or maybe it was a stroke.

"Barrett, what are you doing here?" I asked, doing my best to keep my tone level and professional despite the very last person I ever wanted to lay eyes on standing in the doorway of my office. *He's a client*, I reminded myself, *not your ex. A client.*

He looked around at the other people in my office, quickly losing some of the confidence he'd had only a moment ago, seeing the face of my two best friends. He knew these ladies were my ride-or-die and they'd go feral to defend me. I had to bite my lip to keep from laughing at the sudden fear and trepidation rolling off him.

"Can we talk?" His gaze darted between Ryan and

Tarryn who were both actively trying to melt the skin off his face with their glares. "Um, alone maybe?"

The energy in the room had turned static. It felt like the air could zap me at any moment. Ryan crossed her arms over her chest, the Mama Bear coming out in force. "Anything you have to say to her, you can say in front of us."

I was pretty sure my eyelid had started twitching. "It's fine," I said, resigned to get this over with. The sooner I heard him out, the sooner he'd leave. "You guys can head out. I'll be fine."

Tarryn's head turned in my direction, her eyes filled with concern. "You sure?"

I nodded. "I'm good. Promise."

She studied me closely for a few more beats before seeing something on my face that must have put her at ease. Standing from the chair, she gave Ryan's arm a tug, forcing her to her feet as well. Ryan grabbed hold of the handle on her way out and pulled the door behind her, but left it open a crack, her silent meaning behind that action clear as day. It was the same move my mother pulled any time I had a boyfriend over when I was younger. He was allowed to hang out in my room, but only if the door stayed open. Ryan was giving us some space while warning Barrett she'd be keeping a close eye.

"What can I do for you, Barrett?" I started the moment the two of us were alone.

"How have you been?" he asked as he moved to take one of the chairs across from my desk.

I lifted an eyebrow, and clasped my hands together, resting them on the top of my desk. "I'm fine," I answered flatly. "Are you here to discuss your wedding, or . . ." I trailed off, hoping he'd take the opening to get to it already.

"I just, um . . ." He tugged anxiously at the collar of his shirt, and I couldn't help but notice the white of it wasn't quite as vibrate as Vaughn's. The fabric didn't look as soft, and it wasn't nearly as crisp. His sentences came out stunted and awkward. "I wanted to say thank you. You know, for agreeing to help. With the wedding."

"It's my job."

Barrett cleared his throat. "I know that. But you could have said no. It means a lot to me that you didn't. Leighton appreciates it too."

I was sure Leighton didn't have the first clue that her fiancé was currently sitting in his ex's office, because if she did, her head would likely explode. I also knew the woman didn't have an appreciative bone in her body. But none of that mattered to me. Honestly, as I looked across my desk at Barrett, I was having trouble remembering what it was about him I'd been so drawn to in the first place.

"I didn't do it for you."

"Right." That one word came out clipped. Something moving across his features as he looked at me made my spine go stiff, an anger I'd never seen from his expression before. The guy might have been an asshole and a coward, but he wasn't prone to anger. That shyness he'd carried with him all through school was still prevalent, even all these years later. The man might as well have had a backbone made of gelatin. "*Vaughn*, right?" He said his future brother-in-law's name on a sneer.

"As a matter of fact, yes." There was no point in denying the truth, but I had a feeling Barrett didn't know the real reason behind my decision. He probably thought I did it simply because Vaughn was my boyfriend, when the real reason was so much more profound than that. I'd seen the struggle he was dealing with, the weight he'd been carrying in an effort to take the burden off of his father's shoulders. I had agreed to take the job because of that. Because I respected the hell out of him.

"So that's still happening?" Barrett asked.

I wasn't sure, not after how the night before ended, but Barrett didn't need to know that. "I really don't see how that's any of your business."

"Come on, JoJo, don't be like that," he said beseechingly, the sweetness he infused into his tone setting my teeth on edge. "Just because we aren't together anymore doesn't mean I stopped caring about you. You were important to me. You *are* important." A few months ago —hell, only a few weeks—those words would have sliced me open like a hot knife cutting through butter. But all I felt was . . . annoyed. I didn't miss this man anymore. I didn't want him back or mourn our relationship. I just wanted him to stop taking up my time with hollow words and lies that didn't mean anything.

"I'm only looking out for you. He's not a good guy, Jo."

A stupefied laugh bubbled up my throat. "Oh my God," I said on a manic giggle. "And, what? You think *you* are? I knew you were an asshole, Barrett, but I didn't think you were delusional."

His face grew red as he huffed out an affronted breath. "This guy . . . there's something not right about him. I can't stand the thought of you getting hurt."

I couldn't stop laughing. The hypocrisy was too much. "Really? That's funny." I had to wait until my chuckles died down to pull in a breath. "Because you didn't seem to mind all that much about hurting me when you broke off our engagement for your new fiancée." I held up my hand to stop him when he started to argue. "And don't bother saying you didn't get involved with her until after we were over, because we both know that's a lie. At least do me the courtesy of being honest, for Christ's sake."

"Jolie, I'm sorry—"

I shook my head to stop him. "I don't care. I really and truly mean that, Barrett. I. Don't. Care. Not about you. Not about Leighton. And certainly not about your relationship. For all I care, the two of you can ride off into the sunset together and spend the rest of your lives making each other miserable. But what I won't tolerate is you sitting here and saying things about a man you don't know. There is nothing wrong with Vaughn. What *is* wrong is the fact that you thought you had the right to come to me and talk about him behind his back under the pretense of caring."

"I *do* care, Jolie. If I could go back—"

"Don't finish that sentence."

At that deep, menacing rumble, my head shot up just as my door was thrown all the way open, revealing Vaughn on the other side with an expression like a thunderstorm that was about to crack right open.

"Vaughn? What-what are you doing here?"

When his eyes came to mine, the thunderclouds in them cleared a fraction, and I could have sworn his granite features softened a bit, but that very well could have been the hopeless romantic in me. I might as well have been *every* nerdy girl in an 80's high school romance movie, wishing the most popular boy in school rushes into the crowded cafeteria to declare in front of everybody that he's crazy in love with me. However, when he shifted his focus back to my ex, a shiver went down my spine at the venom in his gaze.

"Is there a reason for you to be in my girlfriend's office right now, Brutus?"

I stifled a laugh as my ex's jaw began to tick. "It's *Barrett.*" Something told me Vaughn really didn't give a shit. "And before she was your girlfriend, she was mine. And we were together a whole hell of a lot longer."

Oh shit. From the way Vaughn's nostrils flared, I knew that was the wrong thing for Barrett to say. "Time for you to go. You said all there was to say to her when you ended it. She doesn't owe you another goddamn second."

Barrett whipped around to me, eyes wide, jaw hanging open. "Seriously, JoJo? *This* guy?"

I opened my mouth, but couldn't get a word in edgewise between these two. "What the hell did I tell you about speaking to her? Get out before I forcibly remove you."

Barrett blustered, his face growing an unnatural shade of maroon. "That's not—this isn't—what Jolie and I have to talk about isn't any of your business—"

Vaughn moved deeper into the office, the energy radiating off him screaming louder than a warning siren. My office suddenly felt half the size it had been a moment ago. "See, that's where you're mistaken. Considering the fact I was buried deeper inside her than any man has ever been less than twenty-four hours ago, everything that has to do with her is *my* business."

I pulled in a broken gasp at the same time my thighs clenched together against the sharp ache that had suddenly formed there.

"And seeing as it was my cock she was coming around and my name she was screaming loud enough to be heard down in the valley, it absolutely is my business. She's mine, Bruno. You were stupid enough to let her go, now I think everyone in this building would agree I'm much smarter than you."

"I agree!" Tarryn's disembodied voice called from the hallway, followed closely by Ryan's "*Shh!*" and a noise that sounded an awful lot like she'd just smacked Tarryn in the arm.

"You *shh!* And stop hitting me, you jerk."

Oh my God. How in the hell was it possible that this whole scene was hilarious and sexy and mind-boggling all at the same time? That tick in my eyelid was getting so much worse. "That's it. This is over. Barrett, it's time for you to go."

He stood from his seat and brushed at the front of his slacks, the look on his face telling me he wasn't happy about being forced out.

"We'll talk later, when we have some privacy. This isn't over."

"That's where you're wrong, Barrett. This is *very* over. From here on out, I don't want to speak or see you, unless it directly involves the wedding my partners and I are being paid to assist with."

Realizing there wasn't a chance he was going to win, he turned on his heel and headed for the door, slowing only as he waited for Vaughn to move out of the way, which Vaughn did after issuing one last, "Bye, Beelzebub."

"It's—" That was all Barrett got out before Vaughn slammed the door in his face.

I barely had a chance to take in a sigh of relief that he was gone before my heart started hammering at being alone with Vaughn. My body didn't seem to give a damn that things the night before had ended so disastrously, because my body was coming to life at just the sight of him. My skin suddenly felt tight, my breathing labored. My fingers itched to dive into his silky hair and yank his mouth to mine. A pulse started low in my belly, growing in pressure as my nipples puckered, the tips hard as diamond.

"You know he's still in love with you, right?" he asked before I had a chance to question what he was doing standing in my office only hours after kicking me to the curb.

I let out a weary sigh as I pressed back in my chair, closing my eyes to massage my temples. "I don't think Barrett knows how to love anyone, honestly." I finally saw that first-hand. For the longest time I questioned what had gone wrong. I thought our relationship had been so wonderful, and I couldn't wrap my head around why he would end it. Now I understood. He was still very much that nerdy kid from back in high school. It didn't matter he'd already had a woman who loved him, who was devoted to him, and wanted to spend the rest of her life with him. The moment someone else showed interest, he hadn't blinked at blowing our world apart. Barrett was still so insecure, he didn't have a clue what he wanted. It was actually kind of sad.

"All right. But he wants you back. That much is obvious."

I opened my eyes, pinning him with a hard stare. "Why are you telling me this? Why are you even here?" I asked exasperatedly.

I saw his throat work on a thick swallow, bobbing over the top of the starched collar of his button-down. A much nicer button-down than Barrett's.

"I'm here . . . The tips of his ears and the sharp ridges of his cheekbones started to deepen with color. "I'm here because I fucked up. I can't stand how we left things last night."

My throat went dry. There was a voice in the very back of my head that wanted to cheer, but I quickly smacked it down, afraid to let myself hope. My voice came out only a few octaves above a whisper as I asked, "How would you have preferred we left them?"

He moved then, coming closer. Each step so slow yet enough to make my heart speed up. "I would have preferred to have you in my bed," he admitted gruffly, his words deep and gravelly. "I would have liked to be able to hold you all night, to feel your skin against mine. I would have liked to be able to press my face into your hair and breathe you in, to have your sunshine scent on my sheets so every time I climbed inside I'd be able to smell you. I would have preferred *anything* over watching you drive away from me last night. It gutted me."

I blinked, his words catching me completely off guard. Goosebumps were spreading across my entire body. At his confession that need coiling deep in my core twisted even tighter. "Then why did you push me away?"

"Because you scare the hell out of me," he confessed

so earnestly the backs of my eyes began to burn. "Because being with you is better than anything I've ever felt before. And I'm not only talking about the sex. You terrify me because nothing I feel for you is fake, baby."

"What—" I had to stop, give myself time to get my thoughts together. "What do you want, Vaughn?" My tongue darted, swiping over my bottom lip as Vaughn closed the last of the space between us and shocked the hell out of me by lowering to his knees right in front of me.

His response was one simple word, but the impact of it was indescribable.

"You."

Chapter Twenty-Five

Jolie

My inner romantic, the one that tended to pop up at the most inconvenient times, was currently swooning to death. As hard as it was, I forced myself to remain seated, clutching the arms of my executive chair in a white-knuckle grip. "What changed?" I needed to know, despite being terrified that his answer might wreck me. "From last night when you couldn't get rid of me fast enough to now, what changed?"

A low growl rattled through his chest. "Not a goddamn thing. From the moment I slid out of you, all I've been able to think about is getting back in." I gave a little jolt at the electric current running from my ankle where he reached out and touched me, all the way up my leg to the apex of my thighs. My breath rushed from my lungs as he slowly dragged his hand up, leaving a path of fire in his wake. "I want inside your body, Jolie." My heart started beating like I'd just run a marathon. "I want in here," he said softly, reaching up with his other hand and brushing a tendril of hair behind my ear, pausing at my temple. "I want in here." His fingertips ghosted down the center of my blouse before pressing deep between my breasts where my heart was rattling around against my ribs.

The hand on my leg traveled upward, past my knee, up my thigh. My breath stuttered past my lips as he slipped beneath my skirt. My legs parted of their own accord, my body's silent way of begging him for more, and he did not disappoint. "And I want back in here more than I want my next breath," he rasped, his large hand cupping my sex. "Christ, I can feel how hot you are, how wet. I can't think straight when I know you want me as badly as I want you."

A whimper worked its way up my throat. "Vaughn," I begged, not even sure what I was begging for. My mind was at war with itself.

"I want everything, Jolie, but until you're there with me, I'll gladly take anything you're willing to give."

His fingertips danced across the sopping wet material of my panties in a feather-light touch that only made my body hotter. "What are you doing to me?" The words came out sounding as frantic as I felt. This man was a hurricane, and I was helpless against him, waiting to get sucked up into the chaos.

"Whatever you want," he assured me, his voice gritty and raw with need. He leaned forward, his height bringing him to the perfect level so his lips could meet mine. When he spoke again, his words ghosted across them like a kiss. "*Anything* you want, Jolie. All you have to do is say the words."

"Touch me," I said insistently. "God, Vaughn. Ease this ache you've created before I go insane."

His tongue came out, dancing across the seam of my lips before slipping past for one swipe against my own. "Good. Now you understand what you do to me." Then his mouth plundered mine as he shoved aside the panel of my panties and plunged two fingers deep inside me. I instantly clamped down around those long, thick digits, a silent scream trapped behind my clenched teeth.

"That's such a good girl," he soothed, driving those skillful fingers in and out, in and out, with perfect precision. "Keeping quiet while your perfect cunt sucks my fingers like it wishes they were my cock." I whimpered again, and he was right there to swallow the sound down. "It's greedy for me already, isn't it? Knows I'll take care of it, give it what it needs."

He curled his fingers upward in a come-hither

motion, the pads dragging across my G-spot. My hands came off the arms of my chair and fisted in the smooth strands of his hair, holding tight as I turned the heat up on the kiss. My hips began to rock uncontrollably, chasing his touch as I got closer to the edge he was driving me toward.

"That's it, Jolie. Hold on to me. Use me. I'm right here, just for you."

"God, you infuriate me," I lamented against his mouth, unable to stop kissing him, stop touching him. Even when I was still so *angry* with him for pushing me away. "I shouldn't want you the way I do after how you treated me, but if you stop, I'll die."

"Never again." His words were a solemn oath. "It won't happen ever again. Hurting you nearly fucking destroyed me. I couldn't stand to see the look in your eyes, and knowing I put it there was a torture I've never experienced."

"Vaughn," I breathed, that pressure inside my core building and building, reaching new heights I'd never felt. "I'm so close."

"Not yet, baby. Not until I taste you. Do me a favor and lift up your skirt."

As hard as it was, I released my grip on his hair and did as he asked, grabbing the hem of my skirt and giving a little shimmy as I pulled it up until it bunched around my waist.

"Christ, you're so pretty," he said worshipfully, his eyes darting all over, like he was trying to take every inch of me in before finally settling on where he was continuing to fuck me with those magic fingers of his. "One of the many regrets I have from last night was that I didn't get to taste you. I don't plan on making that same mistake twice."

He didn't make me wait another second, burying his face between my thighs and feasting from me like I was his favorite meal. I tangled one hand in his hair while I used the other to cover my mouth, desperately trying to keep quiet as his mouth did the most sinful things to me.

His tongue swiped through my slit, lapping up my arousal before spearing into me. "Jesus, you taste better than anything I've ever had. Pure sunshine and honey." He sucked my clit into his mouth, causing me to dig my nails into his scalp. "I'm already addicted."

"Vaughn, I—"

His fingers returned, stroking at my G-spot as he continued teasing my clit with the tip of his tongue. "I know, baby. I can feel you. Give it to me. I want to swallow down every single drop."

On that order, he drove his fingers deep and scraped his teeth over that swollen bundle of nerves, shoving me over the edge into oblivion. He stayed with me through every second of my orgasm, coaxing every last tremor out of me as I struggled to keep my screams locked in my throat.

Before I came back down, he shot to his full height, gripping me under my arms and forcing me to my feet. I barely had a chance to wobble before he palmed the cheeks of my ass and lifted me up, depositing me on the edge of my desk.

"Please, God, Jolie. Tell me I can have you," he panted, reaching down and gripping himself through the material of his slacks. My gaze followed his hand, flaring wide at the sight of his enormous erection straining against the fabric. He was so thick. So ready. "It physically hurts, how badly I want you."

"Do it," I panted on a whisper. "I want to feel you inside me."

A growl worked its way past his lips, making me shiver. "Take your panties off," he ordered as his hands worked to unbuckle his belt. "I want to see that beautiful cunt."

I wriggled free of my underwear, barely getting them over my ankles before he snatched them up and balled them in his fist, shoving them into his pocket. He undid the button of his slacks and lowered the zipper. I couldn't help but gasp at the sight of his hard cock as he pulled it out of his pants, gripping it tighter than I would have dared and giving it a stroke.

"*Fuck,*" he hissed, squeezing his eyes closed and lowering his forehead to mine, letting out a groan of agony.

"What?" I breathed. "What's wrong?"

"No condom," he grunted. "I-I didn't plan on this happening. It isn't why I came here."

He came to get me back, to make up for last night. Knowledge of that created a warmth deep in my chest that spread through the rest of my body like a rock chip spidering out and taking over a windshield.

"I'm on the pill," I admitted, knowing in that very moment that there was nothing I wanted more than to feel this man inside me with nothing between us. "And I'm clean, I promise. I just went to the doctor a few months ago, and there hasn't been anyone . . ."

The black of Vaughn's pupils swallowed up all that beautiful color I loved so much. "You sure, baby? I'm clean. I would never—"

I silenced him with a kiss. "I know. I-I trust you."

His chest expanded on a deep inhale, his eyes falling closed, his expression melting like I'd just given him a gift he would covet for the rest of his life. When they opened again, they bored into me like he was trying to see all the way down to my soul.

He brought a hand up and locked it around the side of my neck while his forehead stayed pressed against mine, locking me to him. "I want you to watch," Vaughn rasped as he fisted his shaft in his other hand. "Watch as I take you. Don't look away."

My breath hitched, but I did as he said, lowering my gaze to where he'd notched the head of his cock with my entrance. My skin was flushed and puffy with my need for him, my arousal making the skin glisten as he slowly worked his hips forward, sliding a single inch inside me. Just that one inch felt better than anything else. I sucked in a gasp, fighting against my body's desire to close my eyes and lean back, basking in the feel of him filling me. But I kept my gaze riveted on where we were connected, refusing to look away.

Vaughn pulled out, his cock slick and shining with my body's response to him before slipping forward again, going even deeper. I was riveted. We both were. It was impossible to look away as that fat, beautiful cock owned me.

"Oh God," I whimpered, my chest shaking, my muscles starting to spasm as that pressure in my core built up again.

"That's right, Jolie. Look how your perfect pussy takes me. Look at how it stretches. Like it was made just for me."

He pushed those last few inches inside, finally bottoming out, and it was so good I couldn't hold my head up any longer. Bracing my hands behind me on the desk, I dragged my tongue across my bottom lip as I met Vaughn's glassy gaze. "I need you to fuck me," I whispered, my voice pleading. "I can't take anymore. Please fuck me."

My request flipped a switch inside him and the wild animal I'd experienced the night before came charging forward. *Thank God!*

He pulled nearly all the way out before slamming back in so hard the bare skin of my ass squeaked as it slid back on my desk. I braced my hands and began circling my hips as Vaughn let loose. Each forward drive of his hips was almost like a punishment. But *God*, it was so damn good. I knew I would never be able to get enough.

"Tell me, Jolie," he grunted against my lips. One hand fisted the hair at the nape of my neck, holding me to him, while the pads of his other fingers were digging into my hip.

"Tell you what?"

"Tell me this feels real for you." He was begging, the need to know how I felt reflecting in his eyes that were locked with mine. "Tell me this isn't fake anymore, that I'm not the only one feeling like this."

His words drove me closer to a release that threatened to undo me completely, or maybe it was the stark desperation for me he didn't bother to mask that did it. I'd never had a man treat me like this, like I had the power to rock his world off its foundation. It was a powerful feeling, consuming, like the highest high.

I lifted one hand, bringing it up to his cheek, relishing the way he nuzzled deeper into my touch like he couldn't get close enough, even as he fucked me brutally. "This isn't fake for me."

His shoulders sagged in relief right before he picked up the pace.

"Oh shit." My fingers curled, scraping gently through the stubble he hadn't bothered shaving off his face this morning. "I'm close."

"Yes, baby," he hissed against my lips. "Fuck, one of these days, in the very near future, I'm going to fuck you in a bed where I can have you completely naked and spread out before me." God, I wanted that too. "In the meantime, I want you to come. Flood my cock, Jolie. Let me know you're mine."

"I am," I panted as the pressure in my core tightened. "I'm yours, Vaughn."

"That's right. *Fuck*, I feel you getting close. You're going to milk me dry, aren't you? You're going to make me come so goddamn hard."

"*Yes!*" I clamped my lips closed, curling them

between my teeth and biting down hard to keep the screams that wanted to escape trapped as I hurtled into the abyss.

"Oh *Jesus*," Vaughn groaned, the muscle in his cheek ticking as he clenched his teeth together and drove himself deep, holding there as the first spurt of his release let loose inside me, coating me from the inside. "*Jesus*! Jolie, nothing feels better than when you come, coming inside you with nothing between us. Never get enough of this."

My nostrils flared as breathes sawed in and out of me, white spots dancing across my vision as I continued to come, Vaughn's release spurring mine on. "So good," I panted, the words ending on a quiet sob. "It feels so good with you."

Vaughn buried his face in the crook of my neck, his teeth pressing into my flesh as he moaned long and low with the last few twitches of his dick inside me.

I felt completely boneless by the time my orgasm ended. Fortunately, Vaughn was strong enough to hold me up or I would have melted into goo and slid to the floor.

His warm exhales danced across my neck as he worked to calm his breathing. Finally, once he'd come all the way down, he lifted his head and looked at me.

"I don't know how you did it."

"Did what?" I asked as I traced his bottom lip with my thumb.

"Made me need you when I made sure I never needed anyone. Made me like you so damn much I want to be around you every hour of every day when I usually hate all people."

An exhausted giggle worked its way up my throat. "I don't think you're nearly as cold and closed off as you claim to be."

"Only with you," he insisted, and I was currently too blissed out to argue. "Does this mean you forgive me?"

"I think it just might."

Then he did something I knew I would never forget, not for the rest of my life. The image would be burned into my brain until I took my very last breath.

At my answer, his lips curled up into the most beautiful smile I'd ever seen, and I knew right then there wasn't anything I wouldn't do for a chance to see it again.

Chapter Twenty-Six

Jolie

My cell started ringing for the third time in five minutes, interrupting the peace I'd been experiencing as I lay in my bed, pressed up against Vaughn's warm, strong body. My hand rested on his chest, my thigh thrown over one of his, and he had an arm wrapped securely around me as we lazed the minutes away after another round of unbelievable sex. It had only been a few days since he showed up at my office, making declarations I'd never expected, but it had been the best few days of my life.

Well, with a few minor exceptions, but I was so damn happy that even those couldn't darken my mood completely. And Lord knew my patience had been tested, especially when Leighton had insisted on scheduling an engagement photoshoot the day after Barrett's unexpected visit. To say she had been a pain in the ass would be putting it lightly. The woman could test the patience of the Pope himself.

Tarryn and Ryan had insisted on being with me the whole time to make sure things didn't deteriorate—meaning they wanted to be sure I didn't do anything that would get me serious prison time. I'd been pretty proud of how I'd handled myself, determined to be a complete professional, but when Leighton saw I wasn't as bothered by her groping Barrett in front of me as she'd hoped, she upped her game. She started in with the passive aggressive insults of not only me, but my family. She pushed all the same buttons she had back in high school, and while she was putting my teeth on edge, I refused to engage.

The same couldn't be said for Tarryn when Leighton made a snide comment about Barrett trading up when he put a ring on her finger. I had worried she was going to beat the hell out of the woman.

But then the most incredible thing had happened. Vaughn showed up out of the blue at the park where Leighton had insisted the pictures would be taken. It had been a complete surprise, and I hadn't been able to wipe the smile off my face.

It was hilarious to see how the dynamic shifted when big brother entered the scene. Leighton was still a pain in the ass, but it was as if she knew her place in the pecking order when Vaughn was around, and it wasn't at the top. Any time she tried hurling an insult, he'd been there to shut it down quickly. All the bravado Barrett had in my office that day was gone, and the man did his best to melt into the background. I had been able to get through the shoot without any more drama. And of course, there was the added bonus that, now that Vaughn and I had drawn the lines thick and clear on what we were to each other, the man couldn't seem to keep his hands off me. I didn't mind one damn bit.

There hadn't been some kind of gargantuan shift in Vaughn's personality, no changes where his Grinchy side disappeared, and I wouldn't have wanted that to happen. I liked Vaughn for exactly who he was, and who he was just so happened to be a grumpy asshole who still wasn't a fan of most people, but *really* liked me for some reason.

His voice rumbled through his bare chest where I was resting my head, doing my best to ignore the outside world a little longer. "Whoever is on the other end of that call isn't going to stop because you're ignoring them."

Oh, I was well aware of that. I knew exactly who was calling and why, and I knew there'd be no stopping her from eventually reaching me. But I was too content to move. "I guess you're rubbing off on me. I've decided I don't like people anymore, therefore, I don't have to talk to them."

He chuckled—that, along with his smile, was a new development over the past few days—making my body shake. I couldn't help but smile at the sound of it. Each smile and laugh I got from him felt like a priceless gift. Even more treasured because of the fact he only did it when it was only the two of us. Like those were meant for me alone and he didn't want to risk sharing them with anyone else.

I cherished each and every one.

"I'm pretty sure it's impossible for you to hate anyone, Calamity."

I stacked my hands on his chest and rested my chin on top so I could look up at him. "Not true. I regularly catch myself daydreaming about punching your sister in her smug face."

"*Half*-sister," he specified, his tone laced with humor. "And wanting to smack the entitlement out of someone isn't the same as hating them. Can you honestly say you hate her?"

I let out an annoyed huff, rolling my eyes dramatically. "I guess not," I grumbled. "Honestly, I don't care enough about her to hate her." Discovering I was basically indifferent about the entire situation that I'd spent far too long letting rule my world was freeing, to say the least.

"You have too good a heart. It's one of the things I like most about you."

I smiled, walking my fingers up his chest and tapping lightly on the end of his nose. "Because it counteracts all your gloom."

He nipped at the tip of my finger, making me giggle before flipping me over onto my back and nestling his hips between my thighs. I could feel him already getting hard for me despite having come not too long ago. I knew men his age were supposed to need a longer recovery time, but Vaughn Cavanagh was a freaking machine. I was actually starting to worry *I* wouldn't be able to keep up with his insatiable appetite.

He dragged his nose along the cord at the side of my neck, making me shiver. I'd discovered over the past few days that the crook of my neck seemed to be one of his favorite places. Any chance he could, he'd bury his face there and breathe me in or kiss me or trail his tongue across my sensitive skin. "You're my perfect balance."

Oh *man*! I liked hearing that *a lot*.

Before I could say so, my phone started ringing again.

"Oh my God," I groaned miserably. "This is my nightmare."

I felt Vaughn's grin against my shoulder right before he rolled over and off the bed, moving in all his naked glory toward the bathroom. "Answer the phone before someone shows up looking for you in person."

With a pout, I pressed myself up against the head-board, pulling the sheet up to cover my chest, snatched the phone off my bedside table, and swiped across the screen. "Hi, Mom."

"Well," she huffed into the phone. "It's about dang time. I've only been calling you all day." I rolled my eyes at her dramatics. "You've called four times in less than ten minutes, that's hardly all day."

She scoffed. "What if it had been an emergency, huh? What if I'd driven my car into a ditch by accident and was pinned inside and I called you and called you for help, and you didn't answer? What would you have done then, huh?"

"I would have pointed out the fact that you wasted serious time calling me when you should have been trying to reach the police . . . the people who could actually help you in that situation."

Vaughn appeared in the doorway, his features soft with humor as he leaned against the door jamb, listening in on my conversation with my mom. I let my eyes travel down his sculpted body as my mother's attempted guilt trip drifted in one ear and out the other.

God, the man really was a work of art. Firm, defined pecs were covered in the thinnest smattering of chest hair that felt amazing against my nipples while he held me close as I rode him. A thin happy trail cut through the abs carved into his stomach and down, leading to the holy grail of dicks. It hung long and heavy between thick, muscular thighs. If he were to turn around, I know I'd see an ass you could bounce a quarter off of, an ass that was currently sporting a bite mark, thanks to me.

I regretted nothing.

"Jolie? *Jo?* My God, girl. Are you even listening to me?"

"Uh, sorry. What?" I blinked myself back into the present, cutting a glare at Vaughn when he shot me a wicked smirk. "I'm listening, I swear. What were you saying?"

"I was *saying* I have dinner in the oven already, but could you be a dear and stop off for a bottle of wine on your way over?"

Okay, I knew I hadn't been tuning her out that badly. "I'm sorry, *what* are you talking about? Why would I need to stop for a bottle of wine?"

My mother's exasperated voice carried through the phone. "Because!" she cried out in affront. "We don't have any here, and on the off chance you and your boyfriend would like a glass while you're enjoying the meal I slaved over all day, I want to be prepared."

As I sputtered, Vaughn chuckled quietly, telling me he'd heard every word the psychotic Lorene Prescott had just spouted.

I closed my eyes and counted to ten, praying for strength as I pinched the bridge of my nose. "Mom, we aren't coming over for dinner tonight."

"Sure you are," she chirped cheerfully. "We discussed it ages ago."

I flipped through my mental files to see if I could place that conversation and came up empty. "I remember you demanding I bring him over, but I never agreed to anything, and we certainly didn't put anything on the schedule."

That was it, my mother had officially lost it. I was going to have to call Dalton and discuss having her committed. Dad could join her if he insisted on putting up a fuss.

"Now, I know I raised my sweet, thoughtful, kind-hearted daughter better than to blow off a family obligation. Especially when I spent *all day* slaving over a hot stove. And in this heat!"

"You have air conditioning," I deadpanned. "And it's been in the high seventies all day. *With* a constant breeze!"

"Oh well, worth a shot," she chirped. "See you at seven! Don't forget the wine." With that, she hung up so I wouldn't be able to say no.

"Oh my God," I breathed, staring down at my phone in bewilderment. "My mom is certifiable."

"Better crazy than evil."

I gave him a flat look. "You say that now, but you haven't met Lorene in person—something you'll apparently be doing later this evening. When you'll be forced to attend family dinner. Because she won't take no for an answer, and if one or both of us don't show, she'll track us down. Damn woman is like a bloodhound."

He walked toward me, all confidence and swagger, bending to bury his face in my neck again. Like it belonged there. "I'm looking forward to it."

I scowled when he pulled back. "Liar."

He grinned unrepentantly. "Okay, so that's a bit of a stretch, but I'll gladly suffer through it for you."

"Careful, I might swoon right out of this bed," I deadpanned to cover up the fact I was actually giddy at the thought of him meeting my family. Even if it did feel rushed.

Yanking the covers from my grip, he bared my body to him and took his time looking me over before climbing on top of me. "The way I see it, we have a couple hours to kill before we have to be at your parents' house. Either you can keep grumbling about it, or you can let me make you come as many times as possible between now and when you have to start getting ready." He lifted a brow in challenge. "What's it going to be?"

The answer was simple. "Option number two, please."

Chapter Twenty-Seven

Vaughn

I would have been lying if I said my stomach wasn't tangled up in knots. I'd never met a girlfriend's parents before. Hell, by the definition, I'd never really had a girlfriend, not in the way most people would consider them. I'd never felt for another woman what I felt for Jolie.

I'd given up the idea of feeling something like this a long time ago. Once I was back under my mother's roof, it was easier not to form any lasting attachments. If she found out there was someone I was interested in, it would be a daily lecture on how all romantic entanglements did was lead a person off the course of the life they were meant to have. I'd hear endless complaints of how miserable she'd been when she was married to my father and, in her words, living a domestic life as a wife and mother, two things she'd never intended to be.

Hearing things like that enough had a serious way of damaging a kid's psyche. Constant ridicule and reminders she'd never wanted me in the first damn place had gone a long way in making me who I was today. Well, who I was *before* Jolie, at least. In the beginning I'd asked her if she was so unhappy being a mother, why had she bothered coming to take me from Hershel at all? Why not let me stay? I couldn't recall her ever giving me a definitive answer, but I eventually realized it was her way of maintaining control over both of us. She might not have wanted to be a wife or a mother, but she sure as hell wanted to control us both.

She thought that by giving birth to me, she had the right to use me when it came to furthering her own career, and that was exactly what she'd done. To the outside world, she might have looked like a loving single mother doing her best, but I knew better. If there wasn't a need for a photo op, I remained at whatever private school she'd shipped me off to until I was eventually old enough to leave on my own. By then, the damage had been done.

As for Hershel, all I could figure was that, even though she didn't love him, she also didn't want to see him happy and thriving. What better way to make that a reality than by plucking his kid away from him?

It was ironic really, how similar Leighton was to Estelle. It was hard to believe that a woman as nurturing and caring as Millicent had raised her. I suppose that was what happened when you raised a child to be a spoiled, entitled brat. No amount of good intentions could undo the damage.

"Are you sure you want to do this?" Jolie asked for the millionth time as I pulled my G-Wagon in front of the well-maintained brick ranch house Jolie had guided me to. She told me during the drive over it was the same house she'd grown up in. It was where she and her brother had been raised, and the walls were full of happy memories from her years there. "I understand if you want to throw the car in drive and take off. I'll make an excuse. In fact, I'll take the blame."

Unbuckling my seatbelt, I twisted in my seat and shot my hand out, gripping her gently by the back of the neck and pulling her across the console so I could fuse my mouth with hers. She didn't hesitate to open on a greedy moan, and I didn't wait to give her a taste of me, sliding my tongue inside her mouth so it could dance with hers.

Her breathing was labored and her eyes were heavy

when I pulled back a handful of seconds later. "This will be fine, you'll see."

I wasn't quite sure I believed that, but if it helped put her at ease, I was more than happy to lie.

She licked her lips and bit down on her plump bottom lip. "This is all moving so fast. If this had been a real relationship—"

I growled, my brows falling into a scowl. "This *is* a real relationship."

She let out a breath and nodded. "You know what I mean. I've just . . . I've never brought a guy home to meet my family this early into a relationship."

My stomach soured at the thought of all the other men who had sat around the Prescott dinner table in the past. The idea of anyone else getting that level of commitment from Jolie made my skin itch and my blood boil. I couldn't control my jealousy when it came to this woman. I didn't know her until recently, but I couldn't help but think it should have been me. It should have only *ever* been me.

I pushed that green-eyed envy to the back of my mind before it made me do something insane like lean across the console and mark her for the whole world to see right before we walked into her parents' house. "Yeah, well, we haven't exactly done things in the most traditional way."

She let out a little snort. "No, we certainly have not."

The fist that had been clenched around my lungs tightened as a worrying thought entered my mind. "Are you okay with that? The fact that this hasn't been like your past . . ." I had to swallow down the bile climbing up my throat to get the next word out. "Relationships?"

Her looking across at me and smiling that big, beautiful smile that lit up my entire fucking world was all it took to calm the storm that had begun to rage inside me.

"I'm very okay, with it," she answered, sincerity wrapping around her words and breathing life into them. "It's us. We're . . . messy and unusual, and I love it. I've had more fun with you in these past few weeks—even when we were fighting—than I ever had with Barrett during our entire relationship."

That was all I needed to hear to settle me.

"All right, then, Calamity. Let's go."

Jolie groaned and leaned into my side, twisting to press her forehead against my shoulder. "Mom, God! Will you please stop?"

My chuckle was low, much lower than the one I'd

been sharing with Jolie lately. My smile was much smaller as well. It was as if I was only capable of giving those to her. But I was still having a great time, watching her mother give her shit and Jolie throw it right back. Her father, Walt, was content to sit back and sip his beer while his girls had it out. The man had been around the block more than a few times already, and I was sure he knew what he was doing.

"Oh, stop your whining. It's just a few photos," Lorene said as she plopped a thick, leather-bound album down in my lap.

"That's the third photo album you've forced my boyfriend to look through."

My chest puffed out at her use of the word boyfriend, and as inconvenient as the timing was, my dick swelled as well.

"And this one's from middle school. Have you forgotten about that unfortunate haircut I had in the seventh grade? It took *months* for it to grow out!"

Lorene didn't look sorry in the least. "I told you that wouldn't be a flattering haircut with your bone structure, but you wouldn't listen."

Jolie crossed her arms from her place beside me on the couch and pouted exaggeratedly. We'd moved into the living room after a delicious dinner so Lorene could torture her daughter in the form of embarrassing childhood photos, and so far I'd enjoyed every second. Sure, Jolie's mother was kind of nutty, but it was obvious where her daughter got her kind heart. She and Walt both had gone out of their way to make me feel welcome. It was a feeling I hadn't experienced since I was thirteen years old.

A feeling of belonging.

"My bone structure wasn't the problem," Jolie grumbled. "It was the fact you insisted on doing it yourself, here at home, when you'd had exactly *zero* hours of professional training. It would have looked fine if I'd gotten it done at a salon like I'd begged you to let me do."

Lorene harrumphed. "In my defense, I didn't think it would be that difficult to do."

"That's not a defense!" Jolie cried. "That's just stating a fact!"

Walt burst into laughter, and I could feel my own chest shaking

"Okay, well . . . then in my defense, it was during that phase where I was clipping coupons and bargain shopping so I could see how much money I could save."

Jolie reared back. "Oh, you mean the phase where you and Jean were trying to outdo each other to see who could get the best deals?"

Walt shook his head. "Worst two months of my life. If I never have to see another can of peaches again it'll be too damn soon."

Lorene looked at me for solidarity. "I'll have you know, I won. Thank you very much. Even though Jean was a sneaky cheat."

I couldn't hold it back any longer. My head fell back on a bark of laughter that sounded nearly as rusty as it felt. By the time I managed to get hold of myself and looked back to Jolie, her gray eyes were sparkling with wonder. Her expression was soft and tender. I wasn't sure I'd ever seen her look so happy. Her beauty took my breath away, and I couldn't help but lean in and press my lips to hers.

"You have a wonderful laugh," she whispered, quiet enough only I could hear. "I'll never get tired of hearing it."

That was the moment I knew for sure I was in love with this woman. Jolie Prescott hadn't just worked herself under my skin and into my bones. She'd burrowed her way into my very soul, breathing life back into the thing that was little more than just a shell.

"Oh, look at them, Walt. They're just the cutest." Lorene cooed, breaking the moment and causing Jolie to roll her eyes good-naturedly. "It's obvious to see how much they care about each other. Warms my heart."

Jolie dropped her forehead against my chest on a chuckle as Lorene shot to her feet, the woman a whirlwind of motion. "Well, now that everyone's had a chance to let their stomach settle, I made dessert! Who likes strawberry shortcake? I made the whipped cream from scratch."

Chapter Twenty-Eight

Vaughn

The following morning, I was still riding the high from the previous evening as I sat in front of my computer. I'd been trying to get work done for the past hour, but my mind kept drifting off, thoughts of Jolie taking up every available space in my brain.

I managed to muddle my way through a conference call and video meeting without letting on that I hadn't paid a damn bit of attention. It was so out of character that if any of my colleagues had noticed, they probably would have called for a psych evaluation. I didn't give a shit. For the first time in longer than I could remember, I was actually happy, and it was all because of her.

After my revelation the night before, I'd decided I was staying in Pembrooke. Moving operations for my company from the city to somewhere much smaller and more rural would be a pain in the ass, but being close to Jolie was worth it. I knew she worried about how fast things were moving between us, so I'd decided to keep that to myself for the time being. However, making the decision for myself had lifted a weight off my chest. It just felt . . . right.

My phone chimed with an incoming text from my father.

Dad: *Just checking to see if you're still available to take me to my final appointment this afternoon.*

That was yet another thing to be happy about. Today was the day, my father's last chemotherapy treatment.

I typed out a quick reply.

Me: *I'll be there.*

I had Jolie. I had this town. And I had a father on the mend. I was convinced there wasn't anything or anyone who could bring me down. I hit send as my doorbell rang. Pocketing my phone, I headed for the front door, assuming it was my weekly grocery delivery. But when I pulled it open, the very last person I expected to see stood across the threshold, and all that light and happiness I'd been holding on to only a moment earlier began to shrivel in her presence.

"Mother. What . . . what are you doing here?"

This couldn't be happening. Not when things were finally starting to go right for me.

Estelle hadn't changed one bit since the last time I saw her. She still wore that hard, unflinching expression that made her look like the unhappiest person on the planet. Her hair was still cut into the same fashionable bob she'd worn for years, religiously colored every six weeks to prevent any gray hair from peeking through. Like me, she didn't have much of a need for casual clothes, choosing to dress in skirts or pants suits worn with heels of a reasonable height. She hadn't changed, no, and that same dark cloud she dragged behind her everywhere she went had currently followed her to my front porch, the goddamn thing big enough to block out every bit of sunshine that had finally started to brighten the dark corners inside of me.

"Is that any way to greet the woman who raised you?"

I lifted my brows, a sound of sarcasm escaping from my throat. "I don't know. Maybe when you find that woman you can ask her, because it certainly wasn't you."

She didn't even flinch, not that I expected her to. She was made of ice, after all. "Are you going to stand there blocking the way or let me in? I traveled quite a way to see you, after all."

I stepped aside, granting her entrance even though

every fiber of my being rebelled against it. Nothing good could come from her being here, but it was difficult not to fall into old patterns.

"I don't recall asking you to come for a visit, so please don't act as if you're doing me a favor by being here." I moved into the kitchen, the clack of her heels against the floor as she followed me, putting my teeth on edge.

"That's where you're wrong. I believe I *am* doing you a favor. It seems your time in this . . . *town*—"she made a derisive curl of her top lip—"has clouded your judgement. I was having lunch with Evelyn Beaumont last week, and she mentioned that you've missed a few meetings. You don't see that as a problem?"

I pulled a glass from the cabinet, my grip so tight it was a wonder it didn't shatter in my hand. I used the time it took to fill it with water and drink half of it down to find my calm. "The only thing I consider a problem is that you've taken it upon yourself to go to members of my board of directors behind my back to ask about how I'm currently running *my* company, and that Evelyn would even discuss it with you. But that's a conversation that should take place between her and me, and you can guarantee, that will be happening *very* soon."

"It's this place," she continued like I hadn't said a word, choosing to tune out every word I'd said. "This place is where things come to die, Vaughn. You've been here too long. It's time for you to come home."

The alarm I'd set on my cell to let me know when it was time to pick up my father went off, cutting Estelle off mid-rant.

"As lovely as this little chat has been, there's somewhere I have to be."

She arched a brow, the extent of emotion the woman showed. "What could possibly be more important than getting your life back on track?"

My molars ground together so hard my jaw ached as I slammed the empty glass onto the counter. "Today is Hershel's last treatment and I've agreed to take him."

"I'm sure someone else can—"

"I'll be taking my father to his appointment," I gritted out, refusing to allow her to finish that sentence. "I don't know if you planned on staying in town for a while or not, but there's a spare room down the hall and to the left. You're welcome to stay, but only if you find a way to seriously shift your attitude in the next few hours. If you don't feel you can do that, there's nothing to stop you from leaving. But I made a commitment, and I'm sticking to it."

With that, I spun on my heel and marched out of the kitchen, my mind reeling after only one interaction.

"Vaughn. Vaughn, son. You okay?" My father's voice broke through the clouds inside my head, pulling me back into the present. I'd been so lost in thought, staring out the window of his little cubical area, I hadn't noticed anything happening around me.

I blinked back into reality, turning around to notice he'd already been hooked up to his IV, a blanket covering his legs to keep him from getting too cold, and the remote to the small television on the arm of his chair at the ready.

"I'm sorry." I did my best to shake myself out of the funk that seemed to be following me around since my mother showed up on my doorstep two hours earlier. "Were you saying something?"

Hershel shook his head, his brow furrowed with concern. "Nothing important." He cocked his head to the side, studying me closely. "You okay, son?"

I massaged at the ache that had started behind my eyeballs and spread through the rest of my skull. "Yeah. Yes. I'm okay. I'm good."

"You know, I might have believed that if you hadn't insisted so many damn times."

I let out a sigh, moving over and sitting in the hard plastic chair provided for the family or friends who came to keep their sick loved ones company so they didn't have to go through these treatments alone. Leaning forward, I braced my elbows on my knees and rubbed at my temples, letting out a sigh that carried the weight of the world.

"Is it your girl?" he asked. "Is there anything I can do to help with that?" He sounded almost eager at the aspect of helping me with my girl problems, and I actually liked the idea of that.

"No, it's not Jolie. She's . . . good. Great actually."

"Then what's got you stuck in here?" He tapped the side of his head, and I had to jerk back in surprise at how well he read me. I was trapped inside my own head like I had been a million times in the past. I was heading down an all-too-familiar road. One I'd been on a million times. My thoughts were spiraling out of control.

"Estelle showed up on my doorstep this morning."

His eyes flared. "Oh. Wow."

I heaved out a breath, sitting back against the chair. "Yeah, that's about the same reaction I had."

He cleared his throat, lifting the cup of water to his mouth and sipping through the straw. "I'm surprised she set foot in this town again after all her talk of how much she hated this place." I hummed knowingly. "What brought her to Pembrooke this time?"

"Same thing that did when I was thirteen years old. She doesn't think I'm living my life the way she approves and wanted to make her displeasure known in person." I shook my head in disgust. "It's like she has a sixth sense whenever I'm happy and has to pop in to ruin it."

"Your mother . . ." Hershel paused, pulling in a pensive breath. "She's . . . complicated."

I let out a scoff. "That's putting it mildly."

"She's always been a certain way, and she can't understand how anyone might think or feel differently. But, son, you have to live your life for yourself. You can't waste your time worrying about what other people expect of you. That'll only lead to misery."

I scrubbed at my face, my chest feeling heavy. "I don't know. Maybe that's what I deserve. I mean. Maybe I don't deserve to be happy?"

My father jerked back in his seat, flabbergasted. "Why on God's green earth would you think that? Of course you deserve happiness. Hell, it could be argued you deserve it more than most."

I shook my head. "How can you say that? I was the world's worst son. I cut you off—"

"Vaughn, no. Son." Sadness washed over his expression as he hung his head, like the pain washing through him was way too heavy to hold. "You've been carrying that on your shoulders all these years, and I blame myself for that. That's my fault."

"I don't understand."

"It wasn't on you to keep the relationship between us strong, Vaughn. That was on me." I opened my mouth to disagree, but he held up a hand to silence me. "You were a kid. I was the adult. I was the *parent*. I shouldn't have let you go in the first goddamn place, then I turned around and made everything worse by not trying harder to stay in your life."

"I understood why you had to let me go with her," I assured him, wanting to take that burden off his shoulders. "She would have fought you, and she fights dirty. I knew that even back then. I never blamed you for letting me go."

He cleared the emotion from his throat, his words coming out raspier than before when he said, "You might not have, but I blamed myself. Millie and I wanted you to stay with us so badly, and you're right, I didn't have the means to fight for custody back then. But I let my sadness over losing you eat away at me. I was in a really dark place for months after you left. By the time I finally pulled myself out, I'd convinced myself too much time had passed, that you wouldn't want to talk to me. I tried telling myself you were better off with your mother, that she could provide you with the kind of life I couldn't. I had no idea I was so wrong, and I'll have to live with that regret for the rest of my life. Truth was, I was only trying to make myself feel better for being a shitty dad."

My throat felt tight, my lungs and eyes burned. "I never thought you were a shitty dad."

His smile wobbled, but he managed to keep it together. "Then you're a better son than I deserve. I know I'm not a perfect father. I let you down; I tried to do better with Leighton and went too far in the opposite direction. I overcompensated for my failures with you, and look how that turned out."

I tried to swallow down the burst of bewildered laughter that rose up my throat and ended up making a choking sound.

"I know I enabled her too much, spoiled her. I know she's a brat, and that's another thing that's my responsibility to fix. The fact is, Vaughn, none of that was ever on you. I want you to let that go right now. We both wasted too many years carrying the blame on our shoulders instead of doing something about it What do you say we let that go and move forward? Starting now. I don't care that it took me getting sick to bring you back here. I'm just grateful you're *here*. I'd do it all again if I had to, if it meant I got to have a relationship with my son."

I let out a raspy laugh past the cotton in my throat. "Can't say I'd wish cancer on you again, but I'm happy I'm here too."

My father leaned over the arm of his chair, reaching across the space between us to place his hand on top of mine. "I know Estelle's sudden appearance probably has you spinning out, but don't let her derail you. I haven't seen you this happy in far too long, and despite what you think, you deserve it. You hold tight to all the things that have healed you recently, you hear me? Don't let her take them away from you. You're stronger than that."

My throat worked on a thick swallow that threatened to choke me as I struggled to force down the lump of emotion in my throat. "Thanks, Dad. That means a lot."

"I'm always here for you. That will never change. Not even when you go back to Denver. I hope you know that."

I let out a chuckle, the sound causing his eyes to light up. "About Denver . . . how would you feel if I decided not to go back?"

His nostrils flared on a sharp inhale, and there was

no way to miss the sudden wetness that turned his eyes glassy. "Like I just won the lottery."

That settled it, then. I needed to get Jolie on board before making everything official. I prayed she felt for me even a fraction of what I felt for her.

Chapter Twenty-Nine

Jolie

"You know, I don't think I've ever seen you like this."

I looked up from the engagement photos for Leighton and Barrett I'd been editing, working magic to make Barrett's wooden smile and Leighton's sneer look normal, to make them appear to be a happy couple despite the strain between them that was clearly evident in every one of the pictures I'd taken. I'd been in this business long enough to know when a couple was going to have a long, happy marriage and when they weren't going to last more than a handful of months. My guess was that Barrett and Leighton would fall into the latter category. That was, if they made it down the aisle at all.

He'd chosen her because she was the shiny new thing he had to have, and she went after him simply for the sport of it. That much was obvious now. But I couldn't find it in me to feel pity for either one of them. They'd eventually reap what they'd sown, and I'd be too busy living my life to care.

"Look like what?" I asked Ryan, rocking back in my chair as she came into my office and sat down across from me.

She smiled knowingly. "Like you're so blissfully in love that, at any moment, a bunch of cartoon squirrels and birds are going to flitter in here to braid flowers into your hair."

My jaw dropped open. "I'm not—that's not—" The denial dried up on my tongue before I could get it out, the lie refusing to pass my lips. It was a reality I'd been fighting from the very start. A truth I'd been determined to ignore even as it niggled in the back of my mind constantly. I thought if I could make myself forget, it wouldn't hurt as badly, but there was no use denying it anymore. "Oh my God." I covered my face with my hands. "You're right. I do. I love Vaughn."

She let out a little laugh. "I know. Looks like you're the only one who hasn't already realized the obvious."

"I tried so damn hard not to fall for him." But he'd made it impossible. That grumpy jerk had worked his way into my heart, etching out a permanent spot for him, and there was no chance I'd ever be able to get him out. He'd seen to that.

"What? Why?"

"Because! He was supposed to be my *fake* boyfriend. He doesn't even live here full-time. He said from the very beginning that staying here was temporary. What the hell am I going to do when he does back to Denver?" I lifted my hand to rub at the ache that had formed in my chest at the thought of Vaughn leaving. This wasn't supposed to happen. It was that damn incurable romantic in me. She'd gone and fallen for another man who was destined to break her heart. Only this time it was going to be so much worse. The feelings I had for Barrett weren't even a fraction of what I felt for Vaughn. When he left, it was going to crush me.

The backs of my eyes began to burn as a painful lump formed in my throat. The sympathy on my best friend's face only made the pain in my chest that much worse. "Maybe before you convince yourself this is hopeless and settle into another heartbreak, you should talk to him about it. For what it's worth, you aren't the only one I've noticed acting differently. Haven't you seen the way that man looks at you?"

I fought back the tears that wanted to fall and sniffled, giving my head a shake. "How does he look at me?"

"Like you're the reason the sun shines, Jo. That man

looks at you like you create the very air he needs to survive. Instead of preparing for the end, why don't you try talking to him? You might be surprised by what he has to say."

It was impossible not to hope, but it was also hope that could destroy me if I wasn't careful. "And if he still decides to leave? Then what?"

"Well . . ." Ryan pushed to her feet, brushing her hands down the front of her skirt. "We'll do what needs to be done. Tarryn and I will be right here to hold you up when you don't feel strong enough to do it yourself. We'll have your back, just like always, and stay right by your side while you heal." She lifted her shoulder in a casual shrug. "It's what we do for each other."

Truer words had never been spoken. "You know I love you, right? Just in case I haven't said it enough lately."

"Love you right back, babe. No matter what happens, we've got this. The three of us can weather anything together."

With that, she turned and walked out of my office, her parting words giving me the strength I needed to do what needed to be done. I'd spent a year trying to safeguard my heart after Barrett hurt me. I'd spent so long trying to protect myself from falling I hadn't stopped to realize I'd never taken the leap. Maybe it was time to jump and hope for the best.

By the time I pulled into Vaughn's driveway later that day, my heart was lodged firmly in my throat. I'd gone over what I wanted to say a million times but it all flew right out of my head like a bird let out of a cage the instant I parked and climbed out of my car.

"You can do this, Jo. Just be honest and real. He cares about you. He's said so himself. This is all going to work out."

Closing my eyes, I sent up a little prayer and lifted my hand to knock.

The moment it opened I launched right in. "Vaughn, I love yo—oh . . ." I started at the sight of the woman standing across the threshold. "You're not Vaughn," I stated lamely, my tongue suddenly feeling thick as I took in the woman whose features closely resembled Vaughn's. She appeared to be around my parents' age, her expression was cold and flat, and her emotionless eyes sent a shiver down my spine. I knew without having to ask, this had to be his mother. "I'm so sorry. I was expecting someone else."

"Yes, I'm aware," she said in a frigid monotone.

My stomach sank down to my feet at the judgmental once-over she gave me, crossing her arms as she stood in the middle of the doorway like she was trying to bar my access. "Let me try that again. I'm Jolie." I held my hand out to her. "You must be Vaughn's mother."

"And you must be the reason my son has recently started throwing away his life and everything he's worked for."

My chin jerked back in shock at her callous words and the ugly tone she used to say them. "I-I'm sorry?"

She huffed out a breath like she was frustrated at having to deal with someone like me. "Might as well come in. I think the two of us should have a talk."

I disagreed wholeheartedly, but the manners my mother instilled in me kicked in, making my feet carry me into the house without any input from my brain.

The click of the front door latching into place echoed through the house like a shotgun blast, giving me a jolt. I followed the ice queen into Vaughn's living room, and I couldn't shake the sense that I'd just walked into a situation I was absolutely not prepared for. At that very moment, I would have given every dime in my bank account to be anywhere else. "Um, is . . . is Vaughn here?"

Estelle took a seat at the end of the sofa facing the front of the house. She waved an elegant hand for me to take a seat on the love seat across from her. She was perched on the very edge, giving off an air that she ruled whatever house she stepped into, including this one. She clasped her hands together and rested them in her lap, crossing her ankles demurely, but there wasn't a single demure thing about this woman. I could sense it, feel it in the air. She was a viper, waiting for her moment to strike.

"He isn't. My son is currently off on some errand he thought was more important than being here and running the company he built."

My brain worked overtime to try and remember what Vaughn told me he had to do today. Then it hit me. My mouth fell open on a sputter and I let out a bewildered laugh. "I'm sorry, did you just refer to Hershel's final round of chemotherapy as *some errand?*" The nerves I'd been experiencing since the moment this woman opened Vaughn's front door quickly dried up in the wake of her unbelievable heartlessness.

Suddenly I could understand why Vaughn was the way he was, and it broke my heart for him that he'd had to grow up with such a vile, insensitive woman.

"My son was raised to keep his priorities straight. Something I see he's slacked off on since returning to this retched place. I'm here to remind him of what's important."

I was right when I told Vaughn I didn't like his mother. And that had been without meeting her. Now that I had, however, I could finally say there *was* a person on this planet that I hate. And she was sitting right in front of me.

"I think your son has done a fine job at prioritizing what's important and what isn't."

"Of course *you* would," she said with a scoff, rolling her eyes like I was being ridiculous. "You strike me as the type of woman who'd get her hooks into someone as successful as my son and dig in deep. I read that on you the moment I opened the door. Well I've got news for you, I wouldn't get too comfortable if I were you. As soon as Vaughn is finished with this little rebellion of his, he'll have no use for you. He's better than this nothing town full of a bunch of people who couldn't manage to find anything better. Your time with my son is coming to an end. I'll see to that; I know what's best for him."

"Wow," I breathed, the anger inside me churning like a pasta pot full of boiling water. "You're a terrible person."

"Excuse me?" she said in affront.

"You heard me." I pushed to my feet, my indignation making it impossible to remain sitting. "You are a *terrible* person. And you're an even worse mother. You don't have the first clue what's best for him, and you don't care enough to try and find out. The only thing you care about is turning him into a carbon copy of you. A miserable, lonely, insensitive robot who doesn't care about anything but yourself."

Estelle rose to her feet as well, taking what she probably thought was a menacing step toward me, but I was too pissed to be cowed. This woman had insulted me, my town, and Vaughn, and I wasn't going to tolerate it. "And you're nothing more than small-town trash my son is using to fill his time while he's stuck in this backwater hole of a town. He'll see you for what you really are and return to where he belongs."

Her words might have been a direct hit to the uncertainty I'd been battling, but I would be damned if I let her see she had any effect on me. This woman wanted a fight? I was here for it, and I would go toe-to-toe with her without blinking.

"Maybe you're right. Maybe what we have won't last, and he'll end up going back to Denver, but at least I'll be able to tell myself that everything I did was *for him.* Vaughn is so much more than you give him credit for. He's more than his money or his job or whatever clout he's able to provide for you. He's the best man I've ever known. He thinks he's this cold, emotionless asshole, but that's only because it's what you've drilled into his head all these years. The Vaughn I got to know has the biggest heart. There isn't anything he wouldn't do for the people he cares about, and that includes uprooting his entire life to come here and take care of his father. That part of him managed to survive *in spite* of having you as a mother. Whether or not I get to be with him for the long run, I'll be happy knowing I made sure he knows he's a good man who deserves happiness. Because that's what you do when you love someone."

"What the hell is going on here?"

I whipped around at the snap of Vaughn's hard, gravelly voice, my heart threatening to beat out of my chest when I saw him just outside the living room. I'd been so lost in my anger at his mother I hadn't heard him come in. And by the flare in Estelle's eyes, I could tell he'd caught her off guard as well.

"Vaughn, I—"

His mother cut in before I could finish. "I was just telling your little plaything here that she's been wasting her time, trying to sink her claws into you. Honestly,

Vaughn. Who in the world have you been associating with while you've been shacking up here? It's time for you to come home where you belong."

"That's enough," Vaughn said on a growl so vicious it made me shiver.

He took two steps in our direction, the energy pouring off him filling the room and making the air thick. His rage vibrated, making the atmosphere feel static. Whatever Estelle saw in her son must not have been something she was used to, because she quickly snapped her mouth shut.

"It's time for you to leave."

My heart sank down into the pit of my stomach as his mother's expression turned smug. "You heard him. You need to go."

I lifted my chin and squared my shoulders, fighting back the burn behind my eyes. I refused to cry in front of her. I wouldn't give her the satisfaction. But before I could so much as take a step, Vaughn spoke again.

"Not her. You."

Estelle rocked back on one foot. "Excuse me?"

"I want you out. I heard everything that was said and you are no longer welcome here." Vaughn's gorgeous eyes moved to me, locking on and growing soft in a way that untangled all the knots twisted up inside me. One look and he eased all my anxieties, because the emotion shining in those deep, beautiful pools was so clear I couldn't believe I hadn't recognized it right away. It was love. Pure and unfiltered.

Estelle's harsh voice was like the crack of a whip. "You can't possibly mean that."

"Oh, I mean it. I won't tolerate anyone coming in here and insulting her."

"But—that's—" She sputtered indignantly.

When Vaughn looked back at her, that icy version I recognized from when we first met had taken control. "You can either leave of your own accord, or I'll have you removed for trespassing. Make no mistake, Mother, I'm done being your puppet. Unless you decide you want to change every aspect of your personality and suddenly become a mother who puts the wellbeing of her child above her own, I have no desire to ever see or speak to you again."

She visibly shook off her son's words, pasting that unaffected mask of hers back into place. "You're confused. We'll speak again when you return to the city. And I'll be expecting an apology."

"I'm not going back. My home is here. With her."

His mother let out a huff of outrage. "You're going to regret this. You'll see."

"The only thing I regret is allowing myself to stay

under your thumb for so long. But that's a mistake I'm rectifying right now."

I vaguely heard the angry click of her kitten heels on the floor as she stomped off, but I was too consumed with Vaughn to register his witch of a mother had left, slamming the door behind her. At his declaration, all the air had rushed from my lungs on a giant gushing exhale. My heart skipped a beat before starting back up even faster than before. "Do you really mean that?" I whispered, my words drowning in hope. "You're staying?"

He moved closer, reaching up and taking my face in his large, strong hands. Every lingering worry, every dull pain that had been coursing through me eased the moment he touched me. "More than I've ever meant anything in my life. *You* are my home. I love you, Calamity. How could I possibly leave when you're here?"

My eyes welled as a smile stretched across my face so wide it made my cheeks ache. "I-I love you too." A bubble of excited laughter slid up my throat. "So much."

His hands traveled down the sides of my neck, his thumbs tracing my jaw as he brought his forehead to rest against mine. "So you're saying you're mine?" he asked against my lips.

"I'm yours. And you're mine. Even when you're a grumpy jerk that drives me crazy."

He graced me with that smile that made my heart flip. "Even when you're being a giant pain in my ass who keeps spilling coffee all over me."

"That's who we are. And I wouldn't have it any other way."

Epilogue

Vaughn

Two months later

I loved my girl, and I felt like I'd done a pretty good job of learning to tolerate her friends over the past couple months, but this was getting fucking ridiculous.

I might have changed for Jolie, but I was still the same grumpy bastard I'd always been, the one who wasn't a fan of most people, and that probably wouldn't change. Not that it mattered, because she loved me and accepted me exactly how I was. She didn't want to change me or turn me into a different man. When I pushed her buttons, she pushed back. We fought, we annoyed each other, but we loved twice as hard.

Currently, I was sitting at the bar at The Drunken

Moose, watching as Jolie and her partners, Ryan and Tarryn, along with two other friends, Eliza and a woman named Lilly, sang and danced along drunkenly to the music coming from the jukebox. And it had to be said that if I never heard another Taylor Swift song for as long as I lived it would be too damn soon.

"Christ. How many songs did they queue up in that damn thing?" Ethan grumbled from beside me. We'd come along as designated drivers, knowing the women wanted to tie one on, but had kept our distance, letting them do their thing while we had a couple beers at the bar. Ethan had brought his buddy Quinn along, Lilly's husband and a local firefighter, and so far he'd turned out to be a pretty cool dude.

Quinn lifted his glass to his mouth and drank. "I think they put the entire album on."

Jesus Christ.

"So, how are things going with you, man? You convince her to move in with you yet?"

I returned my focus to my woman, my chest expanding as I watched her throw her head back and lift her arms in the air, her eyes closed as she sang along—badly—about some anti-hero. "Not yet," I grumped.

A lot had changed in the past two months, and while it took some adjusting on my part, it was easy to see all of those changes had been for the better. I still had a reputation around town for being an asshole, but something had shifted once word spread that I was moving to Pembrooke permanently, all so I could be with Jolie. Apparently my standoff-ish demeanor didn't bother people so much when I was a part of the fabric of the town.

And considering Jolie was beloved by pretty much everyone who knew her, they'd started looking at me as some kind of hero. The man who'd swooped in and healed her heart after it had been broken. It wasn't a title I was particularly comfortable with, but it meant something to Jolie, so I learned to deal.

I was learning a lot when it came to being in a relationship, such as having to accept the people—or in my case, *animals*—that came as part of the package with the woman I loved.

That damned smoosh-faced cat of hers had managed to ruin two more suits, but despite its destructive tendencies, it was still taken with me for some strange reason. Jolie said it was because I was the thing's favorite person, but I was starting to think there were more sinister motives behind it. Like maybe it was just pretending to love me, but it was actually playing the long game when it came to torturing me.

Not that it mattered. I'd take anything the psychotic feline could throw at me. Hell, I was even willing to move the devil cat into my house if it meant getting Jolie there.

Things with my dad were better than I could have hoped for. He was officially in remission, and he and Millie were living their best life. Jolie and I saw them once a month for dinner, and I wasn't the least bit surprised they'd fallen head over heels for her.

Much to Leighton's displeasure.

Speaking of my half-sister, I ended up having to pay Jolie a hundred bucks when she bet me that Leighton's relationship with Barrett would go up in flames before she made it down the aisle. She'd been right. Barrett was currently slinking around town with his tail tucked between his legs, most likely wishing he hadn't been stupid enough to let a woman like Jolie go. Meanwhile, Leighton had taken off for something bigger and better—much like Estelle. She didn't have any skills I was aware of, and after Hershel and Millie informed her they were done enabling her bad attitude and behavior, she didn't have any resources either. It was only a matter of time before she came crawling back, but I wasn't holding my breath. I had better things to focus on.

I'd also grown closer with Jolie's parents and still enjoyed our weekly family dinners in which Lorene got a kick out of torturing her daughter.

We were traveling to Hope Valley the following

month so Jolie could see her niece in person and I could meet her brother and sister-in-law, and, surprisingly, I wasn't dreading it.

I was . . . happy. Every single day, I woke up with a lightness in my chest that hadn't been there since I was a kid, and I knew I'd made the right choice. I finally had a home. A place I was meant to be. A place where I belonged. And it was all because of the woman standing across the bar from me, smiling at me like I lit up her entire world.

"But I'm not giving up," I informed my friends.

Because that woman was my port in the storm, my anchor. She was the lifeline that kept my head above water and stopped me from going adrift.

She was everything, and I fully intended on spending the rest of my life showing her how much she meant to me.

The End.

Keep posted for more Pembrooke to come!

More from Pembrooke

She's a romantic at heart.

Chloe Delaney had three very specific wishes, growing up. She wished to stay settled in the small mountain town of Pembrooke, where she grew up, to one day be her own boss, and to fall in love with a man who would be willing to go to the ends of the earth for her.

With her roots firmly planted in Pembrooke's soil and her bakery, Sinful Sweets, thriving, two of her wishes have already come true. When a handsome single father moves to town, she's certain she's found the man to fill the role of wish number three. The only problem is, you can't force a frog to turn into a prince.

He isn't the Prince Charming type.

When Derrick Anderson moved from Jackson Hole to the small town of Pembrooke, he did it determined to wipe the slate clean. After eight years spent trapped in a miserable marriage, he's made a vow to never take the plunge again. He wants to be untethered, not tangled up in the strings that come with a committed relationship. He has his daughter, his career, and an ex-wife hell bent on making his life unbearable. His plate is already full. The only problem is, he didn't have a plan in place to protect his heart from her.

Neither of them were prepared for the course their lives would take. But once a rollercoaster begins to move, you can't just climb off, now can you?

The only thing they can do is strap in, hold on tight, and enjoy the ride.

She knew what it was like to feel unwanted.

At an early age Eliza Anderson learned a very hard lesson. Sometimes the people who are supposed to love you the most are the ones that cause you the most pain. She learned to guard herself, hesitating to let anyone close for fear of feeling that rejection all over again. Then Ethan came into her life, and what had started as a simple childhood crush morphed into a friendship she eventually came to cherish above all else. He was her safe place. Her rock. A shoulder she could lean on. Until he ripped it all away.

He knew what it was like to feel like an outsider.

Ethan Prewitt grew up learning that you couldn't always trust the people you loved the most to be there. That sense of security he craved had always alluded him, leaving him to feel like an interloper in his own home. He dreamed of escaping the small town of Pembrooke and building a life where he didn't have to depend on anyone but himself. What he never expected was for his friendship with Eliza to grow into something that meant everything to him.

Mistakes were made. Hearts were broken. But now Ethan's home and he's determined to make it right. It was time for their relationship to come full circle.

Because what they had was once in a lifetime.

He's terrified of loving her.

Quinn Mallick already had his happily-ever-after,

and in the blink of an eye it was ripped away from him. Now he's content to walk through the rest of his life carrying the weight of that guilt on his shoulders. He's convinced he doesn't deserve a second chance. But when the town's beautiful dance teacher turns her sights on him he finds himself questioning everything.

She's terrified of losing him.

Lilly Mathewson's once quiet, predictable life has been turned on its head. Feeling alone and adrift, she finds her comfort in the most unexpected of places. Falling for the town widower was never part of the plan, but there is just something about the temperamental man she can't seem to let go of.

What started as two grieving people leaning on each other has quickly turned into something neither of them expected. Lilly is ready to take the next step, but how do you move forward when the man you love refuses to let go of the past?

Especially when the only hope they have of healing their broken souls is if they do it together.

She's a sunny, sassy photographer.

Jolie Prescott has always been in love with love. She spent most of her life walking around with hearts in her eyes and immediately jumped at the chance to start a wedding planning company with her two best friends. So when her own fiancé called off their wedding and immediately started dating someone else, it was a major blow she never saw coming. The gossip about it finally starts to die down in her small town. Then her ex announced he's engaged *again*. And his new fiancée just happens to be Jolie's worst enemy. Which makes it really inconvenient that she can't seem to stop thinking inappropriate thoughts about that woman's moody half-brother.

He is the ultimate grump.

Vaughn Cavanagh never thought he'd set foot back in Pembrooke, Wyoming after moving away when he was thirteen, but when his father gets sick, he uproots his life to try to repair their frayed relationship. The only thing standing in his way is his spoiled brat half-sister, her determination to throw the ultimate wedding, and her beef with a certain wedding photographer he can't get out of his head.

When one impulsive act leads to Vaughn announcing he and Jolie are dating, the two have no choice but to fake their relationship to save face. But when feelings enter the picture and lines start to blur, Vaughn has to decide if he's willing to give up his quiet, solitary life and stay in Pembrooke for a woman he never intended to fall for, or if he's going to risk losing everything because he's too afraid to take that leap.

Discover Other Books by Jessica

<u>ASHLAND SERIES</u>
Dead to Rights

<u>WHITECAP SERIES</u>
Crossing the Line
My Perfect Enemy
Turn of the Tides

<u>THE PEMBROOKE SERIES:</u>
Sweet Sunshine
Coming Full Circle
A Broken Soul
Should Have Been Me

<u>WHISKEY DOLLS SERIES</u>

Bombshell

Knockout

Stunner

Seductress

Temptress

Vamp

HOPE VALLEY SERIES:

Out of My League

Come Back Home Again

The Best of Me

Wrong Side of the Tracks

Stay With Me

Out of the Darkness

The Second Time Around

Waiting for Forever

Love to Hate You

Playing for Keeps

When You Least Expect It

Never for Him

REDEMPTION SERIES

Bad Alibi

Crazy Beautiful

Bittersweet

Guilty Pleasure

Wallflower
Blurred Line
Slow Burn
Favorite Mistake
Sweet Spot

THE CLOVERLEAF SERIES

Picking up the Pieces
Rising from the Ashes
Pushing the Boundaries
Worth the Wait

THE COLORS NOVELS

Scattered Colors
Shrinking Violet
Love Hate Relationship
Wildflower

THE LOCKLAINE BOYS

Fire & Ice
Opposites Attract
Almost Perfect

CIVIL CORRUPTION SERIES

Corrupt
Defile

Consume

Ravage

GIRL TALK SERIES:

Seducing Lola

Tempting Sophia

Enticing Daphne

Charming Fiona

STANDALONE TITLES:

One Knight Stand

Chance Encounters

Nightmares from Within

DEADLY LOVE SERIES:

Destructive

Addictive

Acknowledgments

To my family. You guys make it possible for me to do this job every single day. I'm so lucky to have such an incredible support system.

To Adriana and Dylan, my writing buddies. Thank you so much for keeping me sane through every story I write.

To the author friends I've made along the way. This can be an isolating career at times. Having you guys in my corner means everything.

To Karen and Jan, for taking my words and making them into something understandable, and for not firing me when I blow through EVERY SINGLE deadline.

To my ARC team and all my readers, I wouldn't be here if it wasn't for you. Thank you so much for loving my words as much as I do and sticking with me all this time. Here's to more to come!

About Jessica

Born and raised around Houston, Jessica is a self proclaimed caffeine addict, connoisseur of inexpensive wine, and the worst driver in the state of Texas. In addition to being all of these things, she's first and foremost a wife and mom.

Growing up, she shared her mom and grandmother's

love of reading. But where they leaned toward murder mysteries, Jessica was obsessed with all things romance.

When she's not nose deep in her next manuscript, you can usually find her with her kindle in hand.

Connect with Jessica now

www.authorjessicaprince.com

Jessica's Princesses Reader Group

Newsletter

Instagram

Facebook

TikTok

authorjessicaprince@gmail.com

www.ingramcontent.com/pod-product-compliance
Lightning Source LLC
Chambersburg PA
CBHW020351010826
48973CB00005B/1362